Razor & Helena

A Surviving Red Prequel

Book Two

Jana` Chantel

About Right Media Group | Detroit, MI | 2021

About Right Media Group, LLC.
http://www.aboutrightmedia.com

Razor & Helena: A Surviving Red Prequel
Copyright © 2021 Jana` Chantel

Library of Congress Cataloging-in-Publication Data
Names: Chantel, Jana`, 1988—author.
Title: Razor & Helena: A Surviving Red Prequel/ Jana` Chantel
Description: Detroit: About Right Media Group, LLc. 2021. | Series: Surviving Red; Razor & Helena Book 2
Identifiers: LCCN 2021901310 (print) |
 (ebook) | ISBN 978-1-7330788-4-9 (hardcover) | ISBN 978-1-7330788-5-6 (paperback)
Subjects: | BISAC: FICTION/ Science Fiction/Apocalyptic & Post-Apocalyptic. | FICTION/ Science Fiction/ Action & Adventure. | FICTION/African American/General.
Classification: LCC 2021901310 (print)
LC record available at https://lccn.loc.gov/2021901310

Cover design by Moe Balinger and Fred Evans
Book Design by Jana` Evans

Printed in the United States of America
10   9   8   7   6   5   4

<u>*The Surviving Red Series*</u>

Surviving Red

For my Auntie Daune Daune and Jennifer

My two number one readers.

~*Now*~

Razor

Razor floated in the Detroit River, holding the two people who meant the world to him—Helena and Jade. They both cried in his arms. They all just witnessed the horrific death of the children they'd taken care of—Raina and Levi. Razor fought back his emotions. He needed to focus on the mission, protecting the two women he loved the most. But he couldn't help but feel the painful grief of his loss.

Razor looked after Raina and Levi like they were his own children. He taught them how to survive. He taught them how to fight—how to hide. And whenever they felt anxious or frightened, he always had a way to make them smile. Razor wanted to make the world suitable for them to live in. But none of that mattered anymore because they died at the hands of a psychopath in the end.

The only thing he could think of now was to flee. His sister, Jade, would majorly disagree with his decision, but Razor didn't care. Jade loved the children more than anyone there. They meant the world to her. Unfortunately, she was the focus of Bossman's obsession, so Razor needed to get her out of the country as soon as possible. It was the only way for them to recuperate from their losses and come up with another plan.

This would *not* be their final end.

So, while Helena cried in his arms, and as Jade cursed and shouted threats at Bossman, Razor began to slowly back away toward Canada. A plan was slowly forming in his head. He had an idea of how they would come back, defeat Bossman, and rebuild a new world. Razor just needed to search for him in Canada. He was the key to this whole thing, and Razor knew it.

Jade began to struggle in his arms. She realized what he was doing. Razor tightened his grip on her and Helena and began to swim even faster toward Canada. Jade pleaded and cried the whole way, but eventually, she gave up—too consumed with grief. Razor knew that she would hate him for this decision, but he was confident that he would get her to understand. At the end of it all, it really wasn't about them.

It was about *him*.

~*Then*~

Razor

An 18-year-old Razor towered over his victim—his knuckles bloody. He focused on his breathing—trying to calm his self-down. He couldn't remember what happened. Apparently, he blacked out. This usually occurred when he was angry—correction, pissed. That's been happening to him since he was little. He never thought much of it. If someone was able to get him *that* angry, then they deserved whatever he did to them. And whatever he did to them was usually painful.

Police sirens were in the background. It sounded like they were getting closer. Razor still stood over his victim. He wasn't afraid of the police. He wasn't scared of getting into trouble. On the contrary, he welcomed it. It gave him a rush that nothing else, or anyone else, could make him feel.

Razor tried to recall the argument that he had. He couldn't remember what it was about. He just remembered he and his friend were shouting at each other, and then he was standing over him—his knuckles covered in blood.

As he looked down at his friend, he couldn't shake the feeling of shame that began to slowly creep in. His friend looked up at him with a bloody nose, his left eye was swollen, and random cuts on his face. There were horror and fright in his eyes; he feared for his life. Razor understood the look. If he didn't come to, there's no telling how far he would've gone. They both knew that Razor could've killed him. And that knowledge hung tensely in the air.

His now ex-friend wanted to press charges. So, Razor spent the night in jail. A jail cell wasn't foreign to him. He spent a fair amount of time there. He was the local troublemaker—the side effect of being the only child to older parents. His mother was close to 45 when she had him. His dad was well into his 50s. Reigning in a wild child was hard. They were now well into their 60s and 70s.

Razor spent the whole weekend in jail before his mother eventually came and got him. The car ride home was long and silent. He had made his mother cry plenty of times. It killed him every time. He hated to see her cry. He never meant to hurt her, but he was a constant disappointment.

By the time Razor was 15, she had stopped crying altogether. She became silent—stoned. Due to health reasons, his father didn't get all that worked up about Razor's misfortunes. His father didn't care that the people in town talked about their parenting skills either. They had been trying to have a child for so long that he found Razor to be a blessing—troublemaker and all.

"I'm sorry," Razor said to his silent mother.

"You're always sorry."

"…I just got so angry."

"And you blacked out."

Razor didn't say anything. He's been telling her this since he was a little boy.

"It's fine, Razor. I gave up expecting you to be something I can be proud of a long time ago."

Razor hung his head in disappointment. "You don't know what it's like."

"I no longer care to know."

Razor was a little hurt at his mother's bluntness. This rage *was* him. She didn't care to understand that?

"There's always been this rage inside of me. A rage I can't control."

"A lot of people have rage inside of them, Razor, but they're able to control it." Silence hung in the air. "This is the last time I bail you out."

Something in his mother's tone told him that she meant it.

There was no need for further conversation when Razor got home. He just went straight to his room in the basement. After a while, he heard his parents in the kitchen talking about him. His mother explained that this was the last time they were going to bail Razor out of jail. His father was hesitant to agree.

"Jill, he's all that we have," his father pleaded.

"Don't give me that, Roger. Ryan doesn't care about us. If he did, he wouldn't be getting into so much trouble."

"He's our son."

"And he's an *adult*. Old enough to get out of trouble on his own," Jill disputed.

There was a long pause after her statement. Razor wasn't sure what his parents were doing, but he could hear his father's heavy breathing after some time. Razor knew that Roger was getting his self worked up.

Jill sighed and readjusted her tone. "Besides," she said softly. "His legal fees are dipping into our retirement funds. What are we going to do once that's all gone?"

"You're right," Roger finally calmed down a little and agreed, sadly. "No more bailing him out."

Razor sighed. What a disappointment? He really was letting his parents down as a son. He was determined to accept whatever fate he'd face with this new case. He was going to leave his parents in peace. They deserved that much.

**

Razor stood in the courtroom alone—only his court-appointed lawyer there for support. He was waiting for his sentencing. He pled guilty to the assault and battery charge. Luckily, he was just sentenced to two years of probation and 120 hours of community service.

"Took a lot of finessing on my part," the lawyer bragged.

Razor didn't say anything. He just gave his lawyer a blank stare.

Getting uncomfortable by the eerie stare, the lawyer cleared his throat. "Well, you report to your probation officer first thing tomorrow morning. Don't be late! Or that's jail time for you. The officer will give you your community service assignment."

"Thanks," Razor finally said.

"And do try to stay out of trouble, Mr. Thompson."

Razor didn't respond. He just walked out of the courthouse—determined to put as much distance from the place as possible.

No words were exchanged when he got home. His parents didn't bother to see how his court hearing went. A part of him was saddened by their nonchalant attitude. His behavior really drove them over the edge. Honestly, he couldn't help it. It seemed like ever since he was born, Razor had this unexplainable rage inside of him. It burned deep. It wasn't clear where it came from. He tried hard to suppress it, but whenever he got angry, he just exploded.

His mother, Jill, first sought out counseling. Then came anger management. All of that seemed to upset Razor even more. The attention made him feel different—ashamed. The more they tried to tame or normalize him, the more he rebelled. He accepted the fact that his rage made him who he was. There was no flaw in that. Razor hated that his parents, particularly his mother, saw it that way. But he kept letting his rage guide him, hoping that one day his mother would just accept it.

Razor headed for the basement. He grabbed his cell phone and texted the girl he usually messed around with. A distraction was needed. The time slowly passed while he waited on a response. He occupied his time by playing video games.

Usually, he didn't care for them, but his dad bought a gaming system and some fighting games for Razor when he was 15.

"Another way to fight with your hands," Roger explained.

Although he found it idiotic, Razor gave gaming a try. It was the least he could do for his dad; he rarely asked Razor for anything. He tried to make it work. A couple of months went by, and Razor managed to keep out of trouble—his best record to date. But then there was an incident. Razor couldn't get to his gaming system fast enough, and his hot streak went out the window.

Roger was a little disappointed, but he knew that the gaming system wouldn't keep Razor out of trouble forever.

It was midnight by the time Razor was sneaking in his friend with benefits. His parents were sound asleep.

"I heard you got into trouble again?" she said, sitting on his bed.

"I didn't invite you here to talk."

"No need to get pissy," she took her shirt and bra off. "Was just trying to make conversation."

"We can do that on the phone."

She rolled her eyes as she lay down, and Razor helped her out of her pants. Sex was a stress reliever for him. It was one of the very few things to calm him down. And he needed calming down a lot.

Luckily, Razor didn't have any trouble finding a partner for his stress relief activity. He was very good looking. He stood tall at 6'2, lean, and muscular. His former companions always complimented his physique when they glided their hands across his abs. Tattoos ran down his neck, his right arm, and chest—it was flattering against his fairly tanned skin. He had brown eyes and sandy brown hair. His goatee mostly covered his strong jawline.

Razor climbed on top of his companion and lost himself in his stress relief activity. Every single thought and worry quickly fled from him. He immediately drifted off to sleep once they were done.

The sun had risen when his companion woke him up. "Walk me home," she demanded.

Razor casually rolled over. "You're a big girl. Walk yourself home."

"Asshole!"

"Be sure not to wake my parents on your way out."

She gave him a good push before she stormed out.

Razor paid her no mind. He drifted back to sleep with no problem. He didn't wake until his dad came downstairs.

"You need to see your probation officer."

Razor got up and dressed. Every part of him dreaded the possibility of community service.

*****

The next six weeks went by uneventfully. Razor spent four hours daily, out of the five-day workweek, doing community service. He spent four hours in the morning there and then came home to nap. The rest of the day was spent lounging around in the basement, trying to stay out of trouble. He couldn't afford to get into any more trouble. Determination ran through him. He didn't want to let down his parents again—particularly his mother. He had to prove her wrong.

On the last day of his community service, Razor met with his probation officer. He fought off the urge of irritation as the officer casually flipped through his file.

"Well, Mr. Thompson," he finally said. "I'm impressed. I figured you would've gotten into trouble by now."

"It's Razor."

"Your legal name is Ryan Thompson. That's what I prefer to call you."

Razor glared at the officer. At first, his PO refused to be intimated by him, but he retracted after a few minutes of constant glaring.

"Look," he sighed. "You've been on a perfect streak with staying out of trouble. Do you really wanna ruin that now?"

Razor hated to agree with him, but he reluctantly did. "Fine."

"Now, if you can just stay out of trouble for the next few weeks, I can see about getting your probation sentence reduced."

"Thanks."

"Just continue to stay out of trouble."

Razor left out the office without saying good-bye. He headed home to relax and stay out of trouble. A small part of him was secretly proud of himself. This was going to be the longest streak he's had without getting into trouble. He wondered if his parents took notice, particularly his mother. Lately, he had a strong desire to prove her wrong and make her proud. For once in his life, he wanted to make her smile.

Roger was in the kitchen, making lunch, when Razor walked through the door. Razor greeted his father with a nod.

"How was your meeting?" Roger asked as he continued to make his sandwich.

"Pretty good," Razor sat down at the kitchen table.

"Want a sandwich?"

"Yeah, thanks. So, I'm done with my community service."

"That's good."

"My PO said if I continue to stay out of trouble, he'll see about getting my probation sentence reduced."

"That's excellent son," Roger sat two plates with sandwiches on the table. Razor quickly grabbed his sandwich. Roger sat down. "I'm proud of you. You've never gone this long before."

"I know," Razor said in between bites. "I'm just tired of disappointing you both."

"Razor, I understand that anger. I understand that rage. It's the rage that the Thompson men were cursed with. It only skipped me because of my disease."

Razor sometimes didn't know whether to pity or envy his father.

At the age of 13, Roger was diagnosed with a heart disease called hypertrophic cardiomyopathy. The disease ran on his mother's side. After many very close calls, Roger managed to reel in his anger, reduce his stress, and control his disease (along with the help of medication, of course). But it was because of those near-death experiences that Roger was able to get his anger under control.

Razor didn't have that threat or incentive. He was left to figure it all out on his own. That's why he sometimes envied his father—Roger had *no choice* but to get his anger under control. Razor wasn't sure if he could ever find a reason to rein it in.

"Seems like it affected me more," Razor admitted.

Roger laughed. "Well, it's known to get worse with every generation."

Razor frowned at that notion.

"Don't worry, son. You'll figure it all out."

"Thanks for being so patient with me, dad," Razor looked around for a moment. "Where's mom?"

"Out shopping."

"Oh," Razor got up and put his empty plate in the sink. "I'm about to take a nap. Will you tell her the good news for me?"

"Sure thing."

Razor went down to his room, turned on his TV for background noise, and lay across his bed. It didn't take long for him to drift off to sleep.

The first shake, Razor thought he was dreaming.

The second shake, Razor thought his father was trying to wake him.

When he woke up and saw that his father wasn't in his room, Razor got up only to feel the third shake. What was happening? The whole house was shaking; Razor could feel the rumble underneath his feet. Small cracks were forming on the basement floor.

Was this an earthquake?

It couldn't be. Razor lived in Ferndale, MI. Usually, Michigan hardly ever experienced any earthquakes. Razor panicked when he heard his father yelling upstairs. He ignored all the things that were falling around him and quickly ran up the steps three at a time. He fought to keep his self steady as the house continued to rumble.

Razor found his dad in the living room, still sitting in his favorite recliner chair. Roger's hands clung to the chair's armrest as the house shook violently. Razor quickly helped his father out of the chair, and they sought refuge underneath the living room's doorway.

"Where's mom?"

"At the drug store picking up my prescription."

"Shit," Razor wanted to leave and find his mother, but he couldn't leave his father alone. And he couldn't go while the earthquake was still happening. He had to wait it out.

The house shook for a few more minutes before it finally stopped. Screams and cries began to ring out from outside. Razor quickly helped his father back to his recliner chair.

"Stay here," Razor instructed. "I'm going out to find mom."

Roger looked worried. "Be safe out there."

Razor rushed out of the house, grabbing his car keys along the way. He was shocked for a brief moment when he saw the damage outside. Trees were uprooted entirely from the ground, bringing up the sidewalk along with it. There was a massive crack in the middle of the street, with a minivan stuck inside. Luckily, there was no one inside the van.

A house down the street was utterly demolished. Razor could hear the screams of the people still trapped inside. A group of neighbors rushed to go try and save them. Razor didn't even bother to join the rescue party. He was too worried about his mother. He jumped into his truck and hoped like hell that the roads were decent enough to drive through.

On an average day, the drug store was like eight minutes away from Razor's house. Today, Razor wasn't so sure what his ETA would be. The drive consisted of a lot of swerving. It was a lot of things that he was trying to avoid hitting: debris, fallen trees, and people franticly running around.

Razor grew frustrated. The longer it took for him to get to his mother, the more anxious he became. Razor eventually made his way to downtown Ferndale. The drug store was close by. He relaxed a little as he got closer. He quickly parked his truck at a decent spot; not too much damage was around it, and he rushed to the drug store.

The windows were busted out. The building was slightly slanted, and the roof was caved in. There was a streetlight pole sticking out the door. There were a lot of screams and cries coming from the drug store. Razor broke out into a run. Panic filled him.

"Mom!" he yelled as he made his way through the door. He was able to get over the fallen light pole very quickly and easily. "Mom!"

Razor fought off the panic as his mother had yet to respond. A lot of crying was coming from the back by the pharmacy counter. Razor made his way through the fallen shelves, debris and knocked over merchandise.

"Jill!" he yelled out again, hoping that she would respond to her name.

"Razor! Over here!"

Razor quickly made his way towards his mother's voice.

"Hurry, Razor! Help!"

Razor made it to his mother. She was behind the pharmacy's counter, along with some other customers. The pharmacist was trapped under a bunch of shelves and fallen rubble from the ceiling. Jill and the other customers were trying to help him, but the wreckage was too heavy.

"Razor, please help him," Jill pleaded once she saw him.

Razor gently pushed his mother aside and began lifting the fallen rubble with ease. A few of the customers helped him with the ones he had difficulty with. He was able to get the pharmacist out in no time. Once the pharmacist was all clear, Razor grabbed his mother and led her towards the door.

"What are you doing?" she protested. "We should wait for help."

"Dad is home alone," he said. "We need to get back to him before an aftershock hit."

He wasn't all that familiar with experiencing earthquakes, but he knew that aftershocks were a common thing. And he didn't want to be out when another one occurred.

Razor helped his mother over the fallen streetlamp and led her out of the store. "Where's your car?" he asked once they were out.

Jill gasped and pointed. Razor followed her gaze and saw her car tipped over.

"Do you have anything important in there?"

"A few groceries and some household products."

"Stay here," Razor quickly ran over and retrieved what he could from the car. He ran back over to his mother and led her to his truck. Once they were safely inside, Razor quickly sped off.

Jill looked at the scene in horror. "What on earth is happening?"

Razor continued to weave in and out of traffic—dodging a few things.

"We really should've stayed and made sure he was ok," Jill said to her son.

"We've done all we could."

"You don't know that."

"We can only worry about ourselves."

Jill sighed in disappointment. "That's no way to think, Ryan."

Razor grimaced as he continued to drive. He hated it when his mother used his real name. That always meant that she was angry or disappointed with him. He didn't say anything. His mother was just never going to understand.

During the time of chaos, you had to look out for yourself and your loved ones. That was the only way you could survive. Razor understood that, and he was prepared to make those hard choices in order to keep his parents alive.

Razor felt a little relief as he turned down his street. The quicker he got home, the better. He hated the unknown and what they were experiencing now was just that. He needed some time to think. He needed time to prepare.

Then the ground began to shake.

"Shit," Razor mumbled. "Not again." Razor accelerated, rushing to get home to his dad.

Jill gripped the door handle. "Careful Razor," she mumbled.

Razor ignored her and sped up. He refused to allow his dad to experience this alone. He hated the fact that his mother already had to. Plus, intuition was telling him that being out on the street wasn't good. Jill let out a few screams as he dodged out of the way of falling trees, streetlights, and houses.

Just a little closer.

They were so close to the house. Razor just had to go a little faster, and they would be there. Suddenly, the road in front of them dropped. It lowered about six feet. Razor slammed on the brakes, but not fast enough. They skidded toward the wall of concrete that suddenly formed in front of them.

All Razor heard was his mother's screams before he blacked out.

~2~

Razor

The next few months were even more chaotic and hectic. After a couple of weeks, Razor was able to recover from the crash. He had a concussion and some cuts and bruises. Jill sustained a severe case of whiplash. Overall, they were able to walk away from the crash with no serious injuries. Razor's truck, however, wasn't so lucky. Surprisingly, he didn't care too much about what happened to his vehicle. That wasn't his biggest worry. What worried him the most was the unclear explanations that the government was giving people.

News reports stated that the earthquakes were an uncommon phenomenon. Michigan wasn't the only state to experience the devastating disaster that day. In fact, the whole United States experienced an earthquake. It was one big massive earthquake that was felt around the country. Of course, some states were impacted by it more—like California, Nevada, and New Mexico. Many people died or were severely injured.

The government was scrambling to get control over everything. But it was all too much. There wasn't any kind of plan, or resources for that matter, to handle a scenario where the entire country experienced a natural disaster at the same time.

Razor tried as best he could to prepare him and his parents for the unique experiences. He stocked up on supplies. He boarded up the house—mainly the windows since they were destroyed by the latest earthquake. He begged his parents that they stayed indoors, except for him. Out of all of them, he was the only one capable of handling the chaos that laid outside of their doors.

After the earthquakes, rolling blackouts began to occur. This wasn't limited to the U.S. The blackouts were happening around the world. Crimes such as looting, stealing, and robbing had skyrocketed. Razor was confident that he could deal with these kinds of people. His parents, however, most certainly could not.

Jill gave Razor a hard time with these new rules. She wasn't used to him calling all the shots. Razor tried to be diplomatic with his mother as best he could, but he always struggled with patience. He and his mother argued a lot. He hated it. Especially since it bothered his father so much. Razor didn't want to put too much stress on Roger, especially with his condition.

Razor managed to stock up on a decent supply of Roger's heart medication on his last outing. He didn't tell his parents that he stole them. He wanted to ration out the medicine for as long as he could, so Razor made it a point to avoid any altercations with his mother—for his father's sake.

For the most part, Razor stayed in his room in the basement. Luckily, his space didn't have too much damage done to it after the many earthquakes. After seeing how upset Roger got after Razor's many arguments with Jill, Razor thought it best if he just stayed put in the basement. He only came out to fix them all food, administer his father's medication, or make a supply run.

On this particular day, Razor was napping (something that he did a lot lately) when his mother woke him.

"The electricity is back on," she explained to him. "I want to go out and get some food to cook."

"Make a list, and I'll get it later."

"I wasn't asking. I was giving you a heads up. I'm leaving."

Razor sighed. "Mom, we've been through this; it's not safe for you to leave the house."

"This is my house, Ryan! I'll do whatever the hell I like!"

"Fine," Razor got up and proceeded to put on his shoes. "Then I'm coming with you." Jill was about to protest when Razor glared at her. He was on his last straw with his mother. "That's the *only* way you're leaving this house."

At this point, he was considering locking his mother in her room or something. Roger would just have to get over it. His mission was to keep his parents safe throughout this whole ordeal. He was determined to do that by any means necessary.

The look on Razor's face must have frightened Jill because she didn't say anything else. Instead, she turned around and headed upstairs. Razor could hear her telling his father that Razor was leaving out with her. By the time Razor got upstairs, Jill was silently waiting for him by the door.

Razor said goodbye to his father as he gave Roger his medicine. Then he and his mother left. They were now down to one car, Roger's car. It was an SUV, so it did fine driving through the damaged streets.

Jill gave her son the silent treatment throughout the whole ride. Razor was ok with it. He was quickly learning that no matter what he did, he would never be able to satisfy Jill. Although there were times when he really wanted to please her and make her proud. But as these few months past, he was more than positive that could never happen.

Throughout their many arguments, he explained to his mother that he wasn't behaving that way to be mean but to keep her safe. He loved her and didn't want anything terrible to happen to her. Jill seemed not to listen or didn't *want* to listen. Razor couldn't understand why his mother kept fighting him on this issue. Why was she so resentful? He often wondered if she would've put up so much resistance if it was his father calling all the shots. So, Razor could only conclude that his mother was just bent on being unsatisfied with him.

Razor slowly drove past the grocery store.

"What are you doing?" Jill demanded.

"Scoping out the area," Razor said, looking around the nearby buildings.

Jill rolled her eyes. "I swear, Razor, you can be so paranoid."

"If you're going to be here, you're going to do this my way."

Jill rolled her eyes again but didn't say anything.

Razor drove around the block a couple of times, looking for anything suspicious. Nothing seemed out of the ordinary to him. But he wasn't satisfied with going in just yet. Parking a few buildings down from the grocery store, Razor cut off the engine. Jill went to open her door when Razor grabbed her wrist.

"Not yet," he said, looking at the grocery store.

"What do you mean not yet?"

Razor ignored her attitude and kept looking at the door. He thought he saw a flicker of movement inside.

"Ryan, let me go now!"

Razor tightened his grip. "I said not yet."

"Let go of me!" Jill tried to open the door with her other hand, but Razor pulled her back from the door.

"We don't know if it's clear."

"You're just paranoid."

"I'm just trying to keep us alive," Razor growled. "Now, are you going to wait until I say when it's clear, or should I drive you back home?"

"I'll wait," Jill snapped.

Razor stared at his mother for a moment—reading her face. After a while, he slowly let her wrist go. Jill quickly pulled it back once Razor loosened his grip. She scowled at him as she rubbed her wrist, indicating that he hurt her. Razor ignored her and her theatrics. He looked more intently at the store. He could've sworn he saw movement earlier before. He cursed under his breath. Jill was distracting him with all her drama. Usually, he would've been in the store by now. They've been sitting outside for too long. It seemed suspicious. And if someone else was scoping out the area, they definitely knew he was there now.

He decided to give it a couple more minutes—just to be safe. If someone were scoping them out, he hoped that they would just hold off before doing anything. Jill sighed with impatience. Razor ignored her.

There was a movement in the store again. He was sure of it. Razor quickly turned on the engine and threw the SUV into drive. He was about to speed off when Jill swung open the door and jumped out. She ran toward the store.

"Shit!" Razor slammed on the brakes and threw the car into park. He jumped out of the car and ran after his mother. Fortunately, he caught up to her quickly. He grabbed her arm and pulled her toward him. "We're leaving!"

Jill quickly spun around and slapped him as hard as she could. "Don't *touch* me!"

Razor released her. Taking a deep breath, he quickly reminded his self that this was his mother. But his anger was bubbling over, and his mother wasn't making it easier on him. He watched with resentment as she ran into the store. There was a strong urge to just leave her and let her fend for herself since she was so dead set on doing things without him. But someone was in there. And Razor had a feeling that the outcome wouldn't be pleasant.

Reluctantly, Razor went into the store after his mother. He didn't hear anything, so he figured the occupant was biding their time before confronting them. When he got inside, Jill was gathering up some canned goods at the front of the store. She pretended not to notice him, even though he was in her line of view. She proceeded to make her way to the back of the store.

"We're leaving," Razor said.

"No, we're not. I'm not done."

"Yes, you are. This place isn't clear."

"Look around, Ryan!" Jill gestured. "There's no one here. You're just paranoid."

"Lower your voice."

Jill glared at him. She then turned around and headed toward the back of the store. Razor grabbed her arm again. And again, Jill spun around and smacked him. Razor tightened his hold on his mother.

"You haven't seen what people have become in these past months," Razor said through clenched teeth. He was trying hard not to use excessive force with his mother. "I have. And I'm telling you it's not safe here."

"You just want to use this as an excuse to be in charge," Jill spat. "I don't care what you've seen. I'm not taking orders from a disappointment like you."

Razor was hurt by that comment, but he made sure that it didn't show. Instead, he released her and turned to walk away.

"I'll walk home then," he said over his shoulder.

What was the point of fighting with her anymore? He was getting nowhere. And if they kept it up like this, then Razor was sure that he would end up hurting his mother. He couldn't live with himself if he ended up doing that.

Someone began clapping when Razor was close to the door. He froze. He knew someone was in there. A small part was hoping that they would've stayed hidden until his mother left.

"Excellent restraint," a male voice complimented. "I don't think I could've just simply walked away like you."

To his left, a man walked out of a back room.

"Well," another male voice added. "He seems like he's mommy's good little boy."

Jill jumped at the sound of the new intruder. He was coming down the aisle right behind her. She slowly backed away, coming closer to Razor. Razor closed the distance.

"Does she always give you such a hard time?" the first man asked Razor. He was tall and very lanky.

Razor didn't answer. He just glared at him.

"Too much mouth for me," the second man said. He was shorter than his partner and much more muscular and stockier. "I would've sliced out her fucking tongue a long time ago."

Razor growled as he stood in front of his mother—protecting her.

The second man chuckled. "Oh, don't be like that. I saw your frustration as she was giving you all that lip."

"We'll just leave," Jill whispered. It was barely audible.

The first man looked at her and sighed. "I'm afraid you can't do that. You trespassed on our property. There are consequences for that."

"This isn't your property," Razor stated. He knew the store owner. Neither men were it.

"It is now," the second man said. "And we have certain ways of dealing with trespassers. Especially women," he looked over at Jill and grinned. "No matter how old and mouthy they are."

The first man launched at Razor. Razor quickly punched him in the throat. The lanky man stumbled back, choking. The second man attacked next. Jill screamed out in terror as Razor pushed her out of the way. The stocky man went for Razor's waist. He slammed Razor on the ground.

"Razor!" Jill screamed out, afraid.

The stocky man began punching Razor, but Razor was able to block most of them. He spotted a shelf from a fallen endcap lying next to him. As the stocky man pulled back to deliver another blow, Razor reached out and grabbed the shelf and hit the guy in his face—making sure the pointed edge made contact with his temple. The stocky guy flew back and crashed into an endcap that was still standing. Razor could see that the guy was bleeding from his head.

"Razor!" Jill screamed again. She reached over and threw a can at the first guy who was making his way toward her son.

The lanky guy, still choking, turned his attention to Jill. Razor got to his feet before the guy could get any closer to his mother. Razor hit the guy with the shelf as hard as he could. The guy's neck cracked. The lanky man dropped to the ground.

"Frank!" the stocky man cried out. Frank was dead. His partner knew it. The man jumped up and charged at Razor.

Again, Razor swung the shelf like it was a baseball bat and hit the guy in the face, yet again. The guy flew back once again, landing on the floor. Razor was seeing red. The guy's last comment was ringing in his ears *"...we have certain ways of dealing with trespassers. Especially women, no matter how old and mouthy they are."*

The guy tried to get up. Razor was on him before he could. He hit the guy with the shelf again.

And again. And again. And again. And again.

His rage was spilling over, and there was no way he could control it.

"Razor!"

He hit the guy again.

"Razor!"

He hit the guy again.

"Razor!" Jill gently placed a hand on her son's shoulder. "Honey, please, that's enough."

Razor was breathing heavily as he stared down at what used to be the guy's face. He looked at his hands and the shelf. It was covered with blood. Blood coated his face as well—Razor could feel it. The whole scene reminded him of one of Pollock's paintings. Blood was splattered everywhere, but it somehow looked so beautiful to him. The entire incident made him eerily calm. Was that normal? Razor was starting to wonder if he was losing his mind.

"Honey..." there was terror in Jill's voice. They were silent for a moment. The guy was barely alive; he was making a strange, gurgling sound. It sounded like he was choking on his blood. "Maybe...maybe...you should put him out of his misery?"

Razor looked at his mother with disbelief. He quickly got angry. "You think he would've shown you the same mercy?"

Tears fell from Jill. She knew her son was right. "Please, Razor."

Razor sighed and hit the guy one last time. The guy went silent. Razor tossed the shelf and tried to wipe away as much blood as he could from his hands.

"Hurry up and grab some food," he said to his mother. "Before someone else comes."

Jill stared down at the dead man in disbelief. Unfortunately, she was slowly drifting into shock. Razor could see it on her face. He sighed and quickly bagged up the canned goods that she already had stacked at the front. Then he pulled his mother close to him and helped her walk out of the store. Razor could feel her shaking in his arms. He quickly froze once they stepped outside. A man and two women were waiting just a few feet away. They looked at him with worry.

"Are they in there?" one of the women asked. She appeared to be the youngest.

"Not alive," Razor walked around them once he was sure that they weren't a threat. They appeared to be a family just trying to scavenge up some food. Razor helped his mother into the SUV. It was astounding that it was still there.

"May I?" the woman asked.

Razor wasn't sure why she was asking his permission. It wasn't his store. Then he caught a glimpse of himself in the passenger window. He was covered in blood. His face and neck were caked with it, and his hands looked like they were bathed in blood. The view must've looked scary to them. Razor walked around to the driver's side and opened the door.

"Knock yourself out," he proceeded to get inside the car but hesitated. "I wouldn't be too long if I were you, though."

"Thank you," the man said. And then he and the two women quickly went inside.

Razor sped off once they were out of sight. Jill remained silent through the car ride. However, this silence was different than the one she gave him on the ride over. She was still in shock.

Razor sighed. "I'm sorry," he must've been a bigger disappointment to her. He just killed two men, and he felt no kind of remorse whatsoever. In his mind, the kills were justifiable. The men were trying to hurt his mother. But he wondered if Jill would see it like that. "But from now on, you have to listen to me. Ok?"

"Ok," she whispered in a shaky voice.

**

"He was *born* for this new world," Razor overheard Jill say to Roger when they got back from the grocery store.

Jill was still very shaken up by the time they got home. Roger repeatedly asked her what was wrong. Razor was too ashamed to tell his father what went down at the store. He feared that the knowledge of his son killing two people would send Roger over the edge. Razor didn't want to risk that with his father's heart condition.

Surprisingly, Roger didn't act too bad once Jill told him what happened. He was more upset that his wife was in danger. He also held her accountable for putting herself in that position by not listening to Razor in the first place.

"Trust me, Jill," Roger said after he heard what happened. "Razor knows what he's doing."

"I know, honey," Jill hung her head in shame. "Trust me, I won't disobey him again."

Razor slowly walked into the living room once he heard that their discussion was done. He had been eavesdropping on the conversation as he made them all dinner. As soon as he walked in, Jill looked over at him and gave him an embarrassing smile.

"Thank you, Razor."

Razor handed her a bowl of beans, corn, and rice. "You're welcome."

"No," Jill could see that he didn't understand her gratitude. "Thank you for saving me back there."

Razor looked at her, confused. He was conflicted. On the one hand, he was shocked that his mother was thanking him at all. On the other hand, he was angry that she felt the need to thank him for doing his duty.

"Mom, there's no need to thank me for that. I told you, I love you. I don't want anything bad to happen to you."

"I know, honey," she handed back her bowl of food. "Take it. I'm not really hungry."

"Just eat a little. You're still in shock. It'd be better if you had something in your stomach."

Jill nodded and took two huge portions of the rice, bean, and corn mixture that Razor made. Finding her son satisfied with that, Jill quickly went off to bed. Once his mother was gone, Razor took a seat next to his father and ate his food.

"You alright, son?" Roger asked after a while.

Razor smiled at him weakly. "So much for my good streak."

Even with all the chaos that's been going on, Razor managed to avoid confrontation with people until today.

Roger frowned. "I'll say that this one was justified."

"I feel ashamed."

"There's nothing to be ashamed about. You were protecting your mother."

Razor shook his head. "No, I feel ashamed because I don't feel remorseful about killing them. I killed two people, and there's no inkling of guilt."

Roger nodded—taking in his son's statement.

"Are you disappointed in me?" Razor asked after a long awkward silence.

"Not at all, son. I think your mother may have been right. I think you were born for this new world," Roger admitted. "Some difficult decisions need to be made, and you are the right kind of person to make them. Remorse and guilt. Those are the two things that can keep you down and cloud your judgment."

Razor was a little shocked to hear his father say that. It was so blunt and honest. But Razor saw his point. Now was the time to keep focus and stay on the mission—keeping his parents safe. Emotions got in the way of that. Razor had to be emotionless. Surprisingly, he was good at that.

Razor gave his father his medication. Then the two men spent the remainder of the night watching TV—enjoying the electricity.

The next few months were very easy for Razor since he and his mother were getting along. Jill had no problem listening and following Razor's rules. She was terrified of going back outside. Razor was a little concerned with her fear. He didn't want her to be afraid—just cautious. But Jill was content with never stepping a foot outside. For the moment, Razor thought it best to let her be.

Unfortunately, their time with electricity was short-lived. They had power for about two weeks before another earthquake, and a rolling blackout happened. Razor was finding his self frustrated. The government could not give them a reason as to why this was happening, nor could they provide them with a timeframe on how long this was going to occur. Razor tried to prepare as best as he could, but everything was just too unpredictable.

What he was finding predictable, however, were the earthquakes. So, he spent some time nailing and strapping things down so they would stay in place whenever another quake hit. He got rid of anything that was made of glass or that was breakable. He fixed the cracks that were in the walls and on the roof. He kept his self occupied and busy with chores. Most importantly, he was staying out of trouble.

Although months had passed since he killed those two men, every so often, Razor would suddenly experience a case of paranoia. Sometimes he would be convinced that the police would show up on his doorstep. But they never did. They were too occupied and too spread out to follow up on every single crime that occurred. Razor knew this, but he still couldn't shake the feeling.

There had been more supply runs since the incident. Jill was anxious every time Razor left. She was afraid of him running into trouble again. She was also scared that someone was going to try to break in while he was away. Razor always had to calm her down. He usually left his father with a loaded rifle whenever he went on a supply run—even before the incident. Roger was more than capable of keeping them safe. Jill knew this, but she was anxious all the same. Razor ended up fortifying the house after Jill had a panic attack during his last supply run. With each passing day, he grew more concerned for her.

So, on his very last supply run, Razor made sure that he stocked up on stuff that would last for a long time. Usually, his supply runs lasted for like an hour, tops. But this last run, he spent so much time scavenging in different areas that he was gone for half the day. The supplies should last them until at least six months. That's what Razor was hoping for. And if he rationed them right, the goods might even last longer.

Jill was happy and less anxious now that Razor was going out less frequently.

Razor was now sleeping in the living room. With his mother's fearful condition, he was concerned with being away from her. She felt safe when he was close. He wanted her to always feel that way. And that's where he was when he heard someone trying to break-in through the living room window.

At first, Razor thought he imagined things. He hadn't had a good night's sleep in weeks, so he thought he was getting delirious. But then he heard a voice.

"See if you can get in around back," a male voice commanded.

Razor jumped up and grabbed the rifle that laid on the coffee table beside him. At that moment, he was thankful for Roger's passion for hunting. Although his father hadn't gone hunting in over a decade, Roger still found the need to collect hunting rifles.

Razor quietly walked to his parents' room. Roger met him at the bedroom door with his own rifle in his hand. Instinctively, Jill was directly behind him—the look of fear deep in her eyes.

"Someone's in the back," Roger whispered.

Razor nodded. "I heard them out front too," he whispered.

They all heard someone tinkering around at his parents' window. Jill quickly covered her mouth—trying not to scream.

"They can't get in," Razor assured his mother.

Just then, they heard banging coming from the living room. Someone was trying to get through the window that Razor had securely boarded up. He was confident that they would fail, but he wanted to hide his parents in the rare chance that they did.

Razor motioned for his parents to follow him. They quickly obeyed. As they passed through the living room, Razor could see the silhouette of a person trying to break the boards to get through. Rage bubbled up inside of him. He had to get his parents safely out of the way before he did what he had to do. He led his parents down the basement and into his closet. Razor had turned it into a panic room for just this scenario. There were enough supplies and amenities that his parents could survive in there for weeks.

"Stay put," he demanded. "I'll go run them off."

"No, Razor," Jill pleaded. "Please stay."

"I can't let them get in here."

"He's right, Jill," Roger wrapped his arm around his wife. "They can't get in."

"Then, be sure to make it back to us."

"I will," Razor quickly kissed her cheek and then looked at his dad. "Keep her safe."

Razor secured his parents in the panic room and then went upstairs to deal with the intruders.

The banging increased. The intruders were now trying to get in through the kitchen window. Razor paused at the top of the basement stairs. He was trying to gauge how many were there. There was someone at the kitchen window, the living room window, and his parents' bedroom window. But he couldn't tell if there was any more.

"We know you're in there!" a voice yelled. It sounded like they were at the side door. "Just give us some supplies, and we'll leave you be."

"Yeah, right," another voice whispered.

Razor didn't say anything. He swiftly and quietly made his way up to the attic. He passed the living room and saw that the person was still trying to get in. It was the same view when he passed by his parents' bedroom. The intruders had picked the wrong house. Razor's adrenaline was running high, which made his anger spiral out of control. He was ready to make these people pay.

We'll leave you be.

Razor didn't believe that for a second. How many times did this person make that promise? How many naive people believed them only to fall victim? *They* wouldn't be one of them.

Razor made his way to the secret hatch that he created in the attic. The hatch led him out to the roof. He positioned his self so he couldn't be seen. He scoped out the area around his house. There was one person out front, one person in the backyard, and two by the side door. Razor wasn't satisfied with that number. Something told him that there were more.

After further investigation, he saw that there was one person a few houses down to his right. Another person was a few houses down to his left, and another at the far end of his backyard. They were there on guard in case any of them escaped from the house. These intruders were only here to do one thing: kill.

They had a stable home and an ample amount of supplies. They were a gold mine for marauders.

Razor put the suppressor on his rifle that was stashed by the hatch door. The plan was to take out the guards that were around the perimeter. Then he would focus on the ones closer to the house. He went for the guard on his right first. They went down quickly and quietly. Naturally, Razor was an excellent shot, thanks to Roger. No one seemed to notice that they were a man down.

Then he turned his attention to the guy on his left. Again, they went down without anyone noticing. Next, he went for the guy in the backyard. Razor tried to focus on him, but he was having difficulty seeing him. A tree was in his way. He wanted to wait it out for a moment, but he could see that the person at the front window was slowly making progress. That was unacceptable.

Ignoring the guy for a brief moment, Razor decided to turn his attention to the guy at the front window. He focused in on him—making sure his head was in clear view. Razor held his breath and fired. The guy dropped quickly, but not quietly. Sadly, he went down with a loud thud. So loud that someone on the side of the house heard it.

"What was that?"

"Don't know."

"Go check it out."

Razor watched as someone slowly entered the line of view of his scope. Before they could react to their dead comrade, they dropped. They fell more silently.

"What's going on?" the leader asked when his partner had yet to report the status of the noise. When he still didn't get a response, the leader walked over into Razor's view. "Fuck!" the guy saw the two dead bodies.

Razor fired, but the guy was fast and quickly got out of the way. The bullet only hit the guy in the shoulder. The leader screamed out in pain. Both of the men in the backyard rushed over to see what the problem was.

"Shit," Razor mumbled. He rushed to turn his attention to them.

"Abort! Abort!" the leader yelled before Razor could react. The leader was the first to turn and flee. The others quickly followed.

Razor fired again. He managed to get one of them in the knee. The man fell in the middle of the street, crying. His comrades didn't bother to help him. They kept on running—leaving him behind. Razor quickly climbed down from the roof. He couldn't let them escape. It wasn't clear if they were fleeing or going to get back up. Either way, he couldn't risk them coming back to retaliate.

They had to die.

The guy in the street continued to cry out in pain. Once he saw Razor approaching, he began crawling—trying to put as much distance between them as possible. Razor completely ignored him until he passed him. Then he turned the rifle toward the injured intruder and fired off a shot. The guy's crying instantly stopped.

The two remaining guys were still in his line of view. Razor quickly positioned his self on top of a parked car. The one that was lagging appeared to be the leader. Razor wanted to save him for last. So, he focused on the guy that was further away. He locked in on him and fired. The guy dropped to the ground. It wasn't clear if he was dead or not, but the guy didn't move.

"Fuck!" the leader yelled out again. He ran to the side of someone's house, looking to escape Razor's view.

Razor jumped off the car and proceeded to follow. As he got closer, he could hear the guy crying and frantically looking for somewhere to hide. Razor was at the driveway of the house the intruder fled to when it went silent. He no longer heard the guy moving around. Razor slowly made his way to the backyard—making sure he wasn't heard.

The occupants of the house had left months ago. Of course, looters had picked the place clean. Even the side door was missing. The dark entryway gradually came into Razor's view. He slowly passed it— anticipating someone to jump out.

No one did.

Razor was almost in the backyard when something hard hit him across the back. He fell to the ground. The rifle flew out of his hands and slid across the yard. Razor quickly turned toward his assailant. The intruder had a big piece of wood lifted above his head. He was about to bring it down on Razor, but Razor caught it mid-air. The two men tugged on it for a moment, but since the guy's shoulder was injured, Razor was able to take it from him.

The guy charged at him, but Razor swung the piece of wood and hit the guy in the face. The guy flew back and fell to the ground. Razor got up and strode over to him. Instinctively, he swung the wood and hit the guy repeatedly.

Then Razor blacked out…

…when he came to, he was sitting on the living room couch—the bloody 2x4 still in hand. He couldn't remember how he got there or how long he had been sitting there. Razor didn't see his parents nearby, so he figured they were still in the panic room.

When he opened the door, Jill was sleeping on a cot while Roger was nodding off in a chair.

"Mom. Dad," Razor said, waking them.

Roger slowly opened his eyes, and Jill got up off the cot. They both looked at him in horror. Razor wondered what he looked like. He was starting to regret not looking in the mirror first.

Roger stood up. "You alright, son?"

Razor nodded. "They're gone. It's safe."

"Thank you, Razor," Jill started to cry. She knew what her son did. She knew it had to be hard. And she was very appreciative. Jill walked over and hugged her son tightly.

"You're welcome, mom."

Roger smiled as his son and wife embraced one another. He loved that they were finally getting along. Despite everything that was going on, this was the one thing he was grateful for.

Then there was a tremble. And as usual, a violent shake followed. Razor and Jill suddenly fell to the ground—the force knocking them away from the panic room. The house shook wildly—the worst one yet. Razor could see a huge crack forming in the ceiling. Their home was going to come down at any second. They all needed to get out of there. Reacting instinctively, Razor lifted his mother up and pushed her toward the stairs.

"Go!" he demanded. Razor went to help his dad out of the panic room. The house was coming down. Razor could feel it.

Then everything went in slow motion.

Roger was walking to the door to meet Razor when the storage shelves tipped over. Razor tried to run to his father as fast as he could, but his feet didn't seem to move. The entire unit came tumbling down on Roger. Blood flowed out of his father's head. Razor was close. As he was about to lift the storage shelf off his father, the ceiling came crashing down.

"Roger!" Jill screamed at the top of her lungs.

~3~

Helena

Helena let out a piercing scream as the house violently shook. "Ma! Dad!" she was currently taking cover under the kitchen's doorway. Her parents were upstairs in their bedroom, at least that's the last place she saw them.

"Helena, stay where you are, sweetheart!" her father yelled.

Helena held on tightly to the doorpost—her hands starting to cramp. She hated every moment of this. The earthquakes terrified her. And unfortunately, they were happening more often. It always left their house more damaged and more vulnerable.

Most of the houses in her neighborhood barely stood. Many of their neighbors had to move and seek refuge someplace else. A lot of Helena's friends were among them. It broke her heart when they had to go. She was sure that she would never see them again. A lot of people died due to these earthquakes. She often wondered if they would survive.

Although the earthquakes terrified her, the thought of leaving home terrified her even more. They couldn't leave their home. Not until her older sister Jade made it back to them. Jade ran away from home a year ago after Helena yelled at her to leave. Helena never thought that Jade would actually do it. She only said it in the heat of the moment.

Jade was a teenager and in her rebellious phase. She was causing a lot of grief for their parents. Helena hated it. She hated hearing the arguments. She hated listening to her mother cry. She hated seeing her father fight back his anger. Helena just wanted it all to stop. So, one night, as her parents argued with Jade, Helena screamed at her to leave. The look on Jade's face stunned Helena. Her sister looked genuinely hurt. So, Jade ran away that night and refused to come back.

Both Helena and her parents begged for Jade to come back home, but Jade declined. Sadly, she was enjoying her freedom too much. That hurt Helena the most. She needed her big sister. But Jade would rather hang out with her friends and her boyfriend, Vincent, without any kind of adult supervision.

Despite all of that, Helena still believed that Jade would come back home. With everything that was now going on, Jade couldn't stay out on her own anymore. She had to return home. She had to be with her family. Sadly, it was looking like that wasn't happening anytime soon.

Helena kept her grip on the doorpost, even though her fingers hurt. She waited for the house to stop shaking. She waited for the ground to stop moving. She waited for the fear to leave her body. After what seemed like an eternity, the shaking subsided. Helena let out a sigh of relief. How many more of these did she have to deal with? Will they be without power, yet again, for weeks?

The only thing that scared Helena more than the earthquakes was the darkness. The darkness seemed to bring out the evil in people. Helena remembered the first blackout they had. Someone tried to break into their next-door neighbor's home. They could hear the screams of terror from next door. Helena was terrified. Her father went over to chase off the would-be intruders. Helena was worried the whole time. She didn't want the intruders to hurt her father. But nothing happened. Her father was a big man, and the intruders found him to be very intimidating. The next day, their next-door neighbors moved. They were never seen again.

It took a moment before Helena finally got up from under the doorway. She could hear her parents rushing down the stairs.

"Helena!" her mother screamed out.

"I'm ok," she responded. Physically, she was fine. Mentally, she was drained.

Her mother reached the kitchen's doorway and was instantly relieved to find Helena ok. She took Helena in her arms and hugged her tightly. She kissed Helena's forehead repeatedly. Her mother was always overly affectionate after they've experienced an earthquake. Helena figured that her mother was just very thankful every time they made it through alive.

"I love you," her mother cried.

"I love you too, ma."

Helena's father walked over and embraced them both. Helena stood in the middle of the family's group hug. She was happy that she was with them, but she longed for her sister. She felt incomplete without Jade.

The knocking on the front door broke up the family's loving embrace. They all slowly pulled away from each other. Panicked screams could be heard outside. The screams after the earthquakes were normal to Helena, but something about these screams seemed different. Helena's father went to the door and answered it.

"Oh, thank God," a neighbor from down the street greeted. "We need your help. Ms. Wilson is trapped in her home."

"What do you mean trapped?" Helena's father asked.

"She was in her bedroom when the earthquake hit. Her armoire fell over, blocking the door, and she can't get out of her window because she's on the second floor. Plus, the window is boarded up."

Helena's father sighed. He knew there was no way the old woman could get out by herself. "Ok, let's go."

"We'll come with you," Helena's mother interjected.

They all walked out into the chaos of their neighborhood. As usual, people were scrambling about the streets—assessing the damage that the earthquake has done. Quite a few people lost their homes. Again, Helena was incredibly grateful that their house was still standing. She watched as neighbors tried to help the injured. People were removing debris that was in the way or could potentially cause problems in the future. Helena loved seeing this side of her community. The earthquakes seemed to bring them together more. The darkness, however, seemed to bring out something totally different.

Ms. Wilson was known as the neighborhood's cat lady; she was never married and never had any children. Helena always pitied her. Ms. Wilson was alone, and no one in this world should be alone. Once a month, her parents made her and Jade go down to Ms. Wilson's house to see if she needed help with anything. On the days there wasn't anything to do, the girls would sit and watch TV with her all day. Jade hated it. Helena never minded it too much. It was only one day, and for whatever reason, Helena felt like she owed it to her.

As they approached Ms. Wilson's home, Helena could see that the roof was caving in. Her heart raced. She could tell that it was going to crash through at any second. *Poor Ms. Wilson.* Helena didn't want to imagine Ms. Wilson dying. She had known her since she was born. Ms. Wilson was like another grandmother to her.

"We have to hurry," her father said as he began running. He, too, could see that there wasn't a lot of time left to save Ms. Wilson.

"Dad, be careful!" Helena advised as her father ran inside with a neighbor.

"Stay put right here, Helena."

Helena was shocked for a brief moment. She couldn't handle both of her parents being inside of a crumbling house. "Ma, please, don't."

"It'll be quicker with more people helping."

"But what about an aftershock," this whole situation was too unpredictable. Helena didn't like that.

"We'll be fine, sweetie. I promise," her mother hugged her and kissed the top of her head.

Helena tried her best to calm herself as her mother went inside. A crowd was slowly forming around the house. Everyone kept their eyes on the unstable home, anticipating the worst. Helena was hoping—praying for the best. The minutes seemed to drag on. How long did it take to remove an armoire?

Then she remembered what the neighbor said. The armoire was in the room *with* Ms. Wilson, and it was blocking the bedroom door. Ms. Wilson's bedroom was on the second floor, and her bedroom window was boarded up due to a previous earthquake. Helena remembered. She was the one who helped boarded it up. That meant that everyone inside had to try to push the door open with the heavy armoire blocking the way. Helena wondered how many people it would take to accomplish that.

She was getting antsier by the second. The crowd of spectators was increasing. Helena had the urge to just scream. This situation just didn't feel right to her. Of course, she wanted Ms. Wilson to be saved, but she didn't want her parents in there either. She concluded that they needed more people inside. That was how this could get done quickly.

Without thinking, Helena headed for the front door. She could help them, and she could get her parents out of there. Helena was just about to walk up the front walkway when she felt a rumble. Someone quickly snatched her back as she heard screams coming from inside. They were terrifying screams.

It took a moment for Helena to realize what just happened. She felt like her eyes were playing tricks on her. At first, Ms. Wilson's house was standing—caved in roof and all. Now, the house was a crumbling mess. The shingles of the roof were at direct eye level.

There had been a rumble.

At first, Helena thought that it was an aftershock, but she was now slowly realizing that it was from the house crashing down.

The screams.

The agonizing screams were coming from the occupants inside...and from her.

The person who snatched her back quickly released her and rushed to help the people trapped under the rubble. Helena couldn't stop screaming as she sank to the ground. She didn't have the strength to stand.

This couldn't be happening.

This *can't* be happening, not to her. She needed them to be alive.

Someone came and wrapped their arms around her. It was a boy who looked to be about her age—maybe a year or two older, 15 or 16.

"It's ok," he said. "It's going to be ok."

Helena allowed him to rock her back and forth. She needed comfort. She watched as the spectators rushed to save everyone inside. But as they pulled lifeless body after lifeless body out of the heavy rubble, hope was slowly starting to drain out of her. Helena was all alone. She didn't need to see her parents' bodies to know that.

How was she going to survive in this world all alone?

**

Helena was numb. The days that followed her parents' death was a haze. She couldn't remember when the last time she ate or slept. She couldn't even remember how she got home that day. Did she walk back? Or did someone carry her? Was it the boy who had consoled her? She couldn't even remember if there had been another earthquake or a blackout since then. Helena couldn't bother to feel anything but disbelief and grief. She couldn't be in this world alone. There was no way she could survive it.

She didn't go past the couch in the living room. It was too much for her to make it anywhere that her parents had been, especially their bedroom. Helena had to come up with a plan—quick. She wasn't sure when the next disaster would hit, but she knew she couldn't be alone for it. She needed to find the strength to get off the couch and look for her sister. Jade had to come home now that their parents were gone. There was no way she could just leave Helena alone to fend for herself.

No way.

Helena struggled to push the fear back as she headed for the front door. She had never gone outside without her parents before. Her father had warned her how dangerous it was now. Besides the people in their neighborhood, she couldn't trust anyone. But Helena needed to be brave and press on. She had a hunch about where Jade might be, and she wanted to be back before night hit.

That was what terrified her the most. The night. The darkness. She saw different sides of people during that time.

"I'm coming for you, Jade," she said as she headed out the door.

Her steps were quick and urgent. She wasn't really in the mood to chat with anyone nor in the mood to tell them where she was going. The less information they knew, the better. Helena was aware that the thought made her seem paranoid, but she was on her own. She could only survive if she thought like that.

Luckily for her, her destination was only a half-mile away from her house. Somerset Mall. A lot of people in the Metro Detroit area dubbed it "the rich people" mall. And that was somewhat true. It was "the rich people" mall. But the mall also had an affordable side to it too. It was divided by a skywalk. Sometimes Jade and Helena ventured over to the rich side of the mall from time to time.

"For a little peace and quiet," Jade always said with a smirk. Helena agreed with her. The rich side was vastly more peaceful.

As she approached the mall, Helena paused. It was just a few blocks away, but she wondered if it had fell victim to looters. A lot of stores and businesses were like that now. Rundown. Victimized. Abandoned. Some store owners either left the store to fend on its own or were beaten and had it stolen from them.

Helena remembered her father telling her and her mother how the man who lived around the corner was beaten as looters robbed his store. Her father said they left him with nothing but a bloody face and broken bones. It wasn't clear what the looters did to young girls, but something told her that she should keep her distance.

The mall was in clear view.

Helena hid behind some nearby bushes and watched. The place attracted a lot of people. A large number of people streamed in and out of the building with things in their arms. It didn't seem chaotic and hectic. It seemed like the building wanted to provide people with supplies that they needed to survive.

But Helena wasn't buying it. Something in her gut was telling her that this scenario was off. And one thing about her, she always went with her gut feeling.

That was the thing with the Willer sisters. They always went with their gut feeling.

Jade said that it was their spirit talking to them—warning them about things they couldn't see. Jade told her that they were special because not everyone could listen to their spirit and understand what it was saying. Helena loved it when her sister told her that. She used to think that they were magical.

Sadly, she no longer thought that way. Not since she and Jade drifted apart.

Helena got comfortable behind the bush. She prepared for a long wait. This was as close as she was willing to get to the mall. She was not a fighter, and to go closer to the mall, you had to be one.

The day slowly drifted on with no crazy incidents. A few fights broke out between some looters, but none of them turned deadly. At least, not from what Helena saw anyway. She was going to give her watch a few more minutes before she headed home. Nighttime was a few hours away. She didn't want to cut it close.

A small part of her felt ridiculous. She was honestly naïve enough to think that she was going to find Jade on the first day. At the time, it seemed like an obvious lead. Jade loved going to the mall with her friends and Vincent. Why wouldn't she retreat to something familiar to feel safe?

But as Helena sat there watching different people approach the mall, she started to think that maybe this was a bad idea. However, it was the only idea she had. She didn't feel brave enough to venture any further on her own. This plan had to work. She just needed to keep coming back until she sees Jade.

Helena quickly got up from her hiding spot—making sure she wasn't seen. She headed back home. Once she got back into the safety of her house, she barricaded herself inside and prepared herself for the night.

**

For a week straight, Helena went back to the mall only to come home disappointed. As the days went by, she was no closer to finding Jade. Helena was becoming discouraged. Her plan wasn't working, and she didn't know what else to do. To make matters worse, Helena was starting to run low on food. She would have to go scavenging soon, and she had no clue as to where to start. Her father always went out to find food. Helena had no clue what to do.

As she made her journey to the mall, Helena came up with a plan to scavenge through some houses for food. If she were desperate, she would search through a few businesses.

Helena placed herself in her usual hiding spot behind the bush and watched the mall. The day was very energetic. It didn't take long before fights began to break out.

Usually, Helena didn't really care about the fights, but something about today made her really anxious. The people seemed riled up—vicious. What was making them feel that way? The endless earthquakes? The rolling blackouts? The government's inability to explain why this was all happening? Helena was annoyed with the nation's leaders' failure to understand why all of this was going on. But that didn't make her volatile. It just made her yearn for the truth.

She had been at her hideout for about 15 minutes, and five different fights had already broken out. All of them were very lethal. The last one resulted with a man sprawled out on the ground. Helena was pretty sure that he was bleeding to death. Her gut was telling her that she should get out of there. Helena reluctantly had to cut her day short. She'd promise to resume her search for Jade tomorrow.

Her original plan was to watch the mall for Jade for a few hours and then scavenge for food. But seeing how riled up people were today, Helena was starting to think that the latter part of her plan was no longer a good idea. Just then, her stomach growled, and Helena groaned. She had to scavenge for food. The only thing she had eaten was peanuts, and she ate that for dinner the night before.

Helena waited until she was several blocks away from the mall before she attempted to scavenge through houses.

The neighborhood was still good—in that it was safe. So, Helena figured she would be ok looking for food there. That thought didn't deter her from picking up a piece of wood for a weapon, though. She stood at the end of the block, looking over the houses. She was trying to figure out which house looked promising. Helena wanted to get in and get out as quickly as possible. She didn't want any drama.

The mini brick mansion, a few doors down, looked very hopeful. Helena began making her way to it but came to an abrupt stop. If the home looked promising to her, then it probably looked desirable to looters too. Helena began to look for another house.

The one thing that she always admired about living in Troy was the variety of homes in the neighborhood. You could find a mini-mansion and an old farmhouse on the same block. It amazed and confused her.

Helena made her way to the old farmhouse that was on the corner. She almost missed it because it was blocked by so many trees and bushes. As she approached it, she realized that the house had a storm shelter right next to it. Helena smiled. This was looking like a great idea, after all. Helena went to the storm shelter's door and banged on it. Then she quickly ran and hid on the side of the house. She waited a few minutes to see if anyone would come out. No one did. She repeated the process again just to be on the safe side.

Once it was clear that no one was inside, Helena slowly opened the storm shelter door. Again, she waited to see if anyone was going to approach her. After a while, she finally descended the stairs.

It wasn't much in the storm shelter. There were just a small cot and a shelf with some canned food and bottled water. It appeared someone was living there at some point—the dishevelment of the pillow and blanket on the cot gave that away. But Helena could see the person hadn't been there for a while, considering all the dust gathered on the cans and bottled water.

Helena gathered up everything she could carry in her bag and headed out of the storm shelter. She froze at the entrance.

There was a group of teens waiting for her there. It was five of them—three boys and two girls. They all looked to be around her sister's age. Helena noticed that the guy closest to her was the guy who consoled her the day her parents died. She didn't know how to proceed.

"Hey there," the guy smiled.

Helena hesitated for a moment, looking over each teenager. "Hey."

"How are you doing?" the guy seemed genuinely concerned. "You know, since your parents died."

"I'm fine," Helena snapped. She didn't know why the question bothered her so much.

"Find anything good down there?" one of the girls asked.

"Not really. You can take a look for yourself if you want."

The smile the girl displayed told Helena that she knew she was lying. "No, that's alright."

"We were just about to check out the house, actually," the guy said. "You want to join us?"

Helena nodded. Although she was a little leery about the group, the guy who consoled her made her a little curious. It was his kindness that was throwing her off.

"Alright, everyone," the other girl said in an authoritative tone. "In your positions." She looked over at Helena. "You..."

"Helena."

"Vicky. Helena, you stay here and look out for anyone coming."

"Ok."

"I'll stay up here with you," the guy smiled.

"Wait for our signal before going inside," Vicky continued.

Helena had no clue what she was talking about, but she still nodded. She watched as the rest of the group spread out around the house. Helena couldn't help but envy them; they all seemed like a team—a family. She wanted that desperately. She hated being alone.

"I'm Johnathan, by the way."

Helena gave him a weak smile.

"So, have you been surviving on your own...you know...since your parents died?"

Helena turned away from him, not wanting him to see the tears she was struggling to keep at bay. She tried hard not to think about her parents since their death. Johnathan was making that impossible.

Noticing her silence, he said, "Sorry again,...for your loss."

"Thanks."

"We're clear," the other girl came around the front. "Heading inside now."

Johnathan looked back at her. "Kim, I think Helena and I are going to keep a lookout while you all look around."

Kim looked over at Helena and raised her eyebrows. "Alright."

Johnathan watched Kim go into the house before he returned his attention back to Helena. "So, are you alone?"

Helena sighed. She was trying to avoid answering that question. Still, she could tell that Johnathan was going to be insistent about it. "For now. I'm looking for my sister."

"Your sister? How come she's not with you?"

"She left home almost a year ago."

"How old is she?"

"What's with all the questions?" Helena snapped. She couldn't understand why he was prying.

"I'm sorry. I was just wondering if she was around my age. I might know her. We're all from a group home. We're pretty friendly with the runaways."

Helena began to feel bad for snapping at him. "You're from a group home?"

Johnathan smiled. "Yeah, we all are," he gestured back toward the farmhouse.

"I'm sorry. She's 16. Her name is Jade."

"Jade, huh?" he stared off. It appeared that he was concentrating— trying to put a face to the name. Finally, he wore the look of defeat. "I'm sorry. I don't think I know her."

"That's alright," Helena didn't bother to get hopeful. "I've been searching for her at the mall."

He looked at her wide-eyed. "The mall? You really went over there?"

"I hid and watched from a bush two blocks away."

"But still, that's really brave."

"Well, I'm not brave enough to go any further. That's the only place I've looked for her."

"How old are you?"

"14."

"I'm 15."

"Great."

"Why don't you stay with us?" he suggested. "And I can help you look for your sister in other places."

Helena hated to admit it, but she liked the idea of having someone with her while she searched for Jade. It made the quest less scary. Johnathan seemed alright, but she wasn't so sure about the rest of them.

"I don't know," she finally said. She didn't want to appear too eager for company.

"Oh, come on, you can't expect to survive all on your own."

Helena looked away for a moment. Then she spotted a group of people going into a couple of houses down the street. She and Johnathan couldn't be seen; of course, the trees and bushes did a great job hiding them. But her gut was telling her that if they stayed any longer, the outcome wouldn't be pleasant.

"Looters," she warned.

Johnathan let out two urgent whistles. The group quickly rushed out of the farmhouse. Before Vicky could ask what was going on, they all heard screams coming from down the street. They all ducked down behind the shrubbery.

"We should go out through the backyard," one of the guys said.

"Lead the way, Will," Vicky ordered.

They all followed Will. Johnathan waited for Helena before following them. Once she was near him, he quickly grabbed her hand. She was about to protest when she realized why he took her hand. The group was fast—impossibly fast to Helena. They were already at the end of the half-acre backyard and hopping over the fence. Helena struggled to keep up. If it wasn't for Johnathan, she was sure that the group would've left her by now.

Once they got to the fence, Johnathan boosted her over and then quickly followed. They all ran a few more blocks until the screams could no longer be heard.

"Great job as lookout, Johnathan," Vicky said once they were at a safe distance.

"It was actually Helena who spotted the trouble."

Vicky looked over at Helena. "Thanks."

"No problem."

"I was just telling Helena that she should join our crew," Johnathan said, smiling.

"Sure, she's more than welcome if she wants. We could use another lookout."

"Plus," Kim said, smiling at Helena. "I found this beautiful jacket for her."

It was an old faded blue jean jacket. Helena couldn't tell if she was trying to be funny or what, but she actually did really like it.

"Thanks," Helena said, taking it.

"You welcome." The offer seemed genuine enough.

"I would like to join your crew, but I have one request," the group looked at Helena skeptically.

"What's that?" Vicky asked.

"We all stay at my house."

"We never stay at one location for long. That's a good way to get you killed."

"I'm talking about just for the night."

Vicky raised an eyebrow. "Why?"

"I'm looking for my sister. This will be my last shot before I give up on the notion of finding her at all."

Vicky considered Helena's statement for a moment. "You look pretty young."

"I'm 14."

"Must be very hard surviving out here on your own."

Helena nodded.

"Alright, Helena, you can have your one night. Lead the way."

~4~

Razor

Failure. *Failure. Failure.*

That was the only way Razor could describe himself at the moment. *Failure. Failure. Failure.* He was a bloody mess. Four lifeless bodies were strewn about the floor. And his mother lay still in his arms—the warmth of her body slowly fading away. *Failure. Failure. Failure.* His whole mission—his entire existence since the new world came about was to protect his parents. Razor failed half of his mission when his father died. The other half when Jill drew her last breath.

Failure. Failure. Failure.

After their house was destroyed, life had been more chaotic for Razor and his mother. They could no longer stay in one place. They had to move from house to house if they wanted to stay alive. The state had turned lawless. There were no rules anymore. Anything and everything was now fair game. The unpredictability of people was starting to frustrate Razor. And the more frustrated he became, the more lethal he was toward people.

For a long while, Razor had blamed his self for his father's death. He should've been quicker that day; he should've predicted that the supply shelf was going to tip over. It should've been bolted down. Razor couldn't stop blaming his self; he failed to keep his father safe.

Jill, on the other hand, blamed the earthquake for her husband's death. She had spent weeks consoling her son and reassuring him that Roger's death was not his fault. Jill could see the guilt that was eating at her son. She wanted to take that away from him.

During the passing weeks, after their home was destroyed, Razor implored that they moved from house to house. They both quickly saw that the environment was getting worse by the day. Shelter was the hottest commodity. So, he had to fight to get it and keep it. The only major hiccup to it all was the stability of the home. That was the most challenging part of finding shelter—a building that wasn't severely damaged by the earthquakes. At the moment, there was no such thing as a stable structure.

But on their last week, Razor found a building that was well structured. It was a storefront boutique. They sold unique and custom women's clothing. Like most stores, it was now abandoned. Razor and his mother had just scavenged for some food and supplies when they came across the building. The area had already been scouted, so Razor knew that the building was safe.

They hid out there for the night. It was the most peaceful night that they had in a while. Jill didn't want to leave when the morning came. It was the first time Razor saw Jill happy and stress-free since Roger died. Razor didn't have the heart to make his mother leave, so against his better judgment, they stayed.

They resided at the boutique for a week without incident. It had been the longest they stayed in one place since they left their home. They camped in what used to be the manager's office. Razor stored all their food and supplies back there as well. They rarely left the building. They had enough supplies that could last them awhile.

As the days dragged on, Razor was beginning to find his self bored. He was bored with the situation—bored with the environment. He was tired of scavenging and looking for shelter. It was the end of the world. And through all the unpredictability, Razor was starting to find everything predictable.

Fight to find supplies. Fight to find shelter. Fight to stay alive.

Razor loved fighting but was hating the predictability of it. He would soon regret that thought.

Razor's first mistake: he got too lax.

He was sleeping in the manager's office while his mother was exploring the stockroom. Jill loved the store's clothing, and she was going through the merchandise, picking out the clothes she liked. They both were in desperate need of clothing. The stockroom was right next to the manager's office, so Razor saw no reason why his mother couldn't explore on her own. He had been keeping watch all night and was exhausted. He planned on closing his eyes for like 30 minutes, and then he would prepare dinner.

Razor was falling into a deep slumber when he thought he heard a sound. But he quickly dismissed it—thinking his mind was playing tricks on him.

His second mistake.

It was eerily quiet for a moment, and then Jill let out a short and quick scream. Razor jumped up when he heard it. His heart was pounding. The weirdness of the cry concerned him. It was short and quick, as if someone or something quickly stopped her from alerting him.

Razor thought his eyes were deceiving him when he got into the inventory room. Jill lay on the floor—blood oozing down her throat. Four men stood smug over her.

Razor blacked out.

Jill was lying in his arms when he finally came to—the warmth of her body slowly fading away. Four lifeless bodies were strewn about the floor. Razor was a bloody mess, and he was a failure. His mother was dead because of him. He became too lax—bored. Now his mother paid the price for that. Her eyes glazed over and stared into nothingness.

Razor was a failure—he failed his mission. In this new world, he couldn't keep his parents alive.

Failure. Failure. Failure.

**

Six months later.

Razor approached the makeshift recruiting office with determination. He needed some guidance in his life. The months without his parents were terrible. Razor thought his outbursts were out of control before. It was nothing compared to now. He was ruthless and out of control. It wasn't clear if it was because he was still angry with his mother's death or because he was now free. His parents were no longer holding him back.

Since his mother's death, Razor killed a lot more people. Some of them were justified, and some of them were for vague reasons. After his last altercation, Razor realized what his problem was—the lack of a mission. A mission always seemed to focus him. He was sure that would help control him.

Over the past six months, the army became heavily involved with restoring order. It wasn't complete order. Of course, some things had gone undetected, but it was beginning to get a little civil again. The government still didn't know how long the disasters would last, but they were trying to gain more control—hold on to vital resources. The army was able to help them do that.

Makeshift recruitment places began to open. With the major earthquakes and other disasters, the army had lost a significant amount of people and was in dire need of more. Razor had debated whether he should join or not. He was never that great with following other people's rules, but it made his decision final after his last altercation.

As he walked up to the recruiting office, he recalled the dreadful confrontation.

After his mother's death, Razor wandered aimlessly around the streets. He didn't bother looking for shelter and hunkering down somewhere. It had been months, and Razor saw no desire to seek stability. Instead, he picked fights. It all was for vague and random reasons, but mostly it was to take people's food. As of lately, he couldn't even take it upon his self to scavenge for food. It was way more fun and exhilarating to just forcefully take it from someone else.

On this particular day, Razor was following this big, burly guy for a few hours. The guy was scavenging for supplies at various businesses. The plan was to follow the guy back to his hideout, and then Razor would attack him there. The guy's size excited him. It looked like he would put up a good fight.

The last few altercations left Razor extremely disappointed. It was easy to overpower them and take their stuff that Razor felt like he really didn't earn it. He was really hoping that wouldn't be the case with this new guy.

The man searched three more buildings before heading to his hideout. It was an old, rundown daycare center. Once he was inside, Razor waited a few minutes before sneaking in. Razor found the guy in a big spacious room that looked to be the napping area.

"I'm still unloading," the guy said with his back to Razor. He assumed that he was someone else. When the guy turned around, he looked shocked.

Razor immediately punched the man in the face. He got two hits in before the guy went for his waist. The man screamed as he tackled Razor to the ground. The two men tussled on the floor. The guy still managed to get the upper hand on Razor.

Multiple footsteps were approaching. Then there was the sound of children screaming. The guy looked over—alarmed. Razor took that moment to elbow the guy in the face.

"Greg!" a woman shrieked as Greg flew back and hit the floor. The children screamed even louder.

Razor quickly got to his feet.

There were a woman and two young children standing in the entryway—frightened.

Greg quickly rose to his feet as Razor got closer. The two men both charged at each other. Greg managed to punch Razor a few times in the face. Razor endured the blows as he wrapped his arm around Greg's neck. The woman and the children screamed some more as the man struggled in Razor's arm.

"Please, just take whatever you want and go!" the woman cried.

Razor ignored her; her words couldn't get through to him. He wanted a fight. Nothing she could say would stop him from getting that.

Greg found his strength to headbutt Razor as hard as he could. Razor stumbled back—his hold instantly broken. Blood poured out of his nose. Greg struggled for breath. Razor smiled in satisfaction. He was getting what he wanted. It didn't take long for Greg to turn his attention back to him.

Once again, he went for Razor's legs. He immediately slammed Razor to the ground. Greg got in a few blows before Razor began returning them. One of Razor's punches seemed to have broken Greg's nose. Blood was gushing out of it. Greg fell off Razor. Razor proceeded to get on top of Greg and continued to punch him.

Unfortunately, it appeared that the big man had no more fight in him. This angered Razor. He really needed a challenge, and Greg wasn't giving him one. He started to see red. Razor began punching him furiously.

Then someone ran up behind him.

Instinctively, Razor turned around and pushed them. It took a few minutes for him to realize his terrible mistake.

The children were crying and screaming hysterically.

Greg lay unconscious on the floor.

And across the room, the woman lay on the floor with blood slowly pouring out of her head.

"Mommy!" the children rushed to her side. The woman was unresponsive.

Razor slowly rose to his feet as he came to the scary realization of what he just did. During his rage, he pushed the woman, sending her flying across the room and causing her to crash land into a wooden bookcase.

The children shook their mother to no avail. One of the children, a girl, looked over at Razor with terror in her eyes.

"What did you do?!" she screamed. "You hurt my mommy!"

Razor backed away from them slowly. Guilt and regret washed over him. He made his way out of the building—the children's screams and cries *haunting him.*

Determination coursed through Razor as he entered the recruiting office. This was his last shot at making something of himself.

The office used to be a post office. The P.O. boxes were still lined up when Razor walked in. He was surprised by how well they looked. Besides the dirt that covered them, they were in pristine condition. The office was empty. Razor thought the place would be overflowing with people who wanted to join. Who wouldn't? The army provided you with food and shelter. Who wouldn't want that?

The officer at the desk appeared bored. He was aimlessly drawing on a piece of paper when Razor approached the desk.

"I'm not giving out any food or supplies, so fuck off," the guy said without looking at Razor.

"I'm looking to join."

"Join what?" the guy looked up, surprised.

Razor wondered how smart the guy was. "The army," he said as if it was apparent.

"Really? Why?"

"I didn't know I needed a reason."

The guy scrunched up his face. "Sorry, I just don't get that many people signing up."

Razor looked around the empty office again. "I wonder why."

"It seems like people would rather beg for supplies than serve," the guy gathered up some papers. "Every fucking day, I get people in here begging for food and shit...lazy fucks."

Razor ignored the guy's rant. He looked around again, trying to see if there was someone else he could deal with other than this guy—anybody. To his disappointment, there was no one else there. The guy finished gathering up all the necessary paperwork and handed them over to Razor with a clipboard and pen.

"Fill these out," he instructed. "You can take a seat over there."

Razor followed to where the guy was pointing. A chair was sitting near a window. Razor took a seat and began to fill out the papers. It felt odd to be filling out an application, considering everything that was happening at the moment. It felt oddly strange to him,...and normal. Razor went through the application with no issues. He hasn't done anything so mundane in a while.

Once he was done with the application, he got up and headed back to the desk where the recruitment officer sat. The officer had gone back to doodling on his scrap piece of paper and looked up when Razor was approaching.

"All set?"

Razor placed the completed application in front of the officer. He was a little annoyed with him. The officer liked to point out the obvious.

The guy glanced over the application quickly. "Alright, Mr. Thompson, come around back with me," he opened the half-panel door, so Razor could follow.

They sat down at a desk in the back office. The officer opened a laptop and turned it on. Razor couldn't help but stare.

"Seems like forever since I've seen one of those," he looked at the bulky laptop. "That thing get the internet?"

"A straight satellite feed," the officer was now typing in information into the computer. Razor figured that he was looking him up.

"Glad to know that those are still working."

The officer didn't respond. He kept typing information into the computer. Razor wondered what kind of information the officer was looking for. He pondered what the requirements were to be in the military. Could a criminal record stop him? He worried that they could deny him for that. What would he do if he couldn't join the military? Razor needed saving from his self—he knew this. The army was his only saving grace. It could provide him guidance and a mission for his life. If left wondering, he could be a danger to everyone he meets.

His last altercation proven that.

"Hmm," the officer frowned as he scrolled through the computer. "I see that you were charged with assault."

Razor got uncomfortable. He hoped that he wouldn't see that. "Yeah, that was a little mishap."

"That was almost a year ago."

"Correct. Just a little misfortune of an 18-year-old."

"And a 19-year-old is much wiser?"

"This one is."

"Hmm," the officer frowned again. "Tell me, Mr. Thompson, with all honesty, before the government implemented martial law, have you killed anyone?"

"In self-defense."

"And how many was that?"

"I've...lost count," Razor was ashamed to admit that.

"I see," the officer went back to the computer. "Well, Mr. Thompson, I don't think you will be a good fit for us, but there is a new branch that the government is working on that I think will suit you."

"A new branch?"

"From my understanding, most of our vital resources are depleting. The government is working on preserving them so we can rebuild once everything dies down. One of them is medical care. The government is putting together a task force that will help preserve it and keep away anyone who may try to abuse it."

"And I qualify for that."

"I think you might have what it takes to enforce that law...once it passes, of course."

"Ok...and it offers the same thing that the military does?"

"It does...so are you interested?"

"What's the name?"

The officer frowned. "It's a weird one...the DC task force."

**

A fellow cadet came charging at Razor at full speed. Razor waited for him to get closer before he struck. He couldn't stand the cadet who was attacking him. He had seen guys like him before—boastful, pretending like they were a huge threat. The guy made the other cadets feel intimated. Razor knew the guy was all bark with no bite. He simply stepped aside as the cadet got within reach. Before he could react, Razor had him in the air by his throat and began slamming him repeatedly. The other cadets cheered Razor on.

As the guy was on the ground, he quickly struck Razor in the face with his elbow. Razor had loosened his grip a little, and the guy managed to get out of Razor's grasp. He tackled Razor, and both men fell over. The guy pulled back to punch Razor, but Razor caught his wrist and snapped it. The guy cried out in pain. The cheers grew louder. Razor managed to pin the guy down and was now punching the guy repeatedly.

Then he blacked out.

"This is not how we do things, cadet!" the Captain was screaming when Razor came to. "This is a brotherhood. We do not fight our brothers."

"Tell that to that asshole," Razor still saw red. He barely noticed the other big, muscular guy in the room.

"I don't care—"

"What did he do?" the other guy asked. He was leaning against a bookcase on the back wall.

Razor glanced over at him for a moment. "He was bullying one of the cadets. I got tired of it and said something."

"Bullying, huh..."

"Lies," the Captain said. "I've heard no such thing."

Razor glared at the Captain. "There's been unequivocal evidence. You've just overlooked them because he kisses your ass."

The Captain struggled to keep his composure. "As you can see, Cadet Thompson can be very defiant. I don't think he's fit for this program."

The other guy looked bored and annoyed. "Bring in the other cadet."

"Sir," the Captain began, shocked.

"I said, bring him in."

Razor guessed that this other guy ranked higher than the Captain. The guy's voice was very authoritative and commanding. Plus, the Captain seemed very afraid of him and his presence. The Captain reluctantly went out to get the other cadet.

The two men stood in the office in silence for a moment. The guy looked at Razor with a smirk—appraising him. Usually, the look would make any other person uncomfortable, but Razor was unfazed by it.

The Captain finally came in with the other cadet.

The cadet's face was a swollen, bloody mess. Both eyes were swollen shut, his nose was broken, a few cuts were under his cheek, his bottom lip was split, and his right wrist was broken. The Captain guided him to a chair where he could sit.

The other guy chuckled. "Now I've seen the other guy," he glanced over at Razor with a look of approval.

"Cadet Davis," the Captain began. "Cadet Thompson has made

accusations that you've been bullying some of your other comrades. We brought you in to defend yourself. Care to explain?"

"*We?* Now, who's lying, Captain," the guy smirked. He turned his attention to Davis. "Explain yourself."

Cadet Davis shifted in his seat. "The asshole demanded to know if I attacked another cadet in the showers. I told him he wasn't my commanding officer, and I didn't need to explain myself to him."

"You did it," Razor mumbled.

Davis turned toward him and spat at Razor's feet.

"Attacked him how?" the guy asked Razor.

"It's said that he pinned the guy down and shoved a broomstick handle up his ass."

"That's a lie," the Captain said once again.

"Did you do it?" the guy asked Cadet Davis. The cadet paused, not sure if he should answer or not. "I assure you, cadet, I *am* your commanding officer. In fact, I am the Commander of this whole operation. Now answer me."

"I...I did. But that was because he stole one of my rations."

"That's a lie," Razor interjected. "You found your misplaced ration before you assaulted him."

"Is that true? I must warn you, cadet, it's not wise to lie to me," the guy advised.

"Many people thought he stole from me. I wanted to show them what would happen if they cross me."

The Captain hung his head in shame. The cadet was his favorite, and he went out on a limb for him. He was disappointed in being proven wrong.

Razor couldn't help but feel a little smug. He never liked Davis. He disliked him a little more when he discovered that the Captain favored him. Razor was glad that the truth finally came out. It felt better than beating him to a bloody pulp. The other guy, the Commander, wore a strange look on his face.

"Before you came in cadet, your Captain was just shouting at Cadet Thompson here about how this program is a brotherhood. Do you feel like this program is a brotherhood?"

Cadet Davis hesitated. Razor could tell that he was considering lying but then remembered the Commander's warning. He sighed.

"To be honest, sir, I only see this as a means of survival."

"Hmm," the guy looked like he was considering something. "I appreciate the honesty. I'm not stupid. I know that most of the men have signed up as a means of survival. Still, most of them also understand that for this program to succeed, we have to work as one," he moved away from the bookcase he was leaning on. He stood tall. "You cannot act like those savages out there to one another. Otherwise, what will separate the authorities from those that need to be ruled?"

Razor couldn't stop the involuntary smirk that spread across his face. He could see what the Commander was about to do. Apparently, the Captain and the cadet did not.

The Commander walked behind Davis and placed his hand on his shoulder. He sighed. "Sodomizing a fellow cadet with a broomstick because people thought he stole from you shows me that you don't belong." Without saying anything further, the Commander had his hands on both sides of the cadet's face. He snapped Davis's neck before he had time to react.

The Captain screamed out in shock.

The Commander looked up and smiled. "A piece of advice, *Captain*, choose your favorites wisely. Cadet Thompson, please follow me."

Razor didn't hesitate to follow the Commander out of the office. He approved of his action. If it wasn't for the officers who pulled Razor off the cadet, Razor would've done the same thing.

"I like the way you handled that situation, Thompson."

"Was just doing what was required."

"That's good. I need men like that."

Razor didn't say anything. He was waiting for the question that was sure to follow.

"What's your name?"

"My legal name is Ryan, but I strongly prefer Razor."

"Razor," the guy contemplated for a moment. "What did you do before all this shit went down, Razor?"

"Stirred up a lot of trouble," Razor smirked. He didn't know what it was about this guy, but he was comfortable telling him the truth. He didn't feel judged like he did with other people.

"I have a feeling 'a lot' is an understatement," the guy smiled. "Tell me, Razor, how do you like the program so far?"

They walked out of the office building and was now heading toward a truck. The guy unlocked it and opened the driver's door; he motioned for Razor to get in.

"It's ok," Razor slid into the passenger's seat. "When you remove all the politics."

The guy chuckled. "Politics can indeed snuff out the fun of everything," he agreed. "I've seen the fight. You have severe rage, Razor."

"I've been told," Razor hated when people told him that.

"I like that. I could really use it," the guy started the truck. "I believe you're done with all this training bullshit. How would you feel working beside me?"

"Doing what, exactly?"

The Commander smirked. "More important things than this shit."

Razor liked where he was at, but he hated the Captain. And now that his favorite cadet was killed, Razor was sure that the Captain was going to make the rest of his training hell.

"I'll work with you," he finally said. "Just one thing...you know my name. I think it's fair that I get yours."

"The name's Nick," he threw the truck in drive and sped off. "Nick Sturman."

~5~

Razor

One *year later.*

Two men slammed Razor down onto a bar table, causing the table to snap in half. Razor landed on his back—hard. He quickly grabbed one of the men's legs and managed to break the guy's ankle. The assailant screamed out in pain as he dropped to the ground. Razor grabbed a beer bottle that was nearby and smashed it against the guy's head. The man's cries instantly became silent as he was knocked unconscious.

The second man, looking to avenge his friend, came at Razor with a broken chair leg. Razor took a piece of shard glass from the broken beer bottle and rose to his feet. The man swung the chair leg wildly. Razor dodge out of the way quickly. The guy only hit air. Once the man was close, Razor stabbed the guy in the side and in his shoulder. The man grunted in pain. His movements began to get slower. It didn't take long for Razor to incapacitate him.

Chaos ensued in the bar.

Razor tried to remember what happened as he stared at his bloody hands. All he could recall was that he and Nick were at the bar ordering drinks. They spent all day in-and-out of meetings at the capitol building in Lansing and were looking to have a little fun. Both men had ordered a couple of beers. Razor was finishing off his second beer when Nick went across the room to talk with someone.

The next thing he knew, Nick was tussling with a man in the corner. Razor made his way to Nick's aide when four of the man's friends tried to jump in the fight. Then suddenly, a brawl pursued.

Glancing around the bar, Razor found Nick in the back, fighting off two guys simultaneously. Razor quickly made his way to him. When he was near, Razor grabbed one of the men by the neck and began slamming him repeatedly. Then someone tackled him from behind...

...when Razor came to, just about every piece of furniture in the bar was broken. Some of the non-fighting patrons were cowering in the corner by the bar's entrance. The bartender had a shotgun in his hand. Countless men lay unconscious on the floor, their faces beat and smashed in.

Nick stood in the center of the room, laughing hysterically.

Razor still shook with rage. Two men lay at his feet. It appeared they had been beaten to death. If that were the case, it would explain why all eyes on him look so terrified.

"Bring in the body bags!" Nick shouted with glee. Someone quickly left out the bar. Nick made his way over to Razor. "Thanks for having my back, friend."

Razor nodded. He was still trying to calm his self down.

Nick looked down at a man who was lying on the floor, groaning in pain. The man was beaten to a bloody pulp. "I think now I'll be taking your girl."

Right on cue, a tall blonde walked up to Nick and wrapped her arm around him. She looked at the man, smug.

"Can you believe this asshole, Razor?" Nick looked up at him. "I gave his lady a compliment, and he wanted to be a dick and tried to pick a fight with me."

Razor didn't say anything. Honestly, he didn't care what the reason was; he just wanted a fight. And when he was out with Nick, he usually got one. The best part was that Nick was always excited when he saw Razor's rage. He found it comical. Freeing. Exhilarating. And for once, Razor didn't feel judged or ashamed about it.

A group of men in black and grey fatigues came into the bar and attended to the wounded. A couple of them started cleaning the bar, while a few more began to place the two men Razor fought with into body bags.

Nick walked over to the bartender, the blonde right on his heels. "Sorry for the trouble," he slipped the guy some cash. "This should cover the damages."

The bartender nodded and gave Nick a weak smile. It was clear that the man was afraid of him.

"Well, I'm off to have some fun," Nick turned toward Razor and smiled. "See you in the morning, my friend."

Razor nodded as Nick left the bar. He still couldn't find it within his self to move. He watched as Nick's cleanup crew repair all the damage that they have done. Then someone handed him a towel.

It was a redhead woman. She looked at him, smiling. It was clear that she was impressed with him. "You might wanna clean the blood off your face, killer."

Razor did what she said. He didn't know what he looked like at the moment. But he imagined that it was scary. He wasn't sure if the dry towel would actually clean up all the blood, but he still tried.

The woman looked him up and down, appraising him. "You're sexy," she smirked. "You wanna get out of here?"

She didn't wait for an answer; she headed out of the bar. Razor followed.

**

The woman from the bar was still lying in Razor's bed when he awakened the next day. He was a little annoyed at that. He really didn't like his companions staying over once the deed was done. Razor didn't want them to get any ideas. Relationships, or anything that required permanence, was not his thing. And it definitely wasn't something he was looking for.

The redhead was lying on her stomach with her face turned away from him. She slightly stirred when Razor shook her. It took a moment to get her awake, and when she was, she turned toward him with a smile on her face. Razor didn't return it.

"You need to leave."

Her smile faded a little. "Someone's grumpy in the morning," she reached over and groped him. A sly smile spread across her face. "I can help with that."

Razor quickly pushed her hand away and proceeded out of bed. "I said leave."

"No need to get pissy."

"Now!" he growled.

The woman frowned and quickly got out of bed. She threw him daggered looks as she got dressed. "You're a real asshole, you know that?!"

"Never claimed to be otherwise."

"*Dick*," the woman stomped to the door, opened it, and slammed it shut once she was out of the room.

Razor sighed and glanced over his hotel room, making sure the woman didn't take anything while he was asleep. It was tough for him to trust anyone. Once he confirmed that nothing was missing, he proceeded to the bathroom to take a shower.

He and Nick have been residing at the Capital hotel for a month. Nick was there to finalize the details of the DC task force, and he brought Razor along. Some government officials needed a little convincing as to why the DC task force was necessary in the first place. So, they spent the weeks in and out of meetings, trying to show government officials why the DC task force was needed in today's society.

During his time in the capital, Razor learned that all the nation's capitals were maintained. It was the only place that reminded you of regular times. Of course, it was a place that was heavily guarded. A lot of soldiers secured the area. There was no such thing as looters in the capital.

It still had electricity, water, heat, and other essentials. There were actual businesses there too. Hotels. Restaurants. Bakeries. Clothing stores. And more. The government made sure that the capitals could withstand unexpected disasters. They put all their resources into sustaining them. Their reasoning was if the nation's capitals still stood, then rebuilding civilization was still a possibility.

When they first arrived in Lansing, Razor was amazed and furious.

Amazed that all of it was still around. Furious that these government officials were living lavish lives while their citizens were left to fend for themselves. If his parents were given a chance to live there, they would still be alive. But they were never given that option.

As Razor got out of the shower, he reflected on his year with Nick. He was an impressive man, which Razor quickly learned as time went on. Nick was well respected and feared by those who were in and out of the program. It didn't take long for the two men to become close friends. What Razor respected from Nick the most was the fact that he accepted him for who he was. There was only one other person who'd done that—his father. Because of that, Razor gave Nick his undying loyalty.

Plus, Nick was just as volatile as he was, which was an added bonus for Razor. He didn't feel so alone in that aspect anymore. And because of his interactions with Nick, people were starting to fear and respect Razor more.

Razor absolutely loved it.

There was a knock at the room door once he was fully dressed. Razor opened it. Nick stood on the other side, grinning from ear to ear.

"How was your night?" he asked, walking inside.

Razor shrugged. "Fine enough. How was the blonde?"

Nick scoffed. "Very disappointing. Wasn't worth the brawl after all," he chuckled. "That poor sap took a beating for nothing...oh well, lesson learned, I guess."

"Yeah, that sucks," Razor sat on the edge of the bed.

"I know you're tired of sitting in on meetings with me, but there's someone I want you to meet," Nick sat in the armchair that was across the room.

"Who is it?" Razor was leery with meeting another government official. He didn't care for them. And as far as he was concerned, none of them required his attention when it came to doing his job.

Just then, there was another knock at the door. This time Nick answered it.

"Chase," he greeted. "So glad you could make it."

"Of course, Nick. Anything for you."

Razor quickly rose to his feet as the President entered his room—alone. It was shocking to see him without a security detail.

"Razor, this is Chase," Nick said. "Chase, this is Razor, the promising young man I was telling you about."

"It's an honor meeting you, President Dooms."

"Oh, please, call me Chase when we're alone," he looked over at Nick. "So, I heard you two stirred up a lot of trouble last night."

Nick laughed. "That we did."

"Sounds like old times," Chase smirked, humor evident in his eyes.

"Just a bit deadlier with this one around," Nick gestured toward Razor. He and Chase laughed.

"Well, that'll get you both a lot more fear and respect, so that's a plus," Chase sighed.

"That it will."

Razor stood there silently, not really sure how to process this scene.

The President glanced down at his watch. "We should start heading down."

Nick sighed. "I hate that we have to try to convince these stupid bureaucrats."

"It's all for show, old friend. Trust me, this is happening. You just have to put that ole Nick charm to use. We don't want them to know what's really being done."

Nick laughed. "They'll see what I want them to see," he looked over at Razor. "Ready?"

Razor nodded and followed the two men out of the room.

**

"I just don't see the need of having a task force to patrol the hospitals," one of the Senators stated. "We're trying to hold onto civilization. How is the DC task force going to help us achieve that?"

Razor sat in the back corner of the banquet hall in the hotel. The President was hosting a luncheon where government officials could inquire as much information about the DC task force from him and Nick. The two men sat at a separate table in front of the room so everyone could see them.

"Resources," President Dooms answered. "That is how civilization survives by having the proper resources. We can't do that if everything we need is depleted. And trust me, healthcare is depleting."

"With all due respect, President Dooms," another Senator stood. It was clear that he was opposed to the President's ideas. "But given your previous profession as a healthcare worker, you could see how my colleagues and I are a little apprehensive with this new task force."

"And it is because of my background as a former surgeon that I am aware of how vital healthcare will be in our efforts to rebuild society."

"A former *plastic* surgeon," the Senator mumbled.

President Dooms glared at him. "If I recall correctly, *Senator*, I was nominated and voted in as President by you and your colleagues. I am doing what I can to make sure that America is still thriving when all of this is done. I challenge you to do better…I am not your enemy here."

"But I can show you who is," Nick stood, intervening. He didn't say anything else. Instead, he cued up a video, and the film started playing on the projector screen behind them.

Razor watched as the government officials looked on, horrified. The video showed different hospitals that were being overrun. It captured what was going on inside and outside of the hospitals.

One clip showed the sick and injured trampling over healthcare workers as they all tried to be first to receive aid. Another clip showed a nurse being beaten by a group of marauders as they stole medical supplies. A few clips showed people running out of the hospital with their arms filled with expensive (and now rare) medical equipment. Hospital staff attempted to chase after them but failed to catch them.

The last clip revealed a hospital being torched to the ground; a few healthcare workers ran out of the building as they caught on fire. Their excruciating screams filled the banquet hall.

The government officials let out horrified gasps. The images shocked them, and it infuriated Razor. These people needed to be dealt with. The savagery could not go on any longer.

"Savages," Nick said once the video ended. "That's what they are. Selfish savages that need to be ruled. Just look at how they quickly abused our weakest and most vulnerable system. Healthcare. You can get all that you need at a hospital. Food. First Aide. Hell, you can even get clothing and hygiene items if you're desperate. This is a gold mine for the sick."

"But all of the criminal acts were committed by looters," one Senator said, meekly. "Not the sick."

Nick looked at her with disbelief. "The sick and the looters are one and the same. Did you not see a group of nurses being trampled to death as the sick and injured overpowered them? Did you not see expensive and rare medical equipment being stolen? How can we replace those items? Can we just go online and order them? Can we wait 5 to 7 business days for it to be delivered? No!"

A few of the Senators began to mumble in agreement.

"The world is in a state of uncertainty," Nick continued. "And instead of our citizens coming together and behaving like one, they steal, they kill, and they behave like animals! They come up with ways to scheme and con us. But I say no more!"

"Yeah, no more of this shit!" a government official voiced.

"The army and the national guard cannot do this alone. We need a branch that will focus on protecting our weakest system. Because right now, it is being exploited the most."

The first Senator rose to her feet. "You have convinced me, Commander Sturman, but how do we respond to such savagery?"

"With brutality," Nick slowly looked around the room. He had everyone right where he wanted them. Razor could feel it. "And we put these savages where they belong...in cages."

The vote was unanimous. The DC task force would soon be rolling out to enforce the new medical law. The government officials agreed, the DC task force needed to protect the resources, no matter the cost.

A few hours later, Razor, Nick, and Chase sat at the hotel's bar, celebrating their victory. He didn't think it was possible, but Razor was very impressed with Nick's ability to sway people to his beliefs. Before the luncheon, just about every bureaucrat voiced their opposition on this issue. But as they were leaving, they were all but commending the notion of the DC task force and their mission.

"Well done, Nick!" Chase praised. "That's exactly what we needed."

"It's all about the editing, my friend," the two men laughed while Razor sipped on his beer. Nick took notice of his silence. "Everything alright, Razor?"

Razor nodded. The images of the video consumed his mind. "Just ready for the mission."

The President smiled widely and nudged Nick. "You found us a good one here."

Nick chuckled. "Trust me, my friend. We will be ruling over these savages before you know it."

"Copy that," he looked over at Chase. "So, you used to be a plastic surgeon?"

"In a former life. It's how I met good ole Nick here. He used to be head of security at a hospital I worked at. He was a hard-ass for the rules and safety there."

"The place was a shithole."

Chase took a sip of his bourbon. "It was a hospital in the poorest part of the city. I did a lot of free surgeries there as an act of charity."

"And then you somehow got into politics," Razor couldn't hide the disbelief in his tone.

"Yeah, I had a lot of politicians in my circle, and I had some extreme views about healthcare. One of my politician associates suggested that I try my hand in government, so I ran for US Senator and won."

"And wormed his way to presidency," Nick laughed.

Chase smirked and shrugged. "Thank the fucked-up disasters for that. All the people who were in line for the presidency were killed during all the chaos...lucky pricks. I never even asked to be nominated."

"But you have power, my friend."

"That I do," Chase looked down at his glass and then back up at the two men. "I kind of like it."

"Who wouldn't?!"

"And you two remained friends through it all," Razor couldn't see how Nick rose to be the creator of a new government branch.

"Well, when I became a Senator, there was no one I truly trusted for security. So, I brought on Nick to be a part of my new security detail. And as I rose, so did he. And once I became President, I quickly saw how healthcare was vastly depleting. So, I came up with the new medical law, basically stating that it's illegal to use the healthcare system without a form of payment or service."

"Of course, Chase needed reminding that the law required something to be in place to enforce it."

"So, I entrusted Nick to do it. He's been great from the start."

"Gentlemen, we are making history," Nick raised his beer bottle to toast. All men did. Nick took a sip and looked over at Razor. "My friend, you are lucky to be on the right side of it."

And he was right. Razor felt honored to be a part of it.

~6~

Helena

Six *months later.*

Helena stood in front of the bathroom mirror, staring at herself. 16-years-old. She was now 16 years old, and she was still no closer to finding Jade. It seemed like forever since her parents died. And it seemed like forever since she'd been with Vicky and her crew. She really didn't care for them—except for Johnathan. Helena found the others to be pretty mean. Johnathan was the only one that was nice.

Vicky and the others weren't particularly mean to her; it was more like they didn't care for her. As long as she did her job as a lookout, they really didn't bother to get to know her. Johnathan, on the other hand, wanted to know everything about Helena. It probably was because he liked her. She never had experience with guys liking her before. Helena didn't know how to deal with him besides being nice. She wasn't exactly sure how she felt about him. To be honest, the only thing that occupied her mind was finding her sister.

Helena felt so alone—even though she was a part of a group of six. She knew that she would feel complete once she found Jade. Helena was sure that she would've located her by now. Or that Jade would find her—if she were alive. What would she do if she found out that Jade was dead? Helena would truly be alone. She hated the thought of it.

Helena sighed as she stared into the mirror. She ran her hands through her short, pixie hair; it was freshly dyed mint green, thanks to Kim. They scavenged through an old big box store for supplies when Helena came across many boxed hair dyes. Helena took as much as she could—with the help of the group.

It wasn't until they got back to their hideout that Vicky, Kim, and Helena found out the dye was mint green. Vicky and Kim looked ok with the color, but they allowed it to grow out.

The mint green complimented Helena's golden-brown skin nicely. Her facial structure seemed to work with the color as well. Her heart-shaped face, her small round nose, and almond eyes seem to bring out the color nicely.

The green made Helena feel rebellious. She always viewed herself as a good girl, but once she dyed her hair, it made her feel...adventurous. It was a silly thought, Helena knew that, but she loved the feeling. She never wanted it to go away.

Johnathan took a real liking to her new look. He praised her daily. Johnathan complimented her so much that the other guys, Paul and Will, would tease him about it. He was embarrassed, but not enough to stop.

Helena didn't mind it. She found it flattering and a good distraction from her loneliness.

"Getting ready for a photo shoot in there?!" Kim asked, banging on the door.

"Sorry," Helena quickly snapped out of her trance and got dressed. "Give me another minute!"

It was a heist day.

Helena dreaded them, mostly since their latest target was hospitals. Hospitals became easy targets for the crew. The natural disasters hadn't stopped, and the increase of casualties brought chaos to the medical world. And through all that chaos, the group would slip in undetected and steal the necessary supplies for survival.

Helena never minded stealing supplies from houses, stores, and other businesses, but stealing from the sick and wounded seemed so wrong. So far, they've done four heists from the hospitals, and Helena felt so evil every time. She'd expressed her concerns with the crew before, but they all brushed her off. They told her she was dramatic. But that didn't stop her from worrying.

Plus, a rumor was floating around that a new law was coming into place that imprisoned those who abused the medical system. They would soon be caught for what they were doing.

"Damnit, Helena!" Kim pounded on the door again. "What the hell are you doing?!"

Helena rushed out of the bathroom and almost ran right into Kim. "Sorry," she walked around her. "All yours."

Johnathan was sitting on her bed when she walked into her room. At first, he didn't notice when Helena walked in. He was aimlessly staring at the floor, but finally, he looked up at her and smiled.

"Finally, ready, superstar?"

"Yeah, sorry. I was daydreaming."

"About?"

"Oh, you know, life."

"You're worried."

"When am I *not* worried?" Helena sat down next to Johnathan.

"There's no need to fret, Helena," Johnathan wrapped his arms around her. "This will all go as planned, just like the other ones."

The whole crew told her this since the rumor about the new medical law came out. Helena really wanted to believe them and find reassurance in their words. But her gut was telling her otherwise.

"Let's get ready to head out!" Vicky yelled out from the living room.

Johnathan smiled. "Time to get this show on the road, superstar."

Helena returned a weak smile.

**

They all stopped a block away from the hospital in disappointment. Helena tried to suppress the smug smile that was threatening to creep up on her face.

The hospital was guarded by a few men who looked like soldiers. However, they didn't appear to be soldiers that they were used to. These men looked more lethal—more aggressive. Ordinary soldiers had the appearance of protecting and serving the citizens. These men looked like they were protecting and serving something else, and the citizens were viewed as threats.

Helena was used to the standard green and brown fatigues that the soldiers wore, but these soldiers' uniforms looked scarier. It was just some black and grey fatigues, but the way they were padded, armed, and bulletproofed up made Helena feel like the soldiers were ready for war.

"Shit," Paul grumbled. "That doesn't look good."

"Maybe there's some truth to that rumor after all," Kim admitted.

Will looked over at Vicky. "What do we do now?"

Vicky wore a look of disappointment. Helena could tell that she really thought the rumor wouldn't affect them. At that moment, Helena questioned Vicky's leadership. Vicky met eyes with Helena for a second; an idea sparkled in her eyes. Helena dreaded that look.

"Binoculars," Vicky demanded from Will. He quickly passed them to her. Vicky looked through them for a moment—silence hanging in the air. "It looks like they're running people's names. Helena and Johnathan will go inside."

"But we're the lookouts," Johnathan protested.

"Well aware of your position Johnathan," irritation rose in Vicky's voice. "Helena will ask for them to run her sister's name and see if she's been in," Vicky looked over at Helena, daring her to say that it wasn't a good idea.

"Will they even give her that information?" Johnathan demanded. He didn't like going off book with their plans.

"Have you ever met someone who told Helena no?" Vicky smirked. "Plus, there's a guy up there. I'm sure Helena can charm him." Johnathan was about to protest again, but Vicky cut him off. "I'm not saying she should lose her virginity to him. She just needs to distract him while we lift a few things."

"How will we get in the back?" Paul asked.

"Johnathan will go in before Helena and pretend like he's sick. He will wait by the side door. It's unguarded. While Helena is distracting the staff and the guard, Johnathan will keep a lookout as we break-in through the employee entrance. We will signal Johnathan once we're done."

"I'm not sure about this," Johnathan hesitated.

"I don't give a fuck," Vicky was beyond irritated with him. "We need supplies. So, let's get the job done."

Helena didn't say anything. Honestly, she hadn't really been paying attention ever since Vicky mentioned Jade. Helena had been wanting to acquire information about Jade since they started stealing from hospitals. But Vicky always persisted that Helena was needed as a lookout outside. And it seemed too big of a risk to go back to the hospital they just stole from to ask about Jade.

The crew watched on as Johnathan made his way to the hospital. Vicky looked on through the binoculars. Once he was checked in, Vicky motioned for Helena to proceed on.

Helena fought through the butterflies as she made her way through the hospital doors. It was the first time she actually been inside a hospital since the chaos broke out.

The atmosphere of the emergency room was too much to handle. There was so much going on that it was difficult to register it all. People were crying and in agonizing pain. People were pleading for help and asking to be seen immediately. Some staff members were sympathetic to the injured people, but most of them were nonchalant. It was a hopeless environment.

Helena tried not to make any eye contact with Johnathan, but he did a terrible job not looking at her. She could see him from the corner of her eye. He was shifting back and forth nervously as he inched closer to the side door. Helena focused on the people in line in front of her. They all appeared to be injured. One person had a bloody bandage wrapped around their head. Another person kept saying that they were having severe chest pain. And the person at the front of the line had a broken leg.

The nagging feeling of Johnathan staring at her wouldn't go away. Helena quickly shot an annoyed look his way, hoping that it would convey to him to stop looking so obvious. She knew why he was nervous. They had never been separated as lookouts. Even though they were in the same room, Johnathan didn't like not being right by her side. Helena wasn't sure how she felt about that.

The line steadily moved, and she was getting closer to the front. She took that moment to get a really good look at the staff upfront.

The guy at the registration desk seemed harmless enough—just annoyed.

The guard standing by him, however, made Helena's heart drop to her stomach. The guy looked menacing and yet handsome at the same time. He was tall and lean, yet still muscular. Helena could clearly see his biceps bulging out of his fatigues. Tattoos ran down his neck, and they traveled down to his forearms. His shirt's sleeves were pushed up, and Helena could tell they were the same designs on his neck. For whatever reason, the tattoos frightened her.

The guard had sandy brown hair and brown eyes. The way his eyes glided over everyone in the room terrified her. Helena noticed when his eyes lingered on her. From the corner of her eye, Johnathan shifted uneasily. Apparently, he saw it too. Helena was beginning to dread this plan.

When her turn came up, she'd worked up tears in her eyes. The guy at the registration desk didn't seem to notice, but the guard did. He stood even straighter as Helena approached. The registration guy didn't bother to look up from his computer screen.

"Name."

"I-I don't need medical assistance," Helena stammered.

The guy looked up at her, even more annoyed. "Then, why are you here?"

"I'm looking for my sister," tears began to flow from her eyes. "We got separated a while ago, and she has some health issues. I just want to know if she checked in."

"Can't do that."

"Please, mister," Helena glanced over at the guard. Even though he wasn't looking at her, he appeared to be listening. "Can you please just look?"

"You're holding up my line, kid. Get out of here."

Helena looked at the people behind her. They didn't seem aware of what was going on.

"It's rough out there, mister. Please, don't make me go through all of this alone," Helena choked up a little. "I *really* need my sister."

"The hospital is for the sick and injured. Not to find missing people," the guy looked over at the guard, signaling him to escort Helena out.

"Do it," the guard demanded. His tone was so authoritative and frightening that Helena got the sense that he was the one actually in charge. "Run her sister's name."

The registration guy sighed and rolled his eyes. "Name."

"Thank you, sir," Helena said to the guard. "Last name Willer, first name Jade."

Helena continued to dramatically wipe away her tears as the guy typed in the information. She was aware that the guard's eyes were on her. Now would've been a good time for Vicky and the rest to sneak in.

"She's not here," the guy said with satisfaction. No doubt he was glad to get Helena away from him.

Helena cried harder, making her sobs even more apparent. "Is she at least alive?"

"As of a few weeks ago, yes."

"Oh, thank God," she didn't have to pretend with tears of gratitude. Jade was alive, and she was in this area only a few weeks ago. This was the first solid lead she had on Jade in two years. Helena just needed to be more diligent in her search.

"Check the back," the guard ordered, pulling Helena out of her daydreams about reuniting with Jade.

"Seriously?" the registration guy was even more annoyed.

"Now!"

The guy called over another staff member and instructed them to check the back to make sure Jade wasn't back there. When he looked back at Helena, hatred was apparent in his eyes.

"Can you step to the side, your *highness?*"

Helena gladly obliged, but the guard gave the guy a deathly stare.

"Watch how you treat our guests."

The guy flinched back from the guard's tone. "Sorry, Officer Razor," the guy mumbled.

Helena was about to walk over to where Johnathan was, but the guy gently grabbed her by her elbow.

"You can wait here next to me," he said. Helena didn't bother to protest. Although his tone was gentle, it wasn't supposed to be argued with.

"Thanks again," Helena said. "I really appreciate it."

The guard looked at her—*really* looked at her. He took her all in. It seemed like he was memorizing her face. His stare was so intense that it was making Helena uneasy. They really couldn't get caught. There was no doubt in her mind that this guy would remember who she was. After what seemed like forever, he finally released Helena from his stare.

"You're very welcome, miss."

Helena quickly glanced over at Johnathan. He was glaring at the guard, and he wasn't exactly subtle about it. Helena looked around uncomfortably. She was hoping that he wasn't aware of the daggered look that was being thrown his way. After a few seconds, Helena took a quick peek at the man. He had been looking outside, but when she glanced up, their eyes met. Embarrassed, Helena diverted her eyes elsewhere.

"I like your hair," the guard said quietly enough for only Helena to hear.

To her surprise, she blushed a little. She couldn't understand why. This guard frightened her. The way he looked at everyone else was terrifying—that included other women and children. But when his eyes brushed over her, there was a different look.

"Thanks."

He quickly looked away again.

Helena continued to look around. It was the first time she noticed the way the staff was separating people. After registration, some people were directed to the left while others went right. Helena and Johnathan were on the left. She couldn't understand the reason for the clear separation. Her only guess was that the people on the right were in more dire need of being seen.

Then she felt the guard stiffen up as a group of trucks quickly pulled up. Everyone in the room became alert. Helena could see Johnathan nervously look out the side door. Something was wrong. That was confirmed as the guard gently and quickly moved her behind him—acting as her shield. Johnathan began to take steps toward her when everything went wrong.

First, the registration guy yelled to Helena and the guard that Jade wasn't there.

Next, a staff member in the back shouted about intruders stealing supplies.

Then, a group of soldiers, all dressed like the guard, jumped out of the trucks and rushed in. They immediately started apprehending the group of people who were on the right side of the emergency room. Although the people on the left were safe from these soldiers, everyone began to flee from the hospital.

Just then, Vicky and the rest of the crew burst out of the doors from the back. A nurse was right behind them.

"Thieves!" the nurse shouted. "Stop them!"

Johnathan kicked open the side door as Vicky and the others rushed out. Other panicked people followed, trampling over the nurse that was in pursuit. Helena's stomach was in knots. Johnathan held the door open.

"Come on!" he shouted, looking right at her.

Helena cursed him under her breath. The guard was still shielding her from all the chaos, but he now turned to look at her.

Why would Johnathan acknowledge her? She could've gotten out of there on her own. To her surprise, the guard was fighting off a smile. It seemed like he knew all along.

"I believe he's waiting for you," he smiled at her like he was impressed. It confused her. The guard looked around at the scene. "You better hurry. Otherwise, I'll have to detain you."

Helena gave him an embarrassed and apologetic look. "Thank you so much," she ran to the door but paused at the doorway. She took one last look at the man who terrified and intrigued her.

~7~

Razor

Razor watched as the girl with the mint green hair rushed out the side door of the emergency room. She was beautiful. During the craziness of this whole ordeal, Razor never really paid attention to other women. In fact, *before* all the madness, he never really paid attention to other women. The women that he did have an interest in were only there for stress-relieving purposes. They were usually ok with that arrangement. Razor never experienced any romantic feelings for anyone. And he never had an instant attraction to a woman.

But he felt that now.

It was apparent that the girl with the mint green hair wasn't a woman.

Razor pegged her at about 16–17 at the latest. But he still found her attractive. He was conflicted; he was at least five years her senior. But her flawless golden-brown skin, her beautiful almond-shaped brown eyes, and the fascinating short mint green hair just drew him in. It was something about her that made Razor feel the strong urge to protect and care for her.

It was obvious that she was not alone. The guy that checked in earlier for a minor stomachache couldn't stop staring at her. Plus, the fact that he kept slowly making his way to the emergency door in the waiting room alerted Razor that something was up. The waterworks from the girl didn't fool him either. However, he was sure that the girl really was looking for her sister and was genuinely happy and relieved to learn that she was alive. But the girl seemed so lonely, even though it was apparent that she wasn't on her own.

Usually, he would've never done it, but Razor played along with the act. He looked at her straight on as she pitched her story. He pretended not to notice a group sneaking in through the employee entrance at the side of the building. The stomachache guy was supposed to be blocking the view but was too preoccupied with Razor giving the mint haired girl his attention. He tried really hard not to smile at the obvious jealousy the guy was displaying.

The people that this girl was with were going to get her killed.

Razor resisted the urge to "detain" her when all the chaos broke out. When the guy yelled at her to follow him, confirming that they did, in fact, know each other and that they were up to something, Razor wanted to take her just to show that he could protect her better. But something told him that was a bad idea. She was young and seemed very innocent.

There was no way she could survive in the world he was living in. The people were ruthless. Razor dreaded to think what they would do to her.

Plus, if she were ever to be with him, he would want her to come to him on her own.

So, after a lot of restraint, Razor watched as she ran out the door—back to the guy who would most likely get her killed.

Anger rose in him as she disappeared into the crowd. Once he was confident that she was gone, he turned his rage on those who were in his range.

**

It had been about a month since his encounter with the mint haired girl. Razor was secretly hoping that he would run into her again—without the guy. He tried really hard to focus on the current DC task force mission. Nick told him that it was the task force's grand mission.

A lot of people heard about the new medical law that was being implemented. And as expected, the people thought that it was a joke. Nick seemed happy with that fact. Razor didn't understand why, at first, but as time went by and the people got worse, he understood Nick's reasoning.

The plan was for the DCs to come in aggressive and hard. Nick wanted to strike fear into the hearts of the people. He wanted them all to think twice before misusing the medical care system. This was another way for natural selection.

"Only the strong can survive in this new world," Nick said as he and Razor were staking out a hospital.

They were checking to see how many visitors went to the hospital daily. It seemed like the hospital was being overrun by the sick and injured. Nick was giddy over this.

"What a perfect way to ensure that only the strong will rebuild civilization?"

Razor nodded in agreement. Nick's plan was a solid one. The position he was in was perfect for carrying out his vision. Nick had confided a lot with Razor. He felt privileged to be his confidant.

For someone who had a big vision for the program, Nick had a very hands-off approach. The most important rule was that you weren't allowed to fight with each other. As long as the officers remained brotherly to one another, you were free to do what you want. Any pent-up anger and hostility were to go to the debtors (because medical debt was the only kind of debt that existed now).

Before the new task force's unveiling, Nick held a large assembly for the officers in Lansing. Michigan was the designated area for the trial run. If the numbers were reported strongly, then the DC task force would be rolling out over the entire country, and Nick would oversee it all.

He would have absolute power.

Nick stood on top of a DC truck as the officers surrounded him. Razor stood front and center in the crowd. Nick slowly glanced around at his audience. There was a mixture of officers, government officials, and regular citizens.

"There are some of you here today who are still a little apprehensive of this new task force and its mission. But let me assure you, we *are* necessary. The citizens that reside here in Lansing have been fortunate enough not to witness the real horrors that lie outside of this city. You haven't seen the violence and the terror. You haven't experienced the savagery and the cunningness.

"When it comes to our most vulnerable system, these thugs took no time to exploit and defraud it. But their time for punishment is here! America will show these terrorists that we are still in control. And although we are in a time of uncertainty, we will still fight in order to survive—in order to thrive. We will rebuild our civilization. And we will be stronger than ever! No matter the cost!"

The crowd erupted in cheer.

"No matter the cost! No matter the cost!"

The unveiling of the DC task force was a huge success.

By the time they did the sweep at their third hospital, word had begun to spread around like wildfire. But people began to catch on quickly.

First, Razor noticed that the people became familiar with the separation strategy from the hospital staff. When people were directed to the emergency room's right side, they quickly and slyly snuck out. Razor immediately brought it to the staff and Nick's attention. They decided to switch the directions—this worked for about two sweeps. Again, people caught on, and when they were directed a certain way, they fled.

Nick hid his frustration well, but Razor could see it.

Hospital staff suggested that they direct debtors to the back of the waiting room (the area closer to the doors). Razor opposed the idea. The debtors would be able to catch on and leave even quicker, but Nick agreed to it. Razor could tell that he really wanted numbers. So, the plan briefly worked. But like Razor predicted, the debtors caught on by the time they went to the third hospital with their new tactic.

It was all becoming a headache.

Razor suggested that they had more presence outside of the hospital, instead of the ambush method. If there were more DC officers around the perimeter, they could catch the debtors that attempted to flee. Nick loved the idea and implemented the new plan quickly.

The new plan worked a lot longer than the previous methods. Nick was happy with that. They were getting a lot of debtors with Razor's way, and Nick loved the numbers. But after about three months of this, the debtors caught on.

Now no one came to the hospitals. The emergency rooms slowed down drastically. Staff eventually became bored, and DC officers hated standing around doing nothing.

Most of the officers began to fight among themselves to get assigned prison detail. The way most of them saw it, that was where all the action was. They could do whatever they wanted to the imprisoned debtors. That was more exciting than waiting for them to show up at the hospitals, which they no longer did.

The officers had a taste of blood, and they couldn't turn back now.

Razor needed to think of something quick. He was beginning to realize that a frustrated Nick was not a good Nick at all. His actions were out of control and unpredictable. It seemed like he was losing that cultivated facade that he displayed to everyone else.

Nick was starting to fight with the other officers below him. It usually ended up deadly. The altercations were beginning to make the other officers second guess being there. Sure, the program provided you with food and shelter, but was it worth risking your life with a lethal and unstable leader?

One day, a new idea came to Razor as he drove around a neighborhood near a hospital. It was a well-known poor neighborhood, even before the world ended. He saw a woman and her children walking on the sidewalk. Razor didn't think; he just reacted. He quickly pulled the truck up on the sidewalk, blocking the woman's path.

The woman stood there, frightened. She had two little children, so there was no sense in her running—Razor knew this. He took his time getting out of the truck. He was well aware of the rumors about the cruel treatment from DC officers. It wasn't surprising that the woman stood in front of him, shaking with fear. The children immediately began crying.

"Did I do something wrong, officer?" the woman tried to calm her children down in vain.

"Name?"

She looked up at Razor, surprised. "Excuse me?"

"What is your name?"

"I-I," the woman looked around for someone—anyone who could help her. "I was just walking home."

"I didn't ask what you were doing. I asked for your name," Razor was fighting off annoyance. He didn't plan on doing anything to this woman and her children. He was just testing out a theory.

"Jane Carter."

It was very apparent that the name was a phony, but Razor ran the name anyway just to be sure. Nothing came up—definitely a fake.

Razor sighed in frustration. "Look," he said slowly. "I'm very certain that you are a debtor. It's obvious. I'm not going to apprehend you, but I will if you keep lying to me. I don't think that will work well for you and your children. Now please, tell me your name."

The tears flowed from the woman's eyes. She hung her head in defeat. "Stephenie Gier"

Razor ran it and saw that she was in debt. A million ideas ran through his head on how they could perfect the system.

"Get in the truck," he told the woman.

"But you said—"

"Now!" he growled.

The woman jumped, and the children cried even louder. Stephenie made her way to the truck as Razor opened the back door. She got in, and Razor lifted the children inside. The children screamed when he did this. Their mother did her best to comfort them.

Razor got in the truck and sped off. He listened as Stephenie sung to her children quietly. From the rearview mirror, he could see them drifting off to sleep. He was surprised that she stayed quiet throughout the entire car ride. She finally spoke up as the truck began to slow down.

"May I ask one favor?" she waited for Razor to respond. Once it was clear that he wasn't, she continued. "May my children stay with me in prison? They won't make it on their own."

Razor stopped the truck. "I told you, I wasn't taking you there. Now get out."

She looked out the window and frowned. "Where are we?"

"Somewhere we don't patrol," Razor got out of the truck and opened the back door. "Where the rich lives."

Stephenie got out of the truck slowly. She looked at Razor, confused. "I don't understand."

"Pick a house, stay inside, and if you have to leave out, try to blend in," he handed her a bag of rations. "Some food."

She burst out crying. "Thank you so much, officer."

Razor got the children out of the truck.

"Don't let me see you again," he got in his vehicle and watched as she walked off. Once he saw her pick a house, he drove off toward the DC headquarters.

**

Razor walked into chaos. Nick was yelling obscenities as soon as he stepped into the building. There was the sound of things being thrown around. Razor cursed under his breath. What happened now?

It didn't take much to set Nick off nowadays. The number of debtors being captured was dwindling down massively. Razor knew that Nick was hoping for a bigger splash. The DC task force was feared, but not feared enough to Nick's liking. And the government officials weren't *that* impressed either. Nick's potential power was fleeting.

Razor's new idea was coming just in time.

As he made his way to the top floor, Razor heard more yelling and scuffling. Nick was definitely fighting with someone, but how many? It sounded like more than one. Nervous officers greeted Razor at the door as he entered the briefing room. Nick was savagely beating an officer as two other officers attended to their wounds nearby. It appeared that the two men tried to intervene and obtained some injuries because of it.

"Nick," Razor said gently. It was apparent that the officer was dead, and Nick was beating a corpse. "Nick!"

It took a few seconds for him to snap out of it, but once he did, he looked up at Razor—blood splattered all over his face. He smiled at him.

"Razor, how nice of you to join us. Where have you been, my friend?"

"Out scouting," Razor said. Nick's behavior was familiar to him. None of what he was seeing was a surprise. But it was one thing for him to behave like that when they were out socializing. It's completely different when it involves leadership. "I came up with a new plan."

"That's fantastic," Nick's friendly smile turned into a deadly frown as he kicked the corpse. "The same can't be said for these sac-of-shits!"

"That's enough, Nick," Razor said calmly. Nick immediately stopped. Razor turned to the officer at the door. "Get the body out of here and have these men get looked at."

All the officers quickly obeyed and left out. Razor stared at Nick for a moment. Nick was gazing down at the spot where the body had been.

"Get yourself cleaned up, and then we can go over the plan."

Nick looked up and smiled at Razor again. "That sounds wonderful, my friend."

Razor didn't have to wait long for Nick to get himself together. He was back in the briefing room in less than five minutes. Nick sat down across from Razor and waited silently for him to start. Before he began with his idea, Razor needed to express his concerns to Nick carefully. Razor wrecked his brain on how to proceed but couldn't come up with anything polite. He decided to be blunt. There was no other way to be when it came to Nick.

Razor sighed. "You're fucking this up, Boss."

Nick laughed. "Am I?"

"You made it clear that we are not to fight among each other. That this whole program is a brotherhood, and yet your men see you fight and kill their fellow brothers because things aren't going your way."

Nick laughed even louder in response to Razor's criticism. Razor just waited patiently until he stopped.

"This program will be no good if there aren't men here to carry out the mission. We are the DC task force: protecting resources..."

"No matter the cost," Nick concluded.

"But the cost shouldn't be the loss of our men at our own hand."

"You're right," Nick sighed. "But you know how it is. It's hard to control myself."

"I understand, but let's put that on the debtors instead of our own team."

"Agreed," Nick smiled. "You said you had a plan?"

"First, we need to set up a database system with the hospitals. Instead of running names, they run people's blood. Nine times out of ten people drop aliases when they're registering in. This tactic will help us cut through the bullshit and allows us to identify debtors quickly."

"That's an excellent idea."

"Secondly, we should stop focusing on the hospitals."

"Really?"

"We can be on call when they need us, but we should focus our attention elsewhere."

"Like?"

"Neighborhoods."

"That seems chaotic."

"But it's guaranteed to have people," Razor explained. "People are squatting in just about every livable building, and I am certain that the majority of those people are debtors. If we do neighborhood sweeps, they won't be able to guess any of our tactics. We're less predictable that way."

A satisfied smile spread across Nick's face. "That all seems really promising, Razor. I love it."

"I figured that you would," Razor admitted. "But you're right about it being chaotic. So, we would need to come up with a strategy to deal with it all."

Nick stood up, looking impressed and excited. "Let's get to work."

**

It took over a month to get the database up and going. During that time, Nick and Razor came up with the neighborhoods they would hit for their new trial sweep. They scouted out the area for weeks looking for weak points that they would need to secure. Razor hasn't seen Nick so happy. This was the first solid plan that they had since the hospital sweeps.

It was projected that this plan would bring in way more numbers than the hospitals. It all was exciting for Nick. Razor was glad that he was calm and no longer killing fellow officers. Although he knew that the plan would be a success, Razor still found his self worried. What if this wasn't successful? Razor didn't know what he would do.

The program was fine, and he enjoyed it, but he still found his self lacking a purpose. And he couldn't imagine what Nick would do if this all didn't work out. Razor was sure that he would probably kill most of the men in the program.

"Alright over there?" Nick asked Razor as they sat in the truck.

Razor was sitting in the passenger seat and looking out the window. He could see someone peeking behind a curtain a few houses down.

"I'm good," Razor said. "Just making sure that we didn't miss anything."

"This plan will work."

Razor looked over and saw the confidence on Nick's face.

"It's a great plan," Nick continued. "They won't be expecting it."

"Thanks," Razor noticed the curtains move again. "We should head out. I think we've been made."

Nick quickly started the truck and sped off.

"I've been thinking," he started. "You really take a lot of initiative for just an officer. None of these other assholes take charge when it's needed."

"I'm just doing my job."

"No, you're doing more than your job. That's why I decided to promote you to be my second in command."

Razor was surprised by this news. "Really?"

"You've earned it."

Razor smiled a little. He liked the idea of having so many people under him who he could command.

"I'm honored."

"We're going to do great things, my friend."

"We will indeed," Razor got on the radio. "All clear. Everyone head-in. No matter the cost."

"No matter the cost!" everyone chimed in.

Nick and Razor watched as the trucks rushed in, and the chaos unfolded. Razor smiled in satisfaction at the beautiful view.

History was being made, and he felt like he was on the right side of it.

~8~

Razor

Two *years later.*

There was a quick, urgent knock at Razor's bedroom door. At first, he thought it was a part of his dream, but they became too frequent for it to be an illusion. The tapping at the door increased. Razor stirred; someone was lying next to him. When he opened his eyes, his heart stopped for a brief second.

The woman sleeping next to him had green hair, but this green was different. Instead of the mint green that he loved so much, this green was more of a seafoam. This woman wasn't the woman he truly wanted.

Images of last night slowly came to his mind. He and Nick were at the hotel's bar unwinding from a day of training. They were currently in Sacramento, CA.

After the massive success of neighborhood sweeps, Razor and Nick (now mostly known as Bossman) traveled over the nation training the other officers on this tactic. However, with this new tactic, attempts at uprisings began to follow. So, Razor and Bossman spent their time "interrogating" those who were tempted to fight the system. But really, they spent most of their time beating and torturing people who looked at the program wrong.

They had been in Sacramento for two months, and Razor was beginning to hate residing at the Sheraton Grand hotel. It was a nice enough place. He just hated being in one spot for long. He liked to keep moving. So far, Sacramento had been the lengthiest place that they've stayed. They usually moved from city to city.

To fight off his annoyance, Razor decided to have a drink at the bar, and Nick was all too happy to join him. He spent most of the night listening to Nick complain about his dislike for the new officers they were training. The officers weren't cunning enough for him. Razor barely listened as he finished off his fourth bottle of beer.

Then his heart almost leapt out of his chest.

A woman entered the bar with short green hair. Razor immediately knew that this wasn't the same girl from the hospital. The green was off, and this woman's hair was a bit longer—her hair fell just below her chin. But she was good enough to distract him—even though he knew that it wasn't a good idea.

Razor fought for so long to get the mint haired girl out of his head during their last encounter. Some days, he found himself looking up her sister, Jade Willer, to see if they were ever reunited. From his research, they weren't. He eventually learned the girl's name, though.

After much extensive research on Jade, Razor found out that her sister's name was Helena. Helena Willer. Recently turned 18. He had memorized her birthday—September 30th. It was at that point he realized he was becoming obsessive. So, he fought to stop thinking about her—even though some nights, she visited him in his dreams.

As he watched the Helena-wannabe talk to her friend from across the bar, Razor realized that maybe he could make his dreams come true with this girl. And maybe, just maybe, he could have a night where he didn't dream about Helena. So, as he finished off another beer, Razor approached the woman and her friend. It didn't take a lot of convincing to get both women to leave the bar with him.

The knocking on his bedroom door increased.

"Fuck," Razor slowly sat up. His head was pounding. He and his companions had a few more drinks when they got back to his room. Apparently, he overdid it.

The two women were still sound asleep when Razor got out of bed and walked over to the door. When he opened it, an officer was there wearing a concerned look.

"What?" Razor demanded. His headache was progressively getting worse.

"I'm sorry to wake you, Commander," the officer said apologetically. "But you requested that we kept you updated on that group of looters back in Michigan. Well, sir, they struck again. This time, injuring an officer."

"Shit," Razor sighed.

A month ago, officers in Michigan reported that a group was looting DC trucks during sweeps. At first, the officers were confident that they could handle it themselves. But Razor demanded that he remained updated on the situation. Now that an officer was injured, he saw the need to potentially step in.

"Thanks for the update," he didn't wait for the officer to answer. He immediately slammed the door in his face.

The green-haired woman was awakened by the slammed door. She smiled when she saw a shirtless Razor.

"Well, good morning, sexy," she sat up, the sheet covering up her breasts.

"You need to leave. The both of you," now seeing her with sober eyes, this woman was nowhere close to resembling Helena. That, with the news of the looters, just angered Razor more.

The woman looked a little shocked for a second. It was the sound of Razor's angry tone that threw her off. She nodded and shook her friend awake. It didn't take long for the two women to get dressed and leave out without a word. Razor must've looked scary to them.

Once they were gone, he proceeded to shower and get dressed. It wasn't clear what was on the agenda for today. Razor couldn't recall him and Nick going over it. Both men had gotten so drunk last night, and they both left the bar with companions. So, once he was dressed, Razor headed out to Nick's room.

When he got to the elevators, Nick and Chase were walking out of one. Both men smiled when they saw him.

"Good morning, Razor," Chase beamed.

"Chase," Razor hated calling him by his first name, but the President insisted when it was just the three of them. And it always baffled Razor to see him without his security detail.

"How was your night?" Nick asked.

The men walked into another elevator and called for the lobby. Razor shrugged. He honestly couldn't remember it all.

Nick chuckled. "Must've not been that great if you can't remember it."

"And did you have any entertainment last night, Nick?" Chase asked, amused.

They had reached the lobby, and the three men headed for the banquet hall where breakfast was being served.

"I did...it was...*ok.*"

Chase laughed at that. "Well, you've both had way more action than I've gotten in a while."

"The first lady isn't doing her job?"

"Does she ever?" Chase sighed and rolled his eyes.

Nick laughed as they entered the banquet hall. Razor remained silent. He grabbed a plate and focused on loading it up with food. The other two men did the same. They picked a table to sit at once they were done.

"So, I might need to head back to Michigan," Razor said as they sat down.

Nick frowned. "Why?"

"There's a group looting DC trucks during the sweeps."

"That's a brilliant plan," Chase chuckled. He began eating his scrambled eggs.

"It is, but this last time, left an officer injured."

Nick slowly spread some jelly on his toast—lost in thought. "Later," he finally said. "I believe Chase has a more pressing matter."

Chase nodded as he chewed on his food. It took a few seconds before he spoke. "There's this kid, a biochemist, who's been going around passing out multivitamins for free."

Nick froze, the veins in his neck bulging. "*What?*"

"It's been said that he's targeting debtors," the President continued.

Nick slammed his fist on the table. A few people that were in the room turned to look at them, alarmed. The men didn't pay them any attention.

"I know, he needs to be dealt with," Chase was unfazed by Nick's reaction. He slowly took a sip of his coffee.

Razor ate his piece of bacon with a frown on his face. "Is the guy a debtor?" he finally asked. The President shook his head. "So, what's the problem? There's no law against that."

Both men looked at him in disbelief.

"He's going against our agenda," Chase finally said.

"Our mission is preserving healthcare. If you ask me, this biochemist is helping with that."

"That's not *our* agenda," Nick gestured to the three of them. "Our goal is to ensure that the strong are left to rebuild society."

"It's the only way of this new world," Chase added.

For a moment, Razor felt utterly stupid. Nick had always been spouting his views on how the strong could survive, but he never once thought that he was actually serious about it. And he never once imagined that the President had the same views. Razor always believed that it was all about protecting healthcare. It never once occurred that it was *really* about something else. He wasn't entirely sure how he felt about that.

Instead of voicing his concerns about their beliefs, Razor just nodded.

"We need to interrogate him," Chase continued.

Nick nodded in agreement.

Interrogate. Razor knew what that meant, and questions were not involved. Most of the time, the interrogations didn't really bother him. In fact, he was enjoying an outlet for his rage. After 23 years, Razor was finally getting a sense of his purpose.

The way he saw it, debtors broke the law and deserved to be punished. But as the 5th year of his father's death drew near, Razor was beginning to feel conflicted.

Would his father be proud of what he'd become?

Razor was protecting his country, after all. Protecting their most valuable and vulnerable resource—medical care. The new world couldn't operate without it. Wouldn't his father be proud of that?

But he was now learning that might not be the case.

The men finished their breakfast in silence. It wasn't until they were walking out of the hotel when Nick finally spoke.

"I will send men out to search for the biochemist."

"Good," Chase said with relief.

"I should have him before the end of the day."

**

The biochemist hung upside down—unconscious. It really didn't take long for the officers to find him. The guy's routine was always the same. He canvassed the surrounding neighborhoods that were near hospitals and distributed multivitamins to those who wanted them. That was what the guy was doing when the officers apprehended him.

"Thank God he hasn't gathered a following," Chase sighed as he sat in a chair in the corner of the interrogation room.

They were currently in the basement of an old rundown office building. Whenever Razor and Nick resided in a new city, they quickly sought a place to hold their interrogations. The more beatdown the site looked, the better. The bleak atmosphere always brought a sense of intimidation.

"That would've been unfortunate," Nick agreed. He stood near the captive at the center of the room.

The guy groaned as he came to. When the biochemist was brought in, Razor quickly knocked him out with a swift punch to the face. It was easier to hang someone up when they were unconscious and unable to fight back.

"Oh God," the man cried. "Where am I?! What's happening?!"

They all watched silently as the guy panicked and squirmed around. He was blindfolded, and chains were wrapped around his ankles and wrists.

After a couple of minutes, the President sighed and looked over at Razor. "Shall we begin?"

"Who's there?!"

"What do you want out of him?" Razor inquired. He really wasn't looking forward to torturing the poor guy, but he was given direct orders from his superiors, and at the end of the day, he had to do his job.

"Hello?" the guy tried to turn toward Razor's direction. "What's going on?"

"Make sure that he doesn't have a following," Chase looked at the man with disgust. "I don't want the other government officials to get any ideas about new leadership and empathy."

Razor snorted. "Really? New leadership?"

"Word about how the prisons are being run aren't sitting well with them," it was hard to miss the annoyance in Nick's tone.

"And I'm all for it...there are whispers that they're looking for just about anyone to replace me. Empathy. And a following. That is what they're looking for," Chase stood up and walked to the door. He paused for a moment. "He has one. Let's make sure he doesn't have the other."

"Copy that," Razor pushed over a big bucket of water toward the captive.

"Hey, no, no, no, please," the guy cried at the noise. "What have I done?!"

"Treason," Nick removed the guy's blindfold.

The biochemist frowned at the word. "I've done no such thing! I was just giving out multivitamins."

Nick responded by punching the guy in the gut. He groaned out in pain.

"And that is an act of treason...going against the President's wishes."

The guy was about to object again, but Nick began hitting him some more. Razor stood silently, waiting for his cue to continue the job. After several more hits, Nick finally stopped. He headed for the door.

"Make sure there's no surprise following," he ordered before walking out.

"Copy that," Razor began dunking the guy's head into the bucket of water.

He had been at it for hours with the interrogation. His knuckles were bloody, his hands ached. But it was all a part of a day's hard work. After administering rounds and rounds of torture, Razor was confident that the guy didn't have a following hiding out somewhere. Once he was sure of this, he quickly notified Nick and Chase.

"That's great," Nick stood in front of the guy. Chase lingered in the doorway.

"Please," the guy slurred. His mouth and the rest of his face was swollen from the beating. "Let me go. I've answered your questions. I won't do this again."

"If only it was that simple," Nick sighed. And then, very swiftly, he sliced the guy's throat.

Razor watched as the guy's blood flowed toward his feet. He was standing behind him. For some reason, the guy's death shocked him. At the end of the day, Razor only saw the multivitamins. It wasn't enough to punish the man with death. But that's precisely what they did.

He suddenly didn't feel right.

"Let's go," Nick headed for the door. Razor slowly followed. Chase was right behind him. They came upon a small group of officers. "Clean up that mess in there," he ordered.

The officers quickly obeyed.

When they got back to the hotel, Razor informed the men that he needed to get back to Michigan.

"That we do," Nick sighed.

"Well, I should be heading back to D.C.," Chase smiled. "Until the next time, gentlemen."

Nick turned to Razor. "You handle the looters, and I'll see what kind of trouble I can get myself into," there was glee behind his eyes.

Razor nodded. He was just glad to be getting out of Sacramento.

~9~

Razor

There was a truck—an essential truck. This truck would help resolve the annoying problem that Razor was there to deal with.

When he got to Michigan, officers reported on the status of the looters. Apparently, his officers were having trouble with the looters a lot longer than they initially said. Razor was angry about that. He took it out on some of them. Nick joined in on releasing his anger. Once he was composed, Razor formed a plan of action to deal with the looters.

The plan required him to be out on the field. He rarely worked in the field anymore—not since he and Nick had become the most feared men in the nation. That title brought on a lot of other responsibilities.

Razor purposely planned to be out on the field because he needed a break from Nick. Ever since he joined the program, the two men had been attached at the hip. Razor knew that Nick wouldn't go out on the field. He no longer viewed it as fun. Nick enjoyed the interrogation process too much. And that was precisely what Razor was trying to get away from.

He needed to clear his mind.

They had been back to Michigan for three days now, and Razor was still haunted by the biochemist's death. Sure, he'd killed plenty of people, but this death felt so wrong to him. Most of the people he'd tortured and killed were criminals. This guy found it in his heart to make something that would help people—during a time where helping people was nonexistent. Razor wasn't sure how to process that.

"The bait truck is all set, Commander," an officer radioed.

The truck.

Razor was brought back to his current mission. "Alright," he instructed. "Begin the sweep."

The plan was relatively simple. While his officers performed their sweep, Razor would stake out the bait truck and wait for the looters to show up. He was confident that they will show since the bait truck would be unguarded. The scenario was just too good to pass up.

It didn't take long for the chaos to break out. Razor watched it all unfold as he sat in his truck five blocks away. Many debtors fled by him as the sweep began. Surprisingly, Razor ignored them all. Apprehending the debtors was his officers' responsibility. His primary focus was the looters because they have been roaming free for far too long now. They had to get rid of the group soon, or else it would be open season on the officers.

Razor had to appreciate the ingenious of the looters' plan, though. That was a great way of getting the necessary supplies to survive. The officers were well equipped with supplies for survival since they were generally on the road most of the time. With all the chaos in the sweeps, it's the perfect moment to steal supplies without anyone noticing.

The looters weren't debtors. Debtors were too occupied, trying to avoid prison than stealing supplies. It was a great plan. If some of his officers weren't injured during the process, Razor was tempted to leave them alone.

Then his heart stopped.

Even though there wasn't a clear view, Razor knew that it was her. The mint haired girl. She slowly came into view. It appeared that she was looking around—making sure the coast was clear. Razor pulled out his binoculars to get a better look.

It *was* her—Helena. She looked even more beautiful than he remembered. He was surprised that she was still rocking the green hair after two years. He had mixed emotions.

Of course, she had to be a part of this. That seemed to be his luck. Razor was so ready to extract the appropriate punishment to these looters, but he wasn't so sure if he could do that to *her*.

Even now, as he watched her signal to her crew that the coast was clear, he couldn't alert his officers to move in. His men would show this girl no mercy. In fact, some of his men would even try to have a go at her sexually. Razor struggled to swallow his rage at the thought of that. Why was she having such a significant impact on him?

It was the loneliness from Helena that attracted Razor to her so much. He understood her pain. He felt the same way. Surrounded by countless people and Razor still found himself lonely—even with the occasional companion in his bed. The feeling really hit him when his parents died. He took care of them. He had no one to take care of anymore. But he saw this girl being a recipient of that—if she would let him.

"Shit," the group was unloading the goods as Helena continued to keep an eye out. Razor had to act soon before his men tried to jump in.

"Should we move in on the targets, Commander?" someone radioed.

"Negative," an idea popped into Razor's mind. "I'm going to tail them back to their hideout to make sure that we catch the whole crew."

Razor knew that the whole crew was there, but his men didn't know that. Plus, the group could've recruited more people during the two years since he saw them last.

"Copy that."

Razor watched on with more ease now that his men were at bay. The group emptied out the truck and hurried their way out through the chaos of the sweep. Razor lagged behind for a while. The crew was on foot, and he knew that his truck would be too easy to spot. He kept his eyes on Helena. She was the easiest for him to spot—not because he memorized her face, but because of her hair.

Once they were almost out of his view, Razor began to tail them back to their hideout. It took an agonizing slow amount of time for them to get there. Between the heavy load of supplies and the five-mile walk, Razor barely used the gas pedal.

The groups' getaway plan wasn't exactly the best, especially with the lack of a vehicle. If they were chased, it would've been effortless to apprehend them. It would've also been relatively easy to rob them. Luckily for the group, they had a way of blending in. The only one that stood out was Helena, but Razor was sure that she only stood out to him.

When they finally reached their hideout, Razor parked a few blocks away. He wasn't sure how long he would sit there or if he would be able to keep his men at bay. He peered in the rearview mirror and saw a truck of officers parked a few blocks away. It was very evident that the crew had no more members there with them. It appeared to just only be the six of them. He had just found Helena again. Razor wasn't quite ready to be rid of her yet—if at all.

"Orders, Commander."

Razor sighed. Of course, his men were antsy for action. He couldn't blame them. They wanted these people to pay.

"Stand down for now. I would like to do some more recon on them."

"Commander..."

"You heard my order," Razor was trying not to get agitated with his men. "We need more recon on them before we make a move."

"Yes, sir."

Razor could hear the defiance in the officer's voice. "You all can go back to headquarters."

"Commander?"

"I got it from here," Razor wanted to be alone and was tired of the officers questioning him. "Update Bossman on what's going on."

"Yes, sir. Heading out."

Razor watched them speed off. Once they were clear out of his view, he returned his attention back to the house. He didn't see any new movement in there. It seemed like the group was in for the day. With the supplies they had just stolen, there was no need for them to leave out for weeks.

Razor couldn't tell how long the group had been there. If he had to guess, he would say at the very least a few weeks. He wondered how long they usually stayed in one place. They had survived this long, so they had some idea of what they were doing.

The first time that Razor encountered them, he pegged them to be reckless. Today he confirmed that even further. Not once did someone checked to see if they were being followed. They never checked to see if they were being watched.

The fact that they were looting and injuring DC officers should've made them more cautious and alert. But that didn't seem to be the case. They appeared to be oblivious to the danger that they were in. This pissed Razor off. Because of their carelessness, they put themselves in harm's way. Most importantly, they put Helena in harm's way. He knew that this group would eventually get her killed.

Darkness covered the sky in no time. Razor took that moment to move up the street. After parking the truck around the block, he set up in a house a couple houses down from the groups' hideout. He made sure he was directly across from them. For the most part, the street was abandoned. Razor saw that maybe three houses on the entire street were occupied.

The house he was staking out in was inhabitable. Large parts of the roof were missing. There were barely any walls standing, and it was a maze to walk on the floor. Nature was clearly reclaiming the house. It was the kind of home that no one in their right mind would think to live in, and that was the appeal of it.

Razor set up in the living room. The windows were boarded up, and there was a bush that provided excellent cover for him. It was very easy for him to see the group of looters from his vantage point.

The groups' hideout had sheer curtains hanging from their windows. It was surprising to see that the windows on the house were still intact. The home was well kept up and appeared to be very livable.

Razor watched through his binoculars as the group ate dinner. They all sat around in the living room, talking, and eating. Razor could only guess what they were talking about. His best guess was their next opportunity to loot a DC truck. He would need to bug the place to be sure—that's if they were planning to stay there any longer.

In the morning, Razor planned to bug the groups' hideout to get an idea of what they were up to. He spent the remainder of the night eating some of his rations and watching Helena interact with the group.

It was apparent that Helena was just putting up a good face. The others appeared to be happier than she was. It seemed like she was trying to please the guy from the emergency room. Watching them, it was clear how much the guy was into her. Razor wondered if she was into him, though. He didn't like the idea that she might be.

Razor waited until the group went to sleep before he turned-in himself. He wondered how long Nick would let him be on his own. Nick trusted Razor more than anything in this world; Razor knew that. Still, he knew that Nick would eventually come looking if he stayed away for too long. Especially since they've rarely been apart. And the last thing that Razor wanted was to have Nick stumble across Helena.

Once the group left out, Razor would set up the bugs and cameras and head back to headquarters. Hopefully, it will be in the morning.

**

It was well into the afternoon by the time the group left out of their hideout. They didn't carry anything with them, so Razor guessed that the group was going out on some kind of errand. He waited about 15 minutes before he sneaked inside. He planted listening devices in all the rooms and hid some cameras in the living room, kitchen, and two of the bedrooms.

The house had three rooms and a finished basement. It looked like the basement, and the master bedroom was shared, and the other two rooms were solo. One of the rooms was Helena's. Razor knew that from the strands of green hair on a brush and on a pillowcase. Razor set a camera in Helena's room and the master bedroom (guessing that's where the group's leader slept).

Razor took some more time to look around the house. He noticed the kind of supplies they had gathered. It was a nice amount. The number of rations they had stolen could keep them fed for over three months.

The group even had what Razor dubbed "luxury supplies," like lotion, hair gel, hair dye, notebooks, novels, and more. He also stumbled across some weapons too. Some of the DC officers' issued batons, knives, and tasers were there. How did they get their hands on those? The weapons were usually on the officers at all times. Could that have been the reason why some of his officers got injured?

It appeared that one of the members had a knack for lock picking. There was some lock picking tools and bump keys lying around. There also had to be a hacker in the group. How else could they have the sweep schedules and pictures of the officers (his self included)?

This group was a little more threatening than he thought. The group had an actual plan for what they were doing. They weren't just targeting random officers. They were targeting the well-known (and most dangerous) officers. It was kind of like retribution in some sort of way. Overall, Razor was impressed.

But what he struggled with the most was how he was going to report this to Nick. He had to think of a way to handle this group quickly. The best way, the one he strongly preferred, was to scare them into hiding. There wasn't any need to kill them if he didn't have to, and he really didn't want to harm Helena in any way. He just needed to see what their next move was before he intervened.

By the time the group returned, Razor was in his truck and parked a few blocks away from the house. The group didn't even notice him. It appeared that they had gathered up even more supplies. Razor was impressed, but he didn't understand what all the stockpiling was for. That much supplies were a liability. You couldn't move around freely, and you became an easy target. How long was the group planning on staying there?

The video feed from the living room camera was shown on Razor's tablet. He listened in as they all went over their haul and divided up their goods.

"Can we take a fucking day off now?" the girl named Kim complained.

"Perhaps one," the leader Vicky stated. "Until we figure out our next target."

"I agree with Kim," the guy named Paul said. "We should maybe lie low for a little bit."

"That's a no go. We're making a lot of progress."

"Vicky, if we keep stealing from the DC officers, we're bound to get caught," Paul pleaded.

"Just one more."

"What are you trying to prove here, Vicky?" the guy who liked Helena, Johnathan, asked.

"Nothing," Vicky looked at Helena. "I just want to make sure that everyone can hold their weight."

Helena frowned at her. "What's that supposed to mean?"

"It means we all do the heavy lifting while you just lookout."

"Someone has to do it."

"Everyone can rotate to do it," Vicky refuted. "It's time for you to do more."

"She does just fine," Johnathan intervened.

"Not fine enough," a smirk was playing on Vicky's lips. "Our next target," Vicky pulled Razor's photo off the board, where all the DC officers' pictures and sweep schedules hung.

"You're fucking crazy!" Johnathan objected.

Razor cursed under his breath. This group was *definitely* going to get Helena killed. It was a miracle that she lasted this long with them.

"She's had a run-in with him before," Vicky pointed out.

Helena looked frightened. "He wasn't high up like he is now!"

"But you've encountered him and survived."

"I'm not pressing my luck."

"You're just stealing from him. With your charm, he'll probably just give you what you want."

Razor sighed. He hated to admit it, but the girl Vicky had him there. If Helena displayed her little act like she did at the hospital, he would undoubtedly give her just about everything. She was definitely capable of wooing people.

"I'm not doing it," Helena persisted.

"It's either that or be out on the streets."

"That seems a little harsh," Kim admitted.

"I'm tired of babying her," Vicky glared at Helena. "It's time for you to step up or leave."

Helena looked at Vicky in disgust.

Razor could tell that the two of them had run-ins before. Probably more often than he could imagine. There was a little jealousy, but Razor couldn't tell what for. It appeared that Vicky and the guy Paul were a thing. There didn't seem to be an attraction there with Johnathan. Still, for whatever reason, the way Johnathan treated Helena seemed to really bother Vicky. Razor wondered if Vicky just really wanted to get rid of Helena all along.

"Fuck you, Vicky," Helena walked out the front door, slamming it shut behind her.

From a distance, Razor could see her pacing back and forth in front of the house. This could be his moment. This could be how he saved her. He could pull up right now and tell her to get in—to come with him. He could call his officers to the house and allow them to exact their revenge without any harm coming to Helena.

It could all be over so quickly.

As he was about to put the truck in drive, someone came out of the house. Even from the far distance, Razor could tell that it was Johnathan. He watched as they talked. He couldn't hear what they were saying, but he was sure that Johnathan was doing his best to convince her to stay. That meant that he was convincing her to steal from Razor. To do that, they had to be encouraging her to use some kind of force.

Razor could feel his rage spilling over. This was an idiotic plan that was bound to get her killed. He had to come up with something and keep it off Nick's radar.

"Commander Razor," an officer radioed. "Commander Razor, Bossman is requesting your immediate presence."

Razor watched as Johnathan leaned in and kissed Helena. Anger rose in him. It was best if he left. So, Razor put the truck in drive.

"On the way," he radioed. It took every ounce of strength not to speed toward the house.

~10~

Razor

Nick paced back and forth, screaming obscenities, while occasionally throwing random things. Razor watched on nonchalantly. Nick was more pissed about this new person than the biochemist.

There was a rumor about a pharmaceutical scientist named Dr. Cole Blackwell. He was creating medicine and giving it to the sick. To make matters even worse, he had gathered a following, who helped hide and save debtors from DC officers.

Nick was infuriated when he heard the news. There was no way Dr. Blackwell should've gotten this far. Naturally, he took his anger out on the officers who delivered the information.

Unfortunately, Razor couldn't object to how Nick was handling this. They both have been on the road and haven't been to Michigan in over six months. The officers should've reported this when they first got wind of it. But the officers didn't think that Dr. Blackwell was a threat and didn't have a lot of followers then. The officers only viewed him as a pest.

And during that time, Dr. Blackwell was able to create a lot of medicine and build a massive following. That wasn't a call the officers should've made on their own, and they paid for that error with their lives.

Razor sat at the conference room table watching Nick have his meltdown. He thought it best not to really say anything and let him get all his frustrations out. Nick was only capable of listening to reason once his anger was gone.

What Razor really wanted was to be back out looking in on Helena and her group. But he was happy that Nick was distracted. That way, he wouldn't be inquiring about the group, and he had more time to handle it himself.

"I need recon," Nick said, bringing Razor back to his situation. He had finally calmed down enough to speak.

"On the doctor."

"Yes," Nick never stopped pacing. "I have people out tracking his location. Once they report it to me, I want you to handle it."

"What exactly am I handling?" Razor wondered.

"Intel," Nick paused. "I have a feeling that the doctor will be more complicated to handle than the biochemist."

Razor was relieved. He didn't really like the idea of killing people who were helping others. It wasn't exactly illegal, and it really didn't require the DC task force involvement. The DCs were made to protect the medical care system, not kill those who decided to help.

"My men should be back soon," Nick continued. "Stay here until they return."

"What about the looters?" Razor didn't want to bring Nick's attention back to them, but he really didn't want to spend his time being cooped up at headquarters.

"Fuck'em," Nick spat. "If these fucking officers can't handle them, then they deserve to be robbed and beaten. And that's if I don't kill them myself," Nick stopped his pacing and turned to Razor. "I need you on this. If Chase gets word of this, he's going to lose his shit…you can get back to the looters once you've done some recon on Blackwell."

Razor suppressed a sigh as he stood. "Copy that, Boss," he left Nick to his pacing and headed for his room.

Razor fought off the feeling of irritation. He was feeling conflicted. On the one hand, he understood why Nick was so angry about this Dr. Blackwell person. The doctor was going against how Nick wanted to rebuild the new world.

However, that was a personal matter, and Razor didn't see it fit to use the DC and its resources to execute Nick's and Chase's personal vendetta. But Razor had to put his personal feelings aside. He was second in command. His commanding officer gave him an order, so he had to carry it out, no matter his personal beliefs.

As soon as he entered his room, Razor pulled out his tablet and headphones. He locked his door to ensure that he wouldn't be bothered, and he sat on his bed. Razor sat watching the video feed from the looters' hideout.

The group was in the living room, and they were debating about Helena robbing Razor. It appeared that Helena had given up on the notion of not doing it. However, Johnathan was still arguing the case on how idiotic the whole plan was. Everyone else in the group seemed to agree with him—everyone except for Vicky. And it seemed that her word was the one that really mattered. Razor automatically didn't care for her. After about five more minutes of screaming and shouting, Helena finally spoke up.

"Enough!" Razor watched her get up from the couch. "I already said I'll do it."

Vicky smirked in satisfaction.

"Just drop it already."

"Helena," Johnathan pleaded. "You realize if you do this, you'll more than likely die."

Helena began walking out of the living room. "Then I die," she mumbled.

Razor didn't want that for her. He had to come up with something that could save her. She needed to be saved. That was clear to him. And the jealousy of a group member was going to get her killed. She could no longer be with them.

Razor switched his video feed from the living room to Helena's bedroom. She had just closed her bedroom door and walked over to her bed. She sat down with her head hanging low. She looked so defeated. Razor pitied her. She had to toughen up if she ever was going to survive in this world.

Helena began to cry. "Please," she whispered. "Please, Jade, come find me already."

Razor watched on helplessly as Helena broke down. At that moment, the emptiness inside of him disappeared. She was what he needed. Protecting and caring for her could be his new mission. And he was determined not to fail that.

There was a knock at Helena's door. Razor already knew who it was— even without the camera. Apparently, Helena knew who it was too.

"I'm not in the mood to talk, Johnathan," she sighed.

"Please, Helena. Just let me in."

Helena didn't say anything. Johnathan took that as an invitation to come in. He closed the door behind him and sat next to her on her bed. He wrapped his arm around her and pulled Helena into him. Helena lay there, lifelessly.

Razor could feel his jealousy building up. He couldn't really read her when it came to Johnathan. He couldn't tell if she actually liked Johnathan or was just going along with it to be kind—like she didn't really have a choice. No matter what the case may be, Razor still found himself jealous.

"This doesn't mean you should give up, Helena," Johnathan said.

"I'm not giving up," Helena said as-a-matter-of-factly. "I'm just tired of debating about it."

"I'll spend days training you."

"Yeah, because that will help me defeat a psycho killer."

Razor didn't like the fact that Helena thought of him that way. Compared to how he treated her at the hospital, he had hoped that she would've had a better impression of him. But he understood her feelings. His reputation wasn't exactly a nice one.

"It could help," Johnathan encouraged.

"At this point, I'll take what I can get. I don't really think Vicky's counting on me to succeed here."

Johnathan frowned. "I don't know what's gotten into her."

"I'm not one of you," Helena admitted. "She's never *truly* accepted me."

"Well, let's prove her wrong. We'll start your training in the morning," Johnathan leaned in to kiss her, but Helena turned her head so that he'd get her cheek. Johnathan looked at her, a little surprised.

Helena smiled weakly. "I'm a little tired."

Johnathan slowly got up. "Alright, I'll see you in the morning then."

"Sounds good."

Razor couldn't help but smile a little. He found it oddly satisfying that Helena rejected Johnathan in some small way.

**

Over the next few days, Razor found his self overflowing with frustration. He watched in on Helena's fighting sessions. Johnathan was teaching her how to fight with knives. The sessions were going poorly, according to Razor. Johnathan wasn't a skilled fighter and made many rookie mistakes, and that was what he was passing on to Helena.

If Razor weren't aware of this scheme, Helena wouldn't last a second against him. Razor was thankful that they decided to go after him instead of another officer. Helena was sure to die that way if they did.

Most of his days, Razor spent shouting and cursing at his tablet, and the rest listening to Nick rant on about the doctor. Both left Razor irritated at the end of the day.

It seemed like the spies Nick sent out was taking forever to get back with Blackwell's location. Razor was hoping that they would come back soon. He was ready to do recon on the doctor so he could hurry back to Helena. After watching her last session, a scary thought came into his mind. What if they decided to target a different officer after all?

Just yesterday, Vicky complained that they couldn't get a location on him. Of course, they couldn't. Razor was being cooped up in DC headquarters. And from there, he would be tracking some doctor. Razor had to make his presence known soon. Otherwise, Helena would die trying to go after some other officer.

"How much longer do I have to stay here?" Razor asked Nick, after his fifth day of being at headquarters. Razor had never been there so long.

"Shouldn't be much longer," this was the first time Nick wasn't talking about Dr. Blackwell. "They better report back soon. It wouldn't be good for them if I have to come looking."

"It wouldn't be good for anyone."

Nick laughed. "You really hate sitting still, don't you?"

"With a passion."

"I understand, my friend," Nick sighed. He hated making Razor do things he didn't want to do. "When the information comes, I need you to react right away. There's no one else I trust with this."

"I know," Razor looked out the conference room window. "But if they're not back by tomorrow afternoon, I'm going out and finding the doc's location myself."

"Agreed."

It wasn't until after dinner when Razor got back to his tablet again. Helena and Johnathan were coming back from a run just as Razor was tuning in. It appeared that they were done with their session for the day.

"Another good day," Johnathan said, following Helena into her room.

"Yeah," Helena didn't sound as hopeful as Johnathan.

Johnathan caught onto her tone. "Hey," he grabbed her arm and gently pulled Helena to him. "You can do this. You manipulated him before. I'm positive you can do it again."

"Then, why the fighting sessions?"

"It's all just a precaution."

Helena sighed. "Sure."

"I promise, nothing is going to happen," he kissed her forehead. "And if it does, I'll be there before you know it."

"Thanks," Helena managed to smile.

Johnathan took that opportunity to kiss her on the lips. Helena didn't pull away when he did. Razor could feel his anger slowly building. Johnathan pulled away with a smile.

"Do you need some company tonight?" he asked, feeling brave.

"I actually want to be alone tonight," Helena said. "If you don't mind."

Johnathan smiled, but Razor could see the disappointment in his face. "As you wish," he kissed her again. "Night."

Helena gave him a small smile. "Good night," she watched him leave out, closing the door behind him.

Helena sighed with relief once he was gone. She sat on her bed and stared into space. Razor wondered what she was thinking about. Silent tears began to fall from her eyes. It was clear that she still felt hopeless.

Razor had to admit, her situation was hopeless. She either had to go through with this idiotic plan or be left to survive on her own. Neither one was ideal for her.

If Johnathan truly loved her, he would suggest that they both leave the group and just survive on their own. That was certainly plausible. Razor wondered why Johnathan didn't recommend that in the first place. Did it even occur to him?

Helena quickly brushed away her tears and sighed. Then, she stood up and removed her shirt. Razor was left stunned, watching her in her bra. He didn't anticipate her getting undressed so seeing her in her bra caught him entirely off guard. She was so beautiful. He couldn't help but to admire her flawless brown skin, her ample breast, her flat tummy—he had to look away. A wave of guilt hit him hard. This was wrong. But his eyes diverted back to the tablet as Helena shimmied out of her pants. Razor could see the top of her underwear before his room door flew open.

"Commander Razor," an officer busted in. Razor quickly threw the tablet on the bed. The officer didn't seem to notice. "Bossman demands your presence."

Razor cleared his throat and quickly looked over at his tablet—now faced down on his bed. "For?"

"His men are back with the location on the doctor."

Razor sighed with relief. It was about time. "Good," he stood up and walked out of the room. "Let's go."

~11~

Helena

Everyone in the house was still sleeping when Helena snuck out—

just like she wanted. She just needed more time alone and away from everyone. She was tired of hearing debates from Johnathan and Vicky. She was tired of Vicky throwing her daggered looks on the sly. And she was tired of Johnathan giving her speeches on how "she could do this." Helena was just tired of it all.

What she really wanted was to run away, but she couldn't do that alone. It really felt like she should've found her sister by now. But no matter how hard she looked, she couldn't find Jade.

Once outside, Helena paused for a moment to stretch on the front porch. Ever since Vicky demanded Helena to rob Razor, Helena had taken to running. It was very therapeutic to her. She could clear her mind and forget about everything.

The only downside to her runs was Johnathan. Helena liked him, just not in the way that he wanted. He seemed like a puppy—every time she turned around, he was right there. There have been times when she desperately needed to be alone, and he would be glued to her. She appreciated his friendship, but he seemed to not understand the words "no" or "not right now."

Helena knew that was the main reason Vicky didn't like her—that and she wasn't really a part of "the group home crew." Johnathan was like a brother to Vicky, and Helena was rejecting him. So, to keep the peace, Helena played along and allowed Johnathan to spend time with her, kiss her, and hold her, but that was as far as Helena would let it go. But that didn't seem to please Vicky.

Clearly, she saw right through Helena's charade. Why else would she demand Helena to try to rob Razor? A person she knows Helena can't handle. Helena would more than likely die trying to go through with this plan—and that's what she was trying to make peace with.

Once she was completely stretched, Helena began her run. She knew exactly where she wanted to go. It was a place that she was able to keep secret from the rest of the crew—even Johnathan. It was a place that was near and dear to her heart, and it was only two miles away.

When they first came across their new hideout spot (a couple of months ago), Helena couldn't believe it. She thought that she would never come across this place again, especially since her parents died. Being there also made her feel hopeful that she would find Jade.

It was Crooked Lake.

Her family used to rent a lake house there every summer. Helena and Jade would spend the day in the water—swimming, playing games, telling each other their hopes and dreams. The two never felt closer than when they were out in the water together.

At Crooked Lake, Helena wasn't just an annoying little sister. She was Jade's best friend. Of course, Helena loved that feeling. She loved being her sister's right-hand. Helena always cherished those moments because once they were back home, everything would change. Jade would become preoccupied with her friends and her boyfriend Vincent. Helena wondered if Jade was with him.

By the time she reached the lake, anger had crept in her. Helena was so angry with her sister. She felt abandoned—left all alone. Jade was supposed to be here with her. She was supposed to be taking care of her. Instead, she was out, God knows where, and Helena was here with Vicky and her crew.

If Jade were here, Helena wouldn't be preparing herself to do an impossible task. She wouldn't be coming to terms with the fact that she was more than likely going to die. All this time, Helena has been searching for Jade and coming up empty. She began to wonder if Jade even wanted to be with her.

Tears ran down Helena's face as she walked onto the pier. She was tired. Tired of being afraid. Tired of feeling alone. Everyone has failed her. She wished she could be strong, to no longer need anyone. But that wasn't her. And she didn't know where to begin to become that person.

Helena dropped to her knees and began to scream. It was a hearty scream. A top of the lungs scream. She screamed out in anger. She screamed out in frustration. She screamed out in fear. Before she knew it, she was curled up in a ball, rocking back and forth, crying.

"Why have you abandoned me, Jade?" she stared out to the water, remembering her and Jade laughing and swimming in it. "Why did you leave me all alone?"

Helena stayed like that for a while. She slowly let all her thoughts go. After some time, she drifted off to sleep.

When she finally came to, she stretched and stood up. She was sure that everyone was awake at the house, and Johnathan was probably looking for her, but she wasn't ready to go just yet. She came here to think about her task but got distracted.

With a sigh, she sat on the edge of the pier. There was no way she could rob Razor; it just wasn't practical. She had to sweet talk him into getting what she wanted.

Helena recalled her first encounter with him.

It was weird. The way that he looked at her. She had an eerie feeling that he wanted to take her or something. He was scary. But she also recalled him being attractive. Even in his black and white photo, she could tell that he was handsome. But she heard the rumors about him. The many people he's killed and tortured. The people whose lives were ruined in his wake. She was lucky that she could use her charm on him once. She wasn't so sure if she could do it again.

"Just dazzle him," she said to herself. "That's all you have to do, and he will give you his supplies."

But then a terrifying thought crept into her mind. What if he wanted more?

It was also rumored that Razor was kind of a lady's man. There were actual DC groupies around, and a lot of them favored him. What if he wanted her to become one of them? Helena quickly pushed the idea aside. It was ridiculous. There was no way he would want something like that.

She sighed. It was time for her to go back. If she stayed there any longer, Johnathan would come looking for her. She didn't want him stumbling across her secret place. She stood up.

It didn't feel like she got much accomplished, but she was glad that she could get a good cry out. Most of the time, she muffled her cries because she didn't want anyone to hear her. But not at this place. She could break down as loud as she wanted to. Helena found it a little freeing.

Taking a deep breath, Helena began the two-mile run back home.

The group was huddled up in the living room when she got back in. Johnathan was pacing back and forth—a worried look on his face. He was instantly relieved once she walked through the front door. No one else seemed to notice her entrance. Surprisingly, they were all deep in a debate. Helena didn't know what about. Johnathan walked over to her.

"Thank god," he greeted her. "Where have you been? I was worried."

Helena frowned a little. "Out for a run," she didn't understand why he would be worried. She'd done it before.

Johnathan got closer to her, peeking over his shoulder from time to time. "Vicky's lost it," he whispered. "She wants to go after another officer."

"Helena," Vicky interrupted. "Good, you're back. We have a new target."

"New?" Helena walked further into the living room.

"Yeah," Vicky continued. "We still haven't been able to locate Razor, so I've decided on a way to lure him out."

"And how exactly are you going to do that?" Helena asked skeptically.

"By going after another officer."

"Am I to carry this one out too?" Helena was trying to see where Vicky's head was at.

Vicky smirked. "No, Razor is just for you."

"This is a bad idea," Kim stated.

"Yeah," Will chimed in. "I'm with Kim on this one."

"We are done debating on this!" Vicky snapped. She looked over at Helena. "Get cleaned up. We're heading out tonight."

Helena didn't bother to protest, but she had a sinking feeling as she walked away.

141

Razor & Helena

~12~

Razor

As Razor sat in his DC truck, staking the area out, he understood why it took Nick's spies so long to get back with Blackwell's location. Niles, Michigan. That's where the doctor was hiding out. *Niles, Michigan.* It was just on the border of Michigan and Indiana. No wonder it took the spies so long. No one in their right mind would think to look there.

They learned that Blackwell, his children, and a group of his followers were set up in a warehouse there. Unfortunately, the spies couldn't get the exact location of the warehouse. Still, it was enough intel for Razor to go on.

He had set up in different parts of the town, hoping to catch a glimpse of Dr. Blackwell or one of his followers. On his first day there, he had no such luck. He was hoping that his second day would yield different results.

Razor flipped through the file folder again. He studied the photos of Dr. Blackwell, his two children: Jackson and Beverly, and a few of his followers. He had to come across one of them eventually.

On his first day, he set up on the edge of town, hoping to catch someone coming or going. This time he set up in the downtown area. There were a lot of stores and businesses to scavenge in. He hoped that he would come across someone there. It seemed like a decent spot. But when he looked up and saw that there was still no one in sight, Razor found himself enraged.

He really did not want to be there. Where he wanted to be was with Helena, looking in on her and the group. Instead, he was in the middle of nowhere. To make matters worse, he was too far to check the video feed at their hideout. At least he had that when he was back at headquarters.

He'd better come across someone soon, or else there would be hell to pay. If this were a lousy tip, Razor didn't know what he would do.

A couple more hours passed when finally, Razor saw someone. Or someone's rather; it was Dr. Blackwell's children: Jackson and Beverly. They were leaving out of a store with some supplies.

Razor was thankful that he decided to stake this area out. He waited until they were almost out of sight before he got out and followed them on foot. It didn't take long for him to be unimpressed with them. They were terrible at being able to detect if they were being followed. It was no man's land out there. A simple look around would've sufficed, but they failed to do that.

Razor was confident that this group would pose no threat to Chase, Nick, or the DC, but he had to be sure.

It took about 30 minutes on foot to get to the border of the warehouse location. Razor stayed put, hiding behind some trees and bushes, as he watched Jackson and Beverly meet up with some of the followers. Razor jotted down a few notes in his notebook while Dr. Blackwell's children and followers chatted amongst themselves. He waited until they resumed walking before he began tailing them again.

They met up with more followers at what looked like a picnic area. Razor was stunned when he saw the number of people that were there. From the looks of it, it appeared to be about 50 people. Razor had to get out of sight—quick. He was sure to be discovered if he stayed on the ground. He looked for a tree that was well covered and climbed. With a look through his binoculars, he could see that there weren't any snipers or lookouts in any nearby trees. He was safe there.

With a higher view, Razor could see that there was in fact, around 75 people there. Razor was amazed. There was no way Dr. Blackwell should've gained this many followers, but here he was. Razor wondered why Blackwell hadn't gotten on their radar sooner, but then he took a look around. This was the middle of nowhere. DC officers tended to stick to the cities. No officer came this far.

That was going to change. Razor was sure that Nick and Chase would see to that.

The group gathered around the only picnic table in the area. Razor watched as a man climbed on top of it. It had to be Dr. Blackwell. He looked to be about 5'11, bald with a light salt and pepper beard. He was a lean man. And he wore a black t-shirt and some black cargo pants. In fact, everyone there was in black. Was that on purpose?

The way the people flocked to the man confirmed to Razor that this was, in fact, Dr. Blackwell.

"Ladies and Gents," Dr. Blackwell began. Those that were talking immediately fell silent. "I thank you all for being with me today. Just by showing up, you all are making history."

A few people clapped and cheered.

"By being here today," he continued. "You are saying that you will not stand idly by while the sick are being hunted down like animals. You will not stand idly by as families are being torn apart. You will not stand idly by as this new world becomes cruel and uncivilized. And you will not stand idly by as injustice and corruption unfold."

"No, we won't!" someone shouted.

"I won't do it!" another person chimed in.

"Our mission is to help one another," Dr. Blackwell went on as if no one said anything. "To support one another during these hard times. The world has ended, but that doesn't mean that humanity should end with it!"

More cheers and screams erupted.

Razor sat back, stunned. This man was a leader; there was no doubt about that. He had these people wrapped around his finger. He was giving them hope—a dangerous thing.

"We, the Black Deficit, are determined to bring compassion, empathy, and strength back into this new world. And we will rise and fight against those who wish to abolish that!"

"All hail the Black Deficit!" someone shouted.

"All hail the Black Deficit!" everyone shouted back. "Into the black! Into the black! Into the black!"

The chant filled the forest.

It filled the area.

It filled the town.

It seemed like the numbers grew. This group was on a mission, and the mission was clear— to be the exact opposite of the DC task force. Razor was wrong. This group was a threat. But to what?

There was no law they were breaking. They weren't really a rebel group; they were just helping people. Was there really a crime in that? Their mission was peace. Where was the harm in that?

But Razor knew Nick and Chase. If anything opposes their idea of the new world, then it was perceived as a threat. Razor could see the paranoia now.

But the Black Deficit?

That hardly warranted any paranoia, in Razor's opinion. The Black Deficit. What an oxymoron. A group with that name didn't need to be viewed as a threat or a second thought. The doctor had sway; Razor could give him that, but from what he saw, that was all to Dr. Blackwell. Of course, Razor would have to stay a couple more days to ensure that theory, but there was no need for them to worry.

**

Razor stayed a few more days to get the proper intel on Dr. Blackwell and his group, The Black Deficit. Razor was able to get very close to the industrial warehouse that they resided in. During the night, Razor set up some cameras and listening devices outside the perimeter. There was no way he could get inside unseen. The border would just have to do.

Razor watched as Dr. Blackwell talked and engaged with each member that was there. Almost every day, new members were brought in. And nearly every day, the group grew in numbers.

It was easy to see that the doctor was a compassionate man. Every person that came to them was welcomed with open arms. It didn't matter if the person joining had alternative motives.

One day, a new member tried to run off with some food and other supplies (like a grab and run) when older members stopped them. It was clear that the more senior members wanted to extract some kind of punishment to this person, but Dr. Blackwell stopped them.

"There's no need to steal here," Dr. Blackwell said to the thief. "Take what you need. That is why we are here...to help one another."

A few of the older members began to protest, causing everyone else around them to shout their objections to their leader.

Dr. Blackwell raised his hand casually to silence his followers.

"If we punish those who are in need, then we are no better than the very people we wish to rise against," he looked around at everyone. He made sure to give them some extensive eye contact. "There is no such thing as stealing here. What we have is for everyone."

The thief began to cough uncontrollably. Dr. Blackwell walked over to him and gently picked him up off the ground by his elbow.

"Let's get that cough looked at," Dr. Blackwell suggested, guiding the thief back to the warehouse. "And let's get you some meds. I just made a fresh batch yesterday."

"Thank you," the thief cried. "And I'm so sorry."

"No need to apologize. This is why we're here."

Razor watched on with mixed emotions. On the one hand, he admired and respected Blackwell. It took a lot of courage to stand against the times. No one helped anyone anymore. Usually, it was every man for themselves. So, to be the opposite of what everyone else was being, took courage, and Razor respected him for that.

On the other hand, Razor found Blackwell to be very naïve. That was no way to survive in this world—not for long anyway. Someone was going to kill and take everything the doctor had. And that's if Nick and Chase didn't try to kill him first.

After watching their routines, Razor saw that the doctor was very easy to get to. He didn't have guards around him. Razor wasn't sure if that was by Blackwell's choice or due to ignorance. By Razor's guess, it was probably due to the former. Regardless, his followers should be more persistent in protecting their leader, whether he wanted it or not.

Dr. Blackwell kept his children close to him, teaching them everything he knew. No doubt, grooming them to take over if he was no longer able to lead. He also kept a unique looking teen close by him. Razor learned that the teen's name was Keeper—more likely a nickname. Keeper was good at creating rare gadgets that could conceal things, administer medicine, and do just about anything the doctor wanted. Razor could see why Dr. Blackwell kept him close by.

Razor was confident that he had enough intel to take back to Nick. But before he left, he wanted to make his presence known to the doctor. All things considered, he actually liked Dr. Blackwell. He viewed him as a good man. So, he decided to do something he never does—warn him.

If Blackwell wanted to help clothe, shelter, and feed people, then that was fine. But if he kept providing them medicine, then he would never get off Nick's radar—until he was dead. Razor didn't want to see that for the doc.

If he was frank with himself, the world needed more people like Dr. Blackwell. Unfortunately, it couldn't go on in this chaos for long. Dr. Blackwell could make a great leader in a new, civilized world. It would be a significant loss to lose him.

Once the sun started to set, Razor went back downtown to get his truck. He drove back to the warehouse—unfazed. He no longer cared if someone noticed that he was there. Razor parked his vehicle at the edge of the picnic table where Blackwell gave his speech a few days ago. It was relaxing out. Everyone was in for dinner.

Razor took a couple of rations out of his truck and sat at the picnic table. His radio sat next to him. It had been a while since he heard any news from headquarters. Razor made sure he turned the radio back on.

Nick probably tried to reach him more than once. He would radio headquarters once he was on his way back.

Razor tried not to think about Helena. Usually, when his mind wandered to her, it left him feeling annoyed and irritated. He didn't want to be in a bad mood when he talked to Dr. Blackwell.

It was nighttime by the time Razor heard movement. He was done with dinner and going over his notes by a flashlight when Dr. Blackwell came into his view.

At first, Razor didn't acknowledge him. He closed his notebook and set it aside. Then he got up and walked to his truck. He opened the driver's door and stuck the key in the ignition. He turned on the headlights; the lights shined bright on Dr. Blackwell. It also showed that there was no one else hiding out nearby. They were all alone, just how Razor wanted it.

"So we can see each other properly," Razor said as he sat back in his spot. Dr. Blackwell was already settled in the seat across from him.

"Properly seeing each other is nice," Blackwell extended his hand. "I'm Cole Blackwell."

Razor took his hand and shook it. "I know who you are, doc. You've made quite a name for yourself."

Blackwell smiled. "So have you, Commander Razor," he released his hand from Razor's grip and folded them on the table. "It's nice to know that I'm making a name for myself."

"Not that nice. Unfortunately, you've gained some undesired attention."

"Is that why you're here, Commander Razor?"

"It is."

Blackwell smiled even wider. "Ahh, I see."

Razor didn't say anything. Instead, he watched the doctor intently. He didn't seem afraid of Razor. When most people saw him, they've practically shit themselves. But not the doctor. He looked at Razor like he was every other man, not the one that everyone dubbed to be ruthless. Razor respected that.

"Are you here to kill me?"

"Right now, I'm on a recon mission. Gathering intel on you and your group and reporting it back to Bossman," Razor stated. "But that's right now."

"...a warning," curiosity filled Blackwell's tone.

"It is," Razor was glad that Blackwell was quick to catch on. "Feeding, clothing, and sheltering people, that's all fine. But administering medicine, that's where you're getting dicey. Bossman is not the kind of man to forgive easily."

"Forgiveness is a hard thing to do," Blackwell stated. "Only a strong man can truly do it."

"That may be true, but I'm here to caution you. Right now, I can tell Bossman that you are no threat to him or the DC task force. But if you keep doing this, I won't be able to hold him off for long."

Blackwell smiled again. "I've told everyone that you're not as ruthless as you seem."

Razor was getting annoyed that the doctor wasn't adhering to his advice. "Don't be naïve."

"I know what I'm being, Commander Razor," Blackwell got up and began pacing. He was silent for a moment—thinking about what he was going to say. "Tell me, commander, what is the mission of the DC task force?"

"Protecting resources, no matter the cost."

"But what if I told you that there was no cost?"

"There's always a cost."

"I imagine you joined the task force for a reason."

"To serve my country."

"And how are you serving your country?"

"By protecting our most valuable and vulnerable resource."

"Healthcare."

"Exactly."

Blackwell stopped pacing and leaned across the table. "By hunting down and imprisoning the sick."

Razor didn't say anything at first. He saw what the doctor was getting at. "By hunting down and imprisoning those who are abusing the system."

Blackwell scoffed and resumed pacing. "Oh, come on, don't tell me you believe that bullshit. You are here to carry out one man's agenda, Nick's agenda. The whole Darwinism bullshit. *Only the strong can survive,*" he stopped pacing and turned to look at Razor. "You are being manipulated to carry out one man's vision. One man's personal dream. Are you ok with that?"

"And what are you trying to do exactly?" Razor knew that the doctor was right. It was what he was conflicting with since the biochemist.

"Rebuild," he smiled. "Rebuild civilization. Rebuild humanity. Show everyone that a little human decency still exists, even if the world has gone to shit."

"You're lucky to still be alive with that kind of mentality."

Blackwell laughed. "I'm very well aware of that fact," he looked around and sighed. He sat back down across from Razor and folded his hands once again. "I suppose I won't have much longer."

"Just stay out of our way, and you'll be able to breathe as long as you like."

"Do you really think our paths won't cross again?"

"If you want to stay alive for your children, you won't," Razor hoped that the threat of his children would keep him at bay. But the look in Blackwell's eyes told him that it wouldn't. Razor was about to warn him again when his radio went off.

"Commander Razor, please respond. Commander Razor, please respond."

Both men looked over at the radio that sat beside Razor. Razor quickly picked it up.

"Razor here."

"Commander, Bossman demands your immediate presence."

"I will be there when I can," annoyance hung heavy in his voice.

"The looters struck again, seriously injuring one of our officers. Bossman wants a swift response."

Razor cursed under his breath. This was precisely what he was trying to avoid. With Nick wanting a swift response, it was likely to leave everyone in the group dead.

"I'm on my way," Razor growled. He got up and gathered his things.

"Until we meet again," Blackwell said, getting up as well.

"You better pray that we don't," Razor called over his shoulder. He got in his truck and sped off. He had to think of a way to save Helena.

~13~

Razor

Razor leaned casually on the hood of his truck as Nick read over his notes on Dr. Blackwell. Razor tried to keep his expression as neutral as possible, but deep down inside, he was freaking out. The group of looters, Vicky, and her crew, had done some severe damage during their last robbery. The DC officer they attacked was lying up in the hospital wing now. Some of the nurses weren't sure if he was going to fully recover.

The officer tried to fight off the group, and the group responded back with violence. The officer reported that five people attacked him, while the youngest one, the girl with the mint hair, was the lookout. The officer also noted that she pulled them off, yelling that they were going too far.

Nick was livid when Razor first got there. However, Razor was able to divert his attention with the information on Dr. Blackwell.

Now, he just needed to convince Nick to take a nonlethal approach to Vicky and her crew. Or at least spare Helena since she was the one who stopped them from nearly killing the officer. If he could just spare her, then Razor didn't care what happened to the rest of them.

Nick laughed. "This is good," he flipped through a few more pages in Razor's notebook. "This is really good."

"As you can see," Razor shifted off the hood of the truck. "The doctor really isn't a threat to us or the cause."

"Still couldn't locate their headquarters?"

"Nah, they did an excellent job with hiding it and making sure that they weren't followed," Razor admitted. "Most of his speeches were done downtown or in random neighborhoods where debtors were hiding out."

"Seems like a compelling man."

"Very persuasive."

"He promises these debtors a lot."

"None of them he can deliver," Razor stated. He didn't dare utter the word hope. That was sure to send Nick off the deep end. "Once they see that he's full of shit, the debtors, and his followers, will move on."

Nick sighed. "Agreed, but I still need to notify Chase about this," he threw the notebook on top of the hood. "Now, these looters."

"Yeah, that was unfortunate."

"It was indeed, but I'm the one who took you off them," Nick looked at Razor. "So, did you find out anything?"

Razor sighed. He was afraid Nick was going to ask him that. "Well, I know who their next target will be."

Nick raised an eyebrow.

"Me."

Nick's laughter boomed. Razor never saw him laugh so hard.

"Really?" he asked once he was able to control himself.

"There's a little tension in the group with the leader and the youngest member."

"The one who pulled the attackers off my officer?"

Razor nodded. "She's supposed to be the one to attack me to prove herself to the leader."

"Do you think she'll go through with it?"

"Not sure," Razor shrugged. "But I'm sure they attacked that officer because they couldn't find me. Maybe a way to draw me out."

"Maybe," Nick started to pace a little. "So, what's your plan?"

"Go into the neighborhood they're hiding out in. Make myself known. Once they try to attack me, extract the appropriate punishment."

Nick nodded, liking the sound of the plan. "And if they don't do anything?"

"Get a team to come in and take them away."

"Sounds good," Nick paused and sighed. He rubbed his thumb against his lips. Another plan was forming in his mind. "Take Damien with you. In case they try to sneak up on you."

Razor gave him a puzzling look.

"I'm positive that you can handle yourself, no matter the numbers," Nick assured. "But I want them to receive a swift punishment. Whether they try to attack you or not. I want you and Damien to take them out."

"Copy that."

Nick walked to headquarters' main entrance. "I'll let Damien know the plan," he called over his shoulder.

Razor cursed under his breath. He hated Damien with a passion. Damien was hard to control. Razor didn't like a man he couldn't control. But he had to go along with Nick's plan. If he knew Razor had some kind of feelings toward Helena, then she would be in even more danger.

It didn't take long for Damien to come out with a bag of supplies. Razor didn't move from the hood when he came out. Damien didn't say anything. He walked over to the passenger side of the truck and threw his bag in the back seat. He got in after that.

Razor casually got off the hood and got in the car. He looked over at Damien as he started the truck.

"Let's go get these fuckers," Damien said as a greeting.

Razor nodded and sped off.

**

Surprisingly, the group was still in the same hideout spot. Razor and Damien both called them stupid. After the stunt they'd just pulled, they should've moved to a different location in case they were followed. They were smart—to a certain extent. Overall, they were just reckless.

The men camped out in a house a few houses down from the group's hideout. The two men took turns watching the video feed from the group's home. Razor hated the idea that Damien was watching Helena, but he really didn't have a choice.

They stayed cooped up in the house for three days watching the video feed and spying on the group. On their third day there, Razor decided to tail Helena. He noticed that she would sneak out of the house, alone, every morning. Razor told Damien he wanted to see where she was going and that he should keep an eye on the rest of the group while he was gone. Damien agreed. Razor could tell that Damien didn't care for the group and was ready to take them out.

Like any other day, Helena snuck out of the house, stretched on the front porch, and began her morning jog. Razor followed her. Two miles later, he arrived at a lake. Razor hung back—using a field of trees for cover. Helena stood motionless on the pier. Razor just stared at her in the distance. No matter how many times he saw her, her beauty always stunned him.

Ever since he's been back, he's felt a wave of relief, like he was exhaling for the first time. Only he didn't know that he was holding his breath the whole time. It seemed like he waited forever for this moment—a moment where he could just watch her alone.

It took him completely off guard when Helena began to scream. Razor quickly took the gun off his hip and looked around. He didn't see anyone else around—it was just them two. Helena screamed louder and louder. There were some words that he couldn't make out and then only sounds of frustration. The screams quickly turned into sobs.

"How could you leave me, Jade," she cried. Helena lay down on the pier and curled into a ball. She rocked back and forth. "Why haven't you come back to me?"

It took every ounce of strength for Razor not to go out there and wrap her in his arms. He wanted to console her so bad. If Damien wasn't back at the house, he would've taken her right there. This girl was dying with this group. Razor wanted to save her.

After a while, Helena recollected herself. She wiped away her tears, sat up, and stretched. Once she got back on her feet, she took a deep breath and started her run back home.

For two days, Razor followed Helena and watched her morning routine. It appeared that no one in the group truly knew how she was feeling—not even Johnathan. Johnathan had insisted on going with her during her morning run, but Helena kept telling him no. After she snapped at him for persisting, he finally backed off.

It seemed like her relationship with Vicky hadn't gotten any better either. The tension was even heavier between them. The two women barely spoke or acknowledged each other.

"The leader is a bitch," Damien said one night.

"That she is."

"How much longer until we strike?" Damien was getting impatient. Razor knew he couldn't keep him at bay for long.

"I have an idea."

Damien put the tablet down and looked over at Razor. The group wasn't doing anything besides lounging around.

"Let's hear it."

"There's a lake near here," Razor stated. "I will drive there every day to make myself noticeable and appear vulnerable."

"Ok, then what?"

"I wait for them to follow and attack."

Damien frowned. "I don't like that idea."

"You got something better?"

"I don't like the idea of you going alone."

"They won't bother following or attacking if I'm not alone."

Damien frowned again. He knew Razor had a point there. "I can hide in the truck."

It was Razor's turn to frown. "That's risky."

"It's riskier for you to go alone," Damien said. "I'm going to follow you either way. I don't feel comfortable leaving my Commander vulnerable."

Razor knew that Damien was going to follow regardless. He saw it better if Damien hid out in the back of the truck instead of openly following him.

"Alright," Razor gave in. "We'll start the plan in the morning."

"Copy that."

They waited until Helena was back from the lake to leave out. Razor put on a show, speeding down the street, blaring a CD. This plan went on for about a week. It wasn't until the ninth day that he finally saw that he was being followed. It was two people—Will and Paul. They weren't exactly subtle. Razor wasn't sure if they meant to be obvious or not.

"Fucking amateurs," Damien grumbled from the back. "Can we attack them now?"

"Let's see if they attack first," Razor could hear Damien protesting under his breath.

Razor kept doing his regular routine. He took a swim in the lake, doing a few laps for exercise. Then he would sit on the pier, lost in thought and waiting to air dry. All the while, Damien would be watching the video of the looters' hideout in the back of the truck. He listened to them talk while Razor sat out on the pier as bait.

They were going to attack soon; Razor could feel it. He was just hoping that it would be the two guys instead of Helena.

Most of the time, he thought about her while on the pier. The arguments between her and Vicky had increased now that he's been spotted. It seemed like his presence frightened Helena. He couldn't blame her, really—his attendance generally wasn't a good sign. The others volunteered to carry out the task—mostly the men. Vicky refused their offer. She wanted Helena to do it, or Helena would have to walk.

Razor was followed by Will and Paul for a few more days before she finally appeared. He was standing on the pier when he spotted her from the corner of his eye. His heart stopped. Instantly, Razor wished that she didn't come, even though he and Damien knew that they would make a move today. There would be no way to hold Damien off now that she was here.

Helena fidgeted with her earpiece. Razor pretended not to notice. Instead, he kept his eyes on the lake. Preparing his self mentally for what he had to do.

There was no way he could overlook this. The group made their move. They had to be punished.

Her footsteps got closer. Razor had to calm his nerves. He had to focus on the task at hand because he was being watched. Damien couldn't see how he *really* felt.

"Hello there," Helena greeted nervously. "Mind if I take a swim here?"

Razor looked at her sternly. "Depends," he said.

"On?"

He snatched Helena's arm. She gasped. He pricked her finger and walked over to the truck. He began running her name. Damien was right in front of him—hidden from Helena's line of sight.

"She's going to use a knife," Razor whispered. "Don't do anything until I give you a verbal signal." Her information came up. Both men verified that she wasn't a debtor. "Do I make myself clear?"

"Copy that, Commander," Damien said.

Razor paused at the truck, and he watched Helena from the corner of his eye. Helena took off her jacket and laid it down. She rubbed her hands together and shifted back and forth. She was a nervous wreck; Razor could see it.

"You're all clear, Ms. Willer," he said, walking back toward her.

"I know," Helena walked to the end of the pier and sat down. She took off her shoes and let her feet dangle.

Razor took a seat next to her. "Never seen you here before."

"Never had the chance to come by."

"And why is that?"

"Been too busy trying to survive. Trying to find food. Trying to find shelter. Trying not to get killed in the next natural disaster."

Razor nodded. "I see how that could hold you up."

"It sure can."

They gazed off at the water for the moment—both trying to figure out how to go on.

"Must be nice being a DC officer," Helena finally said.

Razor smirked. He couldn't tell if she was being sarcastic or not. "Yeah, nice."

Helena laughed a little. A quirky, loving laugh. Razor sat stunned. He never heard her laugh before. It was the most magical thing he's ever heard.

"I mean, you all get food, shelter, clothing, and protection. In times like these, that's nice to have."

Razor looked over at her. Unable to control himself, he took his hand and began rubbing her cheek. Helena froze. Shocked at what was happening.

"Is there no one protecting you?" he asked in a caring, loving tone.

"No," Helena managed to say, sadly. "Which leaves me to do what I gotta do to survive." She was so smooth and swift as she sliced Razor's forearm.

Razor quickly moved his hand from Helena's cheek to his forearm. He was sad, angry, and disappointed. Even though he knew it was coming, he was still surprised. Helena sliced at him again. He jumped up. Blood was oozing down his arm profusely, but he knew it wasn't fatal. Razor pretended to get woozy. He wanted to see if she would go in for the kill if he appeared genuinely vulnerable.

There was a voice giving her a command through the earpiece.

"There's so much blood," Helena whispered. It looked like she was about to faint at the sight of his blood.

Then, trying to be dramatic, Razor tumbled into the lake. Helena screamed as he lay there, lifelessly. He must've been putting on a good show because he heard her moving.

"Oh, my God, no!" Helena jumped in after him. "Don't pass out, don't pass out, don't pass out," she kept telling herself as she dragged Razor to shore.

Razor subtly helped her along the way. He felt her rummaging around in her pockets for a while, then Helena began trying to stitch up the cuts on Razor's arm. Her hands were shaky, but she was able to get the job done.

Once she was finished, she got some water to clean off the blood. Helena stood there waiting. Razor realized that she was waiting to see if he was ok, even though she just attacked him. So caring. It did something to him. He let it go on long enough. Razor's eyes fluttered open.

"I'm sorry," she quickly said. She was very apologetic. "I'm so sorry. Please don't hurt me."

Razor looked around for a moment and then down at his arm. She did a good job stitching him up. Considering how shaky her hands had been. He stood up—towering over Helena. There was no way this action was going unpunished. He wanted to take in this moment.

"It's ok, I won't," he began to caress her cheek as he had done before.

Then, feeling brave, he brought his head down to hers. Helena relaxed a little. And then he placed his lips softly on hers. Helena froze underneath him. When he finally pulled away, Razor stared at her for a moment, trying to memorize her face. The dreadful moment was here.

"It's such a shame."

"What is?" She managed to get out. Her voice was breathless. Razor wondered if their kiss was still lingering in her mind.

"That you never got a chance to swim," just then, Damien got out of the truck—looking vicious and scary.

Helena froze once again. This time from fear.

Razor rubbed his forearm. The pain of it all finally sinking in. "You won't like the water now."

"Help! Help! HELP!!!" Helena screamed as Damien dragged her by her hair and into the water.

Damien held Helena underwater. Helena struggled to get out of his grasp. Razor looked away—he couldn't bear the sight. He hoped that Damien would just make it quick. Put them both out of their misery.

Razor was expecting to see the group coming, but as time went on, no one was approaching, not even Johnathan.

Damien was now punching Helena and throwing her around.

"Please stop," she pleaded. "Please, I can't take anymore."

Damien held her back underwater as Razor sat on the shore waiting for somebody to show up and save Helena. Her pleas were killing him. He wasn't sure how much more he could take. His anger was bubbling with each passing moment. The more Helena took her beating, and the longer no one showed, Razor's anger grew.

Helena fell near him. She slowly began crawling away while gasping for air. Damien frowned as he followed behind her.

"What's wrong?" Razor asked. It was taking all his strength not to look at Helena.

"She's not fighting back anymore."

"God," she croaked. "Please forgive me."

The plea nearly killed Razor. She was accepting her fate—she was accepting death. It was clear that her group was leaving her for dead. Even Johnathan, who promised he would be there if something went wrong, left her to die.

Damien smirked. "So it's death you want," he kicked Helena in the stomach. She stopped crawling. "I'm happy to oblige."

Damien began kicking and punching Helena some more. Once she stopped trying to get away, he grabbed her neck and started strangling her.

"Enough," Razor demanded; he couldn't go through with this. It was her group he really wanted. Damien didn't stop. Helena just lay there still—life slowly leaving her body. Razor jumped up. "I said enough!"

"I'm finishing the job," Damien's grip got tighter around Helena's neck.

Razor charged at him, knocking Damien off Helena. They began tussling on the ground. Razor managed to get on top and started bashing Damien's head in on a rock. Blood squirted from his head. Razor didn't stop until Damien's body went lifeless. Razor went still. He slowly took in the scene; he looked over at Helena's unconscious body. Without any hesitation, he went over and picked her up.

"I'm so sorry," he whispered to her. He put Helena in his truck and drove off.

~14~

Helena

Helena was conscious before her eyes opened. The soreness of her body was the first thing she felt. Every single part of her was in pain—even her eyeballs. A small cough escaped her, and it instantly felt like she was dying all over again. Her throat was on fire. She tried to speak, to call out Johnathan's name, but only an incoherent sound came out. It felt like Helena was going to pass out from the pain.

Her mind instantly went to the vicious DC officer who attacked her. She has never been so afraid in her life. The officer was ruthless. Helena could still feel his punches, his kicks, and his callus hands wrapped around her throat. The look in his eyes made her shiver. It seemed like he enjoyed every moment of it. His presence surprised her. And apparently, it shocked the crew too.

Bits and pieces of the crew's argument began to come back to her. They debated whether or not to intervene while she was being beaten to death. They argued back and forth while she was subjected to painful blows. In the end, they abandoned her. They left her to die. That was expected from Vicky, but not from the rest of them—especially not Johnathan. They should've at least stood up to Vicky on this.

Again, Helena was hurtfully reminded that she was not one of them. She was not apart of the "group home" crew. Still, nothing hurt more than being abandoned by Johnathan. She had put her faith in him, and he let her down. That was her punishment for leading him on.

When she finally opened her eyes, Helena realized that she was not in her bed. In fact, she wasn't at her hideout. She wasn't sure where she was.

Helena slowly turned around to get a good look at the room she was in. Instantly, she froze. Razor was sitting in a chair in the corner of the room—staring at her. Ignoring the pain, Helena quickly scurried to the corner of the bed—putting as much distance between them as she possibly could. She attempted to scream for help and instantly regretted it. Only a rasp came out, which was barely audible, and the pain in her throat nearly left her paralyzed.

Terrified, she looked around for some kind of weapon. This was it. This was how she was going to die. No one survived after being left alone in a room with Razor.

It appeared he saw the fear in her eyes because he slowly got up from the chair with his hands up—as if he were surrendering.

"It's ok," he assured her. "I'm not going to hurt you. You're safe here, I promise."

Helena didn't believe him. She looked toward the room door. He told her he wasn't going to hurt her at the lake. And technically, he was right.

It was his friend who hurt her. So, if he was saying it now, then his friend was somewhere nearby. Helena continued to look at the room door, waiting for it to open. Waiting for the torture to begin. She could feel herself hyperventilating; she was going to pass out soon. She could feel it. The unconsciousness would be a warm welcome to her.

"He's dead," Razor said, reading her mind. "I promise he won't be hurting you anymore."

Helena stared at him for a moment. It was odd; he appeared genuine and concerned. After a few seconds passed, she concluded that he was telling the truth. She relaxed a little, but just a *little*.

Razor sighed and slowly sat back down once he saw that she relaxed a bit.

"I'm really sorry about what happened," he began picking at the arm of the chair. He looked nervous for some reason. "You really didn't leave me any choice. Once you attacked me, there was no way for me to call him off."

Helena attempted to swallow her saliva. Her throat was dry and burning.

"Did you kill him?" she rasped. She wondered if he understood her.

"I did. Like I said, there was no way for me to call him off."

Helena didn't understand why he saved her. He wasn't known for protecting people, more like the opposite. She noticed that Razor was staring at her. It seemed like he was expecting something. A thank you, maybe?

"Where are we?" Helena rasped as she looked around the room again.

"A safe house."

She nodded and rubbed her throat. The pain intensified every time she talked. She was badly in need of some kind of relief.

"Are you in a lot of pain?" Razor asked. Helena noted the concern in his voice.

She nodded.

He abruptly left out of the room. Helena noticed how swift he was. He came back quickly with a bowl of soup. It was like he had it prepared for her already. Helena's heart raced when he walked toward her. She wasn't ready to be so close to him. Razor gently handed the bowl to her. Helena took it, making sure she didn't touch him.

"Eat," he encouraged, backing away from her. "It will help with your throat."

Helena took a spoonful of soup as she watched him take his seat in the corner of the room. She was comfortable with him there. At least she could see him coming from that position. Their eyes met after he took his seat. Helena quickly looked away. She couldn't handle watching him for long. But he never took his eyes off her.

It seemed like he didn't care if he was caught watching her. Helena looked at everything in the room beside him. After a few more spoonfuls of soup, Helena cleared her throat. It felt a little better now that it was lubricated.

"Why did you save me?" the question was barely a whisper.

Razor sighed and finally avoided eye contact with her. He was quiet for a moment. So silent that Helena thought he wasn't going to answer her. Finally, he shrugged. Helena realized that was all that she was going to get. He had his reason for saving her. Helena just wondered why he was lying about it.

"I knew you were going to attack me," he stated instead. "I've been spying on you all for weeks. I knew I was your next target, and I knew you all were looking for me. You and your group weren't exactly stealth about it."

Helena was afraid, knowing that he was spying on them for so long.

What were the things he's seen? Or heard?

"Attacking you wasn't my idea. I was forced to," she explained. She feared Razor might go back on his promise of not hurting her.

"I know," he said calmly. He smiled a little. "I just wanted to see if you had it in you to go through with it."

Helena sat there, stunned. She ate the rest of her soup in silence. It appeared that he was testing her. Trying to see what she would do—what she was capable of. The notion bothered her. She could still feel Razor's eyes on her.

"So, on the pier," she began after she finished her soup. "Was any of that real?"

"I'm afraid not," he said casually. "I just wanted to see if you could really get dirty."

Irritation rose within her. It seemed like everyone wanted to see if she could get dirty. Why did she have to be that way? What was wrong with the way she was? Helena just wanted to live her life without having to hurt anyone. It seemed like you couldn't live that way anymore. Not in this new world anyway. Being herself was a surefire way to get herself killed—or alone.

"How did you know about the lake?" she asked. She could feel the tears coming—hanging on the brim.

"I followed you there one day."

That information caused Helena to look over at him. She had been doing good, avoiding his gaze until now. The action made her feel violated. Crooked lake was her secret place, and he ruined that.

"You're such a cruel asshole," she cried. The tears were spilling over. Every good memory of her family that she associated with the lake was now wiped away. And it was all his fault.

Razor frowned at her reaction.

"That was my special place, my safe haven. And now, because of you, it's ruined. That was the only good thing I had left in this world."

The tears wouldn't stop flowing. Helena's throat began hurting again from her crying and trying to scream at Razor. Helena knew being angry at him was a bad idea. It was an excellent way to get herself killed, but she couldn't help herself. It had been a rough day.

Razor got up and walked to her. Immediately, Helena froze but then caught the look on his face. He looked sad, disappointed, and apologetic. He sat on the edge of the bed and gently took her hand in his. Helena held her breath; his reaction surprised her. She looked down, unable to meet his eyes. Helena focused on his hands; they were firm but very warm. The warmth was pleasant to her. Razor gently lifted her chin, forcing her to look at him. He held his gaze on her for a moment. It seemed like he was memorizing her face.

"I am deeply sorry," he said, sincerely. "I wasn't aware how much that place meant to you."

Helena slipped her hand out of his. "Oh, you didn't learn that from your weeks of spying?" She was surprised by his reaction and the way he was treating her. It was all so confusing that she wasn't thinking clearly.

He chuckled. "You all were robbing my officers," he retook her hand. "Did you really expect me *not* to spy on you?"

Helena instantly felt stupid when he asked that question. Why didn't it occur that someone would come looking in on them? After what they were doing, how could they not? She realized how naïve they had been. They were seriously over their heads with all of this. They were never a match for the DCs.

"We were foolish," she said quietly. She hated to admit that.

"You were making a bad name for yourselves," Razor stated as-a-matter-of-factly. "You all needed to be punished."

Helena frowned at his words. "But I'm the only one who was punished."

"Because your group abandoned you."

Those words stung. Helena removed her hand from his again. He was right, though; Vicky and her crew did abandon her. They left her to die. That was the harsh reality.

"I'm sorry for my bluntness."

Helena looked at Razor again. His kindness was baffling. She wasn't sure how she should feel around him anymore.

"What are you going to do with me?" she figured he had to have a plan, right?

"Nothing, I just wanted to make sure that you were ok before I send you back to your group...if that's what you want," Razor didn't wait for her to respond. He took her empty bowl and left out of the room again.

Helena stared at the empty doorway.

Did she want to go back to Vicky and her crew? They did just leave her to die. They've proven that in the face of trouble, they would abandon her. Is that the kind of people she really wanted to survive with? But what other choice did she have? She knew she couldn't survive alone. They were her only option.

Razor came back in with a cup of tea. He handed it to Helena.

"That's going to help with your throat, too," he said, sitting back on the edge of the bed. "But let it cool down some."

Helena nodded and looked down at the tea in her hands. Her fingertip aimlessly circled around the brim of the cup.

"So," Razor began. "Are you going back to your group?"

There was curiosity on his face. That really surprised Helena. Why did he want to know? It seemed like he was expecting some kind of answer. Helena shrugged.

"I have no one else," she hated admitting that.

"What about your sister? Jade?"

"I don't think she wants me around," Helena brushed away the tears that escaped at the mention of Jade. "If she did, she would've found me by now."

Razor nodded and then looked at the cup of tea. "Drink."

"You're not what I expected," Helena blew on her tea before she took a sip. She could taste the lemon and honey in it.

Razor frowned at her remark.

Helena drank her tea some more. "Do you like being a DC officer?"

"It has its perks," he smirked.

"Like hurting people...do you like that?"

"With some."

Helena looked down at her tea—too afraid to look at him. "Will you hurt me?"

"No, you're safe with me."

Helena sipped on her tea some more. She was about halfway done with it. The lemon and honey were doing wonders for her throat. It wasn't hurting nearly as bad as it was before. Finally, she looked back up at Razor. As expected, he was looking at her. It seemed like he never took his eyes off her—except when he left the room. Surprisingly, she no longer felt intimidated by his gaze.

"What will happen to the crew?" she asked. "If I go back to them?"

"They will get a warning. If they rob or attack another DC officer, then I will have no choice but to kill them."

Helena knew that he was telling the truth. She nodded, satisfied with his answer. She felt lightheaded when she nodded.

Razor abruptly got off the bed and began packing a bag with supplies.

"What are you doing?" Helena's head was spinning. It was hard for her to focus on him. She saw three Razors.

"Giving you some supplies before I take you back."

He was giving her supplies, even after she tried to rob him. It was all too much for Helena to handle. She didn't deserve this rare kindness that she was receiving from him.

"Thank you," she noticed that it came out as a slur. Confusion was flowing through her. She looked over at Razor, concerned. "Something's wrong."

"I slipped some sleeping pills into your tea," he stated as he walked over to her. "Your body's been through a lot. You need to rest."

Helena instantly felt betrayed. The kindness she was feeling now vanished. She frowned at him.

"You said you wouldn't hurt me," she wasn't sure if he understood her as she passed out.

**

The bright sunlight woke Helena up the next morning. When she opened her eyes, she automatically knew she was back in her room. Her heart sank a little. She wasn't so sure if she wanted to be there anymore.

The bag of supplies was lying next to her in bed, with a note attached to the top flap.

It read: *Be safe. And no more robbing my officers.—Razor.*

It surprised Helena to see Razor's handwriting. It was surprisingly neat.

"How did you get here?"

Helena was startled at the sound of Vicky's voice. Vicky and Johnathan were standing in her doorway. Apparently, she didn't notice them because her body was hurting. Helena hoped that Razor had packed some pain medication in her bag of supplies. Otherwise, she was in store for a world of pain.

"I guess he brought me here," Helena finally said.

"Razor?" Vicky was shocked.

Helena nodded. The burning in her throat slowly crept in. She was dreading it.

"Oh, Helena," Johnathan rushed over to her. "Look at what he did to you. You're black and blue."

"He never touched me," she stated.

"No, he just sicced that asshole on you," Johnathan tried to touch her, but Helena recoiled from his touch.

"How does he know where we stay?" Vicky asked, ignoring her and Johnathan's interactions.

"He's been spying on us for weeks. He knew everything. Him being a target. Me attacking him. He knew it all. It was a trap."

"Why did he let you go?"

"I don't know. He never told me."

"We need to leave, quick," Vicky left out of Helena's room, screaming code red. Everyone scrambled around, trying to pack.

"I tried to come for you," Johnathan began.

"But you didn't," Helena cut him off. She didn't want to hear any bullshit excuses. "None of you did."

"None of it was how we expected," he got up and started packing her things.

Helena was in too much pain to move, and she no longer cared about anything. She made the wrong decision. She shouldn't have come back. She should've stayed with Razor; that was ridiculous. There was no way she could stay with him. Besides, it wasn't like he was offering. The whole thought was absurd. She should've just survived on her own. She should've told him to drop her off somewhere safe. Because in the end, that's all Helena had—herself.

"But you promised that you would be there no matter what," Helena pointed out. She couldn't help the anger that seeped through her tone.

Johnathan stopped packing and looked over at her. Helena could see the tears forming in his eyes.

"I know, I failed you. We were all just so afraid," he walked over to her. He took her hands in his. Helena noticed that they didn't feel as warm as Razor's. "But I promise I will spend the rest of my days making it up to you."

Then they heard Kim scream. It was incoherent and terrifying. Everyone rushed out the front door. Johnathan quickly ran out of the room to follow. Then Vicky yelled her name. Helena rushed as fast as she could. Her body was tremendously sore. When she got to the front door, she stopped. Razor was standing a few feet away from the porch. He didn't look or acknowledge anyone else, just her.

"Do you want to come with me?" he asked. "I promise I will keep you safe, and you will never have to worry about surviving again."

Helena was stunned by the offer. She was even more stunned by the look on Razor's face. He looked afraid. Like he feared her rejection. She thought he wasn't capable of that. The look made her view him in a different light, and suddenly the offer felt right.

Without any hesitation or any more thought, Helena walked to him. Johnathan grabbed her in protest, but she quickly brushed him off. This was it. This is how she would survive in this new world—with the most ruthless man in the nation.

And she felt perfectly safe by his side.

~15~

Razor

Razor must've looked over at the passenger seat about 20 times during the short ride back to the safehouse. He was in disbelief. He couldn't believe that Helena actually went with him. None of it was planned. He had dropped Helena off back to her group's hideout. When she was asleep, he snuck her inside and placed her in her bed.

The original plan was to leave Helena and head back to headquarters. But once Razor got back to his truck, he couldn't bring himself to leave. Razor watched Helena sleep soundlessly in her bed from his tablet.

None of the others in her group had a clue that she was there. Something inside of Razor told him to leave, but before he knew it, the sun was rising. Not too long after that, Vicky approached Helena's room and was shocked to find Helena in her bed. Johnathan shortly came after.

They were both stunned by the discovery. Razor noticed that Helena was waking up. At first, she didn't see them. Her attention was on the bag of supplies and the note that he attached to it. If he wasn't mistaken, he could've sworn that she smiled.

Vicky asked Helena how she got there. Helena told them everything. Razor expected her to. How else were they going to get the message? His warning.

And as expected, he watched as they all frantically ran around packing their things. But what hurt Razor was watching Johnathan pack up Helena's things. This was the dreaded moment. She was leaving him—possibly forever.

Razor was prepared to do it—to let her go. But then he caught the look on her face. She was second-guessing her decision; he could see it. This was his moment to offer her safety—relief.

Before he thought about it, Razor was walking up to the house.

One of the members, the girl named Kim, was walking out the front door as he made his way to the porch. She let out a scream. Razor couldn't tell if she was screaming for help or to warn the others. Either way, the message was clear. She was terrified of his presence.

The others ran to the door. The leader, Vicky, shouted Helena's name when she saw him. They were all terrified. But Razor ignored them. Once Helena came to the door, Razor could've sworn that she was relieved to see him. The words had left his mouth before he could think.

"Do you want to come with me?" he asked. "I promise I will keep you safe, and you will never have to worry about surviving again."

Razor waited in agony for her decision. He never really felt that way before. He actually feared her rejection. He wasn't sure what he would do if she told him no. Would he just walk away? Pretend like it never happened? Could he look at her the same way after her rejection?

To his surprise, Helena walked to him, her eyes never leaving his. There was no hesitation when she did it. Of course, Johnathan tried to stop her, but Helena quickly brushed him off. The action just reassured that she was actually choosing him. Razor found himself to be delighted—another feeling he never experienced.

Now she was sitting in the passenger seat as he pulled up to the safehouse. He looked over at her one last time before he got out of the truck—confirming that she was really there. Razor led her to the front door and walked her inside.

"Here we are," he stated. He watched Helena walk in. She took a look around—analyzing everything in sight.

"You really were close," she mumbled.

He smiled a little. "I had to do my recon."

Helena nodded. She picked up a few things that were on the coffee table. "Been here long?"

"Just for a few weeks."

"Doing your due diligence, I suppose."

"This will be your room," Razor led her to the room that she was in before. "I'm sure it looks familiar to you."

Helena looked inside the room. There was no expression on her face. Razor wasn't sure what she was thinking.

"I'll sleep out here," he pointed to the couch in the living room. "It's a pullout."

"Where did he sleep?" her voice cracked. She looked him in the eyes. "Your friend?"

"He wasn't my friend, just a colleague. He slept out here."

"Good," she sighed. "Will we be here long?"

Razor frowned. That part he wasn't sure on. None of this was a part of his plan. He wasn't sure what to do now.

"I don't know," he admitted. "But I need to report back to Bossman."

"Bossman?" there was fear in Helena's eyes.

"It's ok," Razor tried to reassure her, but he wasn't so sure if it really was ok. "I just need to let him know how the mission went."

"And the dead DC officer?"

Razor shrugged. That part, he wasn't worried about. "I'll tell him it was self-defense. The officer wasn't known for following orders. I'll tell Bossman that I gave him an order, he disobeyed, he attacked me, and I killed him in self-defense."

"I can't imagine that he'll believe that."

"Trust me, he will."

Helena bit her bottom lip. She was still afraid. "Will you tell him about me?"

"No," Razor said sternly. He promised he would keep her safe. She wasn't safe if Nick knew about her.

Helena sighed and nodded.

"I shouldn't be gone longer than a day...two tops," Razor put out some supplies for her.

"You're leaving me," the fear in her voice was unmistakable.

"Not for long. Like I said, I need to report back to Bossman," Razor looked over at Helena. The look on her face surprised him. She looked concerned for him. "I'll be ok, trust me. Just stay put and don't go outside."

Helena nodded.

"These supplies should hold you. I'll be back soon," Razor didn't want to do it, but he left. He had been away from headquarters far too long. Nick was bound to send someone out to this location if he didn't report back soon.

Razor listened to the radio intently as he made his way back. He wanted to make sure that Nick didn't give out the order to check on Razor while he was on his way to HQ.

He needed to figure out what he was going to do about Helena. It had been so long since he was responsible for someone else. Not since his parents died. One thing was for sure, he couldn't allow Helena to become a DC officer. She didn't have the heart for it—that much was clear. And that was one of the things that he liked about her. She had this innocence about her. And he was drawn to it like a moth to a flame.

There was one way he could see this working—if he married her. That was going to be a hard sell, but if he married her, she could receive the benefits and the protection of the DC task force. Razor just needed to hide her as long as he could. He might be able to convince her of marriage if enough time had passed. It was a plan. A sliver of a plan, but Razor knew he could make do with it.

Razor made it back to HQ in record timing. The sun was just setting when he pulled up. Determination ran through him as he walked inside. There was no doubt that Nick was going to notice that he was a man short.

When he got inside, he spotted Nick walking into the lobby. There was a travel bag in his hand. Nick smiled when Razor walked in. The smile dropped as his eyes lingered on the door.

"It looks like you're a man shy," Nick noted, a smile still playing on his lips.

"There was an incident."

Nick raised an eyebrow.

"He refused an order and attacked me."

"Dead, I presume."

"That is correct."

"Was this before or after you've dealt with the looters?"

"Kind of during."

Nick laughed, to Razor's surprise. "Well, I knew only one of you would come back. I was hoping that it was you."

Razor grimaced. The whole notion that Nick did it for kicks bothered him.

"Oh, don't give me that look," Nick sighed, then smiled. "I had great confidence in you. Besides, Damien was a pain in my ass with all of his insubordination."

"Then why not get rid of him?" Razor tried not to sound annoyed.

"I believe I just did," Nick looked at Razor like it was apparent. "Now, what happened to the looters?"

"They've been dealt with."

"How?"

"The youngest member took a beating while the others watched."

"The one that pulled the others off the officer?"

Razor nodded. He hated that he had to refer to Helena in such a callous matter, but it all needed to appear cruel. The shocked look on Nick's face reassured him that he made the right decision.

"That was a bit harsh," Nick admitted. "I thought you would've spared that one."

"I wanted to show them that was the punishment for the lookout. The punishment would be worse for those who attacked my officers," Razor paused. "But Damien took it too far and nearly killed the poor girl."

"Naturally," Nick didn't seem bothered. "So, you killed him in front of them too."

"Scared them shitless."

Nick boomed with laughter. "Well done, my friend."

"I'm sure we won't be hearing a peep out of them."

"I'm positive about that," Nick grabbed his bag and resumed walking out of the building. "Nonetheless, I would like for you to stay behind and keep an eye on the looters and the doc."

"Going somewhere?" Razor tried not to sound too relieved.

"Off to a few places. One is to D.C. to talk to Chase about Blackwell. I should be back in a few months, but I need you here to report back."

"Copy that."

"I'm sure you'll keep everything in order."

"That I will."

Nick stopped at a truck. Razor watched as a few more officers loaded in. They all briefly acknowledged him.

"You'll just have to make do with torturing people here," Nick teased.

Razor smirked. "I think I'll manage."

"See you in a few months."

"See you then."

Razor watched as the trucks drove off. Nick was off to resume his "interrogations." Usually, Razor would be upset about being left behind, but now he was relieved. At least he didn't have to look over his shoulder for the next few months. He hoped that it would be longer.

Once the trucks were out of sight, Razor went inside of HQ for a moment. He restocked on supplies and packed some more clothes. He snuck a few things for Helena to wear as well. It wasn't clear what her clothing situation was like, but it was better to be safe than sorry. Once he packed all that he could, Razor alerted his officers that he will be out on the road for a while.

"Only contact me if you've failed to handle the situation yourself," Razor warned. The last thing he wanted was one of his officers coming to look for him. He dreaded the thought of someone accidentally stumbling across Helena.

15 minutes later, Razor was out the door and back on the road. He

hoped to make great timing on the trip back. If he timed it right, he should be back at the house by morning. Razor found his self anxious as he drove back. What if she left? What if she came to her senses and decided she didn't want to stay with him after all? Could he really blame her? He wasn't exactly known for taking care of people—just the opposite.

Without thinking about it, Razor eased off the gas pedal. He wasn't so sure what to expect when he got back. He began to prepare for the scenario of coming back to an empty house.

He never felt so stupid. He allowed himself to believe this fantasy, and now he didn't know what he would do if it shattered. Would he become more ruthless? Is that even possible?

The entrance to the subdivision was approaching. Razor's many questions would soon be answered.

The sun was already up when he parked in the backyard. Razor sat in the truck for a moment—watching the house. There wasn't any movement inside, but that wasn't suspicious. Helena could still be asleep. It was still early, after all.

Razor watched to make sure there wasn't any movement in the nearby house. The last time he checked, the day of the pier, the surrounding homes were still vacant. Someone could've moved in by now. Someone might've come around scavenging.

The anticipation was killing him. It was time to rip off the Band-Aid. Razor gathered all the supplies and got out of the car. He made his way to the back door—walking quietly and deliberately. Before he opened the door, he peeked in the bedroom window. His heart stopped. Helena was lying in bed, sleeping. At this point, he was expecting to come back to an empty house. He was relieved that she stayed.

Razor walked into the house silently, making sure not to disturb Helena. He then unloaded his supplies in the living room. Everything was organized into neat piles. The food rations were stored in the kitchen cabinets. A few cooking supplies were on the kitchen counter. The First Aid kit sat in a basket underneath the coffee table. Hygienic items sat in a cupboard in the bathroom. And different kinds of weapons were laid hidden in various spots around the house, in case of an attack.

Then Razor sorted through the clothing, separating Helena's from his'.

By the time Helena got up, Razor was in the kitchen making oatmeal. When she first walked out of her room, she gasped—surprised to see someone there.

"Do you have to be so scary?" she complained, lingering in her bedroom's doorway.

"Sorry, didn't mean to startle you," Razor began putting the oatmeal into two bowls. He could hear Helena walking through the living room.

"How did it go?" she asked.

"Good, Bossman will be out of town for a few months, so we won't have to worry about him. No one will be coming to look for you. As far as he's concerned, you've been dealt with."

Helena sighed with relief.

Razor placed the bowls of oatmeal on the kitchen table. "Breakfast," he announced as he sat down.

Helena still lingered in the living room. It seemed like she was avoiding him. She stared out the living room window, biting on her bottom lip. Maybe she was second-guessing her decision. Razor frowned at her leeriness. Although he couldn't blame her. She glanced over at him and saw the frown on his face. Razor looked down at his bowl of oatmeal. She slowly made her way to the kitchen. She pulled out the chair across from him and sat down.

When he looked back up, Helena had the spoon in her hand but was frowning down at the bowl. She looked back up at him.

"Did you put anything in it?" she asked. "Like drugs?"

Razor sighed and rolled his eyes. He instantly regretted slipping her sleeping pills, even though it was for her own good. He reached over and took a spoonful of her oatmeal, and ate.

"I won't do anything like that again," he stated.

Helena stared at him—not saying anything. He could tell that she was trying to figure out if he was telling the truth or not. Razor ate his oatmeal, trying to ignore her gaze. It was something about her judging him that made him feel uncomfortable. After a few more minutes, she began to eat her oatmeal too.

Razor was the first to finish. He went over to the kitchen sink and washed the dishes. Helena walked over to the sink when he was cleaning out the pot.

"Thank you for breakfast," she said as he took her bowl from her.

"I brought back some clothes for you," he said without looking at her. "They're just a few fatigues, t-shirts, a jacket, and a pair of boots. I wasn't sure what your clothing situation was like."

"I could use a few more items, thanks."

"They're sitting on the couch," he sat the dishes on the counter to dry. "Hopefully, they'll fit."

Helena walked over and gathered up the clothes. Then she went into her room—closing the door without saying a word.

**

If he didn't know any better, Razor could've sworn that he was living alone. The next few days were dreadful. Helena avoided him as much as possible. She only came out of her room to eat and go to the bathroom. Razor gave her space. It all had to be a lot to process, but the silence was killing him. Usually, he preferred it. But for whatever reason, he couldn't accept it from her. The only time she spoke was to say thank you for the food he prepared. But the most agonizing thing was that he had to taste her food first to assure that he didn't drug it.

"You know, at some point, you're gonna have to trust me," he said on the fourth day. He had just taken the first bite of her tuna fish and rice.

Helena didn't say anything to him. She stared at her plate of food, frowning like she always did when he placed something in front of her.

Razor sighed in frustration. "I promised that I would keep you safe. Why would I drug you?"

Helena continued to give him the silent treatment. She ate her food without looking up at him.

Razor pushed his plate aside. He suddenly lost his appetite. He watched Helena as she ate. She ignored him as much as possible. He sighed again and began to pick at his nails. What was he going to do with her? How could he get her to trust him? It frustrated him, even more when he couldn't come up with anything.

"Why did you save me that day?" Helena asked. It appeared that this was the source of her problem.

Razor looked up to see her eyes narrowed. Some of her bruises were healing. That was a huge relief to him. It killed him to look at her.

"I don't know."

Helena pushed her empty plate away. "And this is why I don't trust you. You're lying to me."

"I'm not lying."

"Withholding information is the same thing as lying," she quickly rose from her seat, causing her chair to fall. "You know why, you just won't tell me."

"Does it really matter?" he could feel his anger slowly rising. "You're getting food, shelter, and protection without doing anything. Most people would be grateful for that, no questions asked."

"I'm not like most people."

"I'd say using someone to get what you want makes you just like most people."

Helena looked offended. "You offered."

"And you came, so why are you treating me like shit?!" Razor kicked the table, and it toppled over. He instantly regretted that.

Helena jumped back, startled. She looked scared and then angry. She stormed off to her room and slammed the door.

"Fuck," Razor mumbled. He spent the remaining of the evening cleaning the food off the floor and fixing the table.

When he lay on the pullout that night, he listened as Helena cried herself to sleep. She was still unhappy. Razor knew that she cried herself to sleep every night when she was with Vicky and her crew. He hoped that would stop once she was with him. He was naïve to think that could ever happen. There was no way he could make her happy, not like this. He had to think of something else. Anything else.

The next morning, Razor went out to his truck and checked in with his officers over the radio. All was well. The sweeps were going accordingly. They were doing well with the number of debtors they apprehended, and the prisons were running smoothly. There was nothing that needed his immediate attention, and there was nothing that required Nick's presence. Everything was fine.

Razor sat in his truck well into the afternoon, preparing his notes for Nick. He wanted to give Helena as much space as he could after last night's incident. After he frightened her, he was convinced that she would never let her guard down with him. It was probably better if he ran some errands or something. The more space he gave Helena, the better.

By the time he went back into the house, Helena was in the bathroom. Razor went and sat on the couch. He took inventory of the supplies. They weren't close to running out of anything, but there were a couple of things he could stock up on.

When Helena came out of the bathroom, Razor was going over the list he created. Helena stood in the doorway, watching him. After a few seconds, she walked into the living room.

"Hey," she was never the first to speak.

"I need to get a few things."

"You're leaving?"

Razor looked up when he heard the fear in her voice. "For a little bit."

"Oh," she looked over at the kitchen. Her voice dripped with disappointment. "Ok."

Razor sighed; he really couldn't pin her emotions. She was all over the place. He was convinced that she would be happy to have the place to herself for a few hours. But here she was, face full of disappointment.

"I could stay if you want," he said. "The things that I need aren't that urgent."

Helena nodded and walked into the kitchen. Razor watched her go through the cabinets, looking for something to eat. She found what she wanted and started preparing it.

The silent treatment again.

"I'm sorry about last night. I didn't mean to lose my temper with you."

She kept her back to him. "It's ok."

"None of this is easy," he admitted. He wasn't sure what he was expecting from her. "I'm trying to figure it all out."

Helena still didn't say anything to him. She began to spread the peanut butter on her piece of bread. Razor watched her back; his eyes followed her movements. She was giving him nothing.

"I have an idea," he said after a while. He watched as Helena silently sat at the table. She took the chair that faced him. Although, she didn't look up from her plate.

"It's a compromise, really. I can find you a safe place to live, and I will just pop in to restock your supplies. You won't have to deal with me…you won't have to live with a monster," Razor gave her a weak smile at the last part.

Helena froze at his statement. "I don't think I want that," she whispered.

Razor nodded at her statement—relieved that she didn't want him gone completely.

"It's been a while since I looked after someone else. Not since my parents," Razor sighed and leaned back on the couch. He was trying his hardest not to get frustrated, but this whole situation was frustrating. "My parents were older when they had me. And even older when the world went to shit. My dad had some medical issues, so I had to look after them even more."

Helena still sat frozen at the kitchen table. He was wondering if she was even breathing.

"It was hard, but taking care of them gave me purpose. They were my mission. I tend to do better when I have a mission," he closed his eyes. "I don't even think they survived the first year…shit, it all seems so long ago."

"They died."

Razor nodded. "My dad died during an earthquake. My mom was killed months later. I felt like a complete failure," he sighed. Reliving his parents' death always put him in a bad mood, but he was already in a bad mood. "Time got really blurry after that. My anger was out of control. I can't even tell you how many people I've killed."

Helena gasped at that. Razor blocked it out. Usually, everyone viewed him as a monster. He shouldn't expect anything different from her.

"Then, one day, I realized how out of control I was and decided to join the army. I was denied, of course, but I was offered to join the DC task force. I had a purpose again."

"So, why do you seem so sad?" Helena got up from the kitchen table and sat in the armchair in the living room. "Why did you save me?"

"Because I still feel empty," he admitted for what seemed like the first time. "The DC was fun for a while, but it's aimless. And I feel aimless with it...then I saw you."

Helena frowned at that. "What do I have to do with anything?"

"The moment I saw you walk into that hospital, my heart stopped. You reminded me so much of my mother, especially when she was younger," Razor looked over at Helena and smirked. "She was difficult to live with too."

Helena rolled her eyes. "I'm sure she had her reasons," she mumbled.

Razor chuckled and then sighed. "You looked lost, sad, and hurt. It was even more apparent when you mentioned Jade. I felt so drawn to you then," he looked over at her—trying to read her face. It was hard to read her. "I admit, I looked into you way before I got wind of you and your group robbing and attacking my officers...I was a little obsessed with you."

"So, when you were spying on us?" there was a hint of anger creeping in Helena's voice.

"I had a camera in your room," Razor stated. There was no point lying to her.

"...do you not understand how *creepy* that is?!" she was shaking with anger, and a few tears were threatening to escape her eyes.

"I apologize for my behavior," he understood her reaction. It was a massive violation, probably more significant than drugging her. "I was excited to be reunited with you. You gave me a new purpose, and I just wanted to save you. Of course, none of this excuse my behavior."

"Did you see me undress? Did you pleasure yourself to me?" she was going into hysterics. "You *sick, perverted freak*!"

"Of course not," Razor frowned, insulted by her accusations. "It was nothing like that. I just wanted to see what you were like. How you interacted with the others. It all confirmed my theory, you needed saving. You were dying with that group."

Helena sat in the armchair, frowning at the floor. She was processing this information. She brushed away a few tears that escaped.

Razor wasn't sure how this was going. He wasn't sure if she would ever be able to trust him. At this point, he completely understood. He just thought that it was best to be honest with her instead of lying.

"As I said, I could take you somewhere safe and only show up to give you supplies. I could leave."

Helena sighed. "I don't want that," she frowned at him. "But no more of this creepy shit!"

"Again, I apologize for that. It was a huge violation."

Helena stayed silent—her eyes refocused on the floor.

"It's just," she paused for a moment, struggling to figure out what she was going to say next. "I hate the fact that you took one look at me and instantly knew that I needed saving. That seems to be what all people see when they look at me...but I do need saving."

"You're not helpless," Razor encouraged. "I also find you very brave."

Helena scoffed and rolled her eyes.

"I'm serious. Not everyone has the guts to attack me," he pointed out.

"That's because I fear being alone more than I fear *you*."

Razor chuckled. "I fear that too."

"Well," she looked up and smiled at him. "At least we have that in common."

Razor was stunned by her smile. It took him a moment to respond. "At least we have that."

~16~

Razor

Three *months later.*

"I need to start training you on how to fight properly," Razor greeted as he walked into the house. He had just come back from headquarters.

Nick reported that he was going to be on the road for a little while longer. A few more people tried to move against the DCs in Georgia, and Nick wanted to pay them a visit. He reported that he should be out for at least another month. Razor made no complaints about the new development.

Helena was sitting on the living room couch, staring out the window. Razor took her surprise out of his pocket. They had been getting along over the last few months, ever since he laid everything out on the table.

She wasn't avoiding him like she used to. And he no longer heard her crying herself to sleep at night.

Helena frowned. "Why...holy *crap*, peanut M&M's!"

Razor laughed at her reaction. He was hoping that she would like her gift. Helena jumped off the couch and ran over to him.

"I got lucky and found them in one of my MRE packs," he handed her the pack of candy.

"For me?"

Razor nodded.

"Thank you," she smiled. Helena tore open the packaged and grabbed a single M&M. She placed it in her mouth and closed her eyes as she chewed. "Mmmm. Chocolate. My God, it's so heavenly."

"Loves chocolate. Noted," Razor laughed as he walked past her. He placed his things on the coffee table and sat on the couch.

Helena turned around and faced him. She ate another M&M. "My dad used to call me and Jade the chocolate monsters," she took a seat in the armchair. "Anything that consisted of chocolate was devoured almost immediately."

Razor declined her offer of an M&M. "You never really mention your parents. What were they like?"

"They were the best parents anyone could ask for," Helena looked down at the package of M&Ms in her hand. Razor could see the sadness creeping in her face. He hit a nerve. "My mother was a passionate, strong, and fearless woman. Jade was so much like her, which was why they butted heads so much. I grew up wishing I was half as strong as them."

"You're strong."

Helena laughed breathlessly at Razor's comment. "No, I'm not. I'm more like my father. He was a very caring, empathetic man. He hardly ever got angry. The only time I saw him mad was the night Jade ran away.

This was before the new world."

"Jade wasn't with you before?" this was news to him. Razor always assumed that Helena lost her sister through the chaos from the natural disasters.

"No, she was 16 at the time and was in the rebellious stage, mostly against our mother," Helena looked out the window, lost in thought. "She had this boyfriend, Vincent, and she would spend every moment with him. My mother never liked him. I didn't either. He didn't seem like he could be trusted...anyway, she came back late past curfew, and she and my mother were having their shouting match. Then my father got angry...my calm, sweet, caring father. Jade drove him there."

Razor sat quietly, listening to her story. She was missing them; he could see that clearly. But he could also see the guilt on her face—guilt he couldn't understand.

"I hated Jade for that. She made our father angry,...*our father*. I was so pissed that the words just came out. I told her to leave...well, shouted, rather," she smiled weakly. "I told her to leave. It was clear that she didn't want to be there, so she should do us all a favor and just...go. And she did. She never came back, no matter how much we begged and apologized to her after that."

"I'm sorry."

"Don't be. I was hopeful that Jade would come back once all the natural disasters began. But then our parents died. They were trying to help our elderly neighbor who lived down the street when her house collapsed with them still inside...I can still hear their screams. They haunt me."

Razor watched as Helena resumed eating some more of her M&Ms. Occasionally, she would wipe away the tears that had fallen. He finally understood where all the loss and sadness was coming from. Her family hasn't been on good terms when the world started to end. And her parents died without being able to reconcile with their lost daughter. And as Razor watched Helena, he could tell that she feared dying without reconciling with her sister too.

Helena sighed and looked over at Razor, shocked. "I think I hate my sister."

"I'd say that's a valid feeling."

"I think she might hate me too," she frowned.

"Well, I don't think that's true."

"Why else hasn't she found me?"

"She's a debtor," Razor stated. "She spends her time hiding out from me," he flashed her a devious smile. Helena shivered. Razor frowned at her reaction; he wondered if he frightened her.

"I guess that's true," she bit her bottom lip. "Is she deep in debt?"

Razor nodded. "Very much so."

"I guess she has a lot on her hands then."

"It's alright to still be angry with her," Razor could still see the conflict on her face.

Helena sighed. "Thanks again for the M&Ms. That was very sweet of you," she smiled at him. "So, why do you need to teach me to fight?"

"In case someone comes when I'm not here," Razor almost forgot about his original subject.

"Well, that won't happen if you don't leave me alone so much."

"True, but I still have duties to attend to."

"I know," she frowned. "I've been taught how to fight already."

"I said *properly trained.*"

"Have I not been properly trained?"

Razor laughed. "Not even close."

"Did you see my training?"

Razor tensed. He could hear the teasing in Helena's tone, but he was still leery about mentioning the time he spent spying on her. "I did."

"Not to your satisfaction, huh."

"I'm surprised you survived so long with them."

"They were that bad?"

"They came up with a plan that nearly got you killed. If you had attacked any other officer, you'd be dead."

"Point taken."

Razor smiled at the frown on her face. "I don't understand how you ended up with them in the first place."

"Well, Johnathan was there when my parents died," Helena noticeably got uncomfortable. "He comforted me after the house collapsed."

"And that's when you met them."

"No, that was weeks later. I was out looking for Jade, but I was running low on food, so I decided to scavenge for something. I found this storm shelter and stocked up on food. When I came out, they were there. Johnathan suggested that I stay with them, and Vicky agreed. And I've been with them ever since...I was 14 at the time."

"How old are you now?" Razor knew it already, but he didn't want to freak her out even further.

"18," she frowned at him. "How old are you? 43?"

Razor laughed. "I look that old?"

"Well, you do have a wild beard, old man."

"I'm 23."

"You're aging terribly," she teased.

"Maybe I should shave," Razor rubbed his beard.

"No, I like it. It works for you."

"Really? For an old man?"

Helena laughed. Razor was stunned once again. This was the second time he heard her laugh. The first time she briefly looked happy. He felt hopeful—something he has never felt. He was enjoying her conversation. He was enjoying getting to know her better. This was something he had to protect—no matter the cost.

"I should make you some real food," he said, getting up from the couch.

"Real food sounds nice."

Razor could feel Helena's eyes still on him as he walked to the kitchen. A few seconds later, he heard her walk into the kitchen and take a seat at the table. She was silent for a moment. Something was on her mind; Razor could feel it. He moved around the kitchen, biding his time.

"Got a new flavor in the MRE this time...BBQ pork ribs," he joked.

"Sounds delicious," Helena sighed. "So, training?"

Razor turned around to see her looking down at the table. Her fingers aimlessly doodling on the tabletop. "We'll start tomorrow."

"Will it be intense?" there was fear in her voice.

The bruises on her face were all cleared up. Razor assumed the same could be said for the other bruises on her body that he couldn't see. It killed him to look at her and know that he was responsible for them. He didn't want to be responsible for another bruise on her body. It was clear that she was afraid that he would put some there.

"It's just some simple moves and combinations. You'll be doing all the hitting," Razor smiled, hoping to reassure her.

Helena nodded. "Ok," she looked up at him and smiled. "Can't wait to eat."

**

Training went fine over the next couple of weeks. Razor taught Helena a few self-defense moves along with some offensive moves. He was mindful not to scare her. He didn't know how she would react if she saw the *real him*—the *vicious him*. That was something he hoped she would never see. It was something he never wanted to be around her.

Along with combat moves, they did strength exercises. Razor wanted to ensure that her physical strength improved as well. Although he was extremely against it, he conceded on running for stamina. Naturally, Helena was delighted about that. Razor couldn't blame her. She was cooped up in the house for months.

Razor was being overcautious about her not being seen by anyone. But Nick was still out of town, so he could at least be a little lax about her going out for a run. Of course, Razor joined her on the runs.

Only one time, he allowed her to run by herself, and he drove his self crazy. He tried to spend the time checking in on his officers, but he could hardly pay attention. Worse case scenarios kept entering his mind. After that, he suggested that he accompany her on the runs. He could even lag behind if she wanted. To his surprise, she agreed to it.

"I know you worry," she teased. "I didn't even think that was possible for you."

Helena had been teasing him a lot lately. Razor wasn't sure what to make of it, but he was glad that she felt comfortable enough to joke with him.

They didn't usually talk during their runs. Razor was ok with that. Some days he would lag behind on purpose. He didn't want to smother her with his presence; that could be annoying. He knew he would hate it. But whenever he did that, Helena would stop and wait for him to catch up. Razor hated to admit it, but he found himself flattered by this action. Especially since he knew that she used to take these runs to avoid Johnathan.

It was odd that Razor still found his self jealous of him. The group was long gone—back to scavenging for supplies and hiding out in different houses. They were still doing little heists, but they did it to other people and not his officers. Razor tailed them a few times to assure that they were on the straight and narrow. It didn't seem like Helena missed them.

They both avoided the lake during their runs. It had become an unspoken rule. Their usual route was to the park in the neighborhood that was three miles away. They took a brief break there and ran back. They did this every other day. Although Razor thought it was too often, they would have to cut down on the runs once Nick returned. He hoped that it wouldn't disappoint her.

"So, how am I doing, Mr. Commander?" Helena asked one day when they reached the park. She made her way to the park bench, which was abnormal for her. She turned around and smiled at him.

Even though he saw her smile more often, Razor couldn't get over how beautiful it was. It left him breathless, even more than the run.

"I'm confident that you can hold your own."

"Your seal of approval means everything to me."

Razor took a seat on the bench. "Glad to give it."

Helena stretched out on the bench beside him. "I'd imagine that I'd be slowing you down."

"This isn't about me."

Helena leaned forward, resting her elbows on her thighs. She frowned, suddenly deep in thought. "...I've never been much of a runner."

"You seem like it to me."

"It's my escapism."

"From life in general? Or someone in particular?"

"I guess both," she frowned deeper. "When Vicky demanded that I rob you or leave the group, I felt trapped. I just wanted to run away from everything. From the group. From my fear. From my life."

"And now?"

"Well, I still feel trapped," she looked over at him and smiled. "Not by you, by this world, but I don't feel the need to run anymore...although, I now understand the meaning of a runner's high."

"And your fear?"

"How can I be afraid with the most ruthless man by my side."

Razor chuckled. He appreciated her attempt at flattery.

"I haven't felt safe since my parents died."

"You didn't feel that way with the group?"

"Nah, although Johnathan tried."

Razor looked down at his hands and cleared his throat. For whatever reason, the mention of Johnathan made him uncomfortable.

"Well, I think making you feel safe is part of a boyfriend's job...from what I've been told, anyway."

Helena frowned briefly. "It wasn't really like that. Honestly, I don't know what we were. I was just going with the flow of things. I never had a boyfriend before, so my knowledge on what to do is very limited," she looked down and smiled shyly, the embarrassment clear on her face. "Plus, I was just being nice. I never really liked him in that way."

Razor knew all of this, of course, but he still didn't know how to process this information. Instead, he decided to change the subject.

"We should head back," he sighed. "I need to make sure you have enough supplies for a few days."

"You're leaving?"

"Tomorrow. I need to check in on someone."

"Can I come?"

"That's not a good idea."

"Oh, please, Razor," she grabbed his arm and pouted her face. "I've been cooped up in that house for months. I follow all your rules, and I've been a much more pleasant roommate. Can I please tag along?"

"It's too risky. You could be seen," Razor noted that this was the first time she touched him.

"I can hide in the back," she quickly suggested. Apparently, she's thought about this before. She poked out her lip even more and batted her lashes. "Please, Razor, I've never been in one place for so long."

Razor sighed. It was way too risky, but he couldn't endure her pouting. She was pulling out the big guns, and it was working on him. Although he hated that she referred to them as roommates, he didn't want to let her down. He stood up.

"Alright, you can come along, but you have to stay hidden."

Helena jumped up and hugged him tightly. "Oh, thank you, thank you, thank you."

Razor noticed how wonderful her hair smelled as he hugged her back. He made her happy. He was doing good with his mission.

"You're welcome."

Helena pulled away and smiled. "So, where are we going?"

"Niles," Razor headed in the direction toward home.

"Where the hell is Niles?"

~17~

Razor

Once they were out of the Metro Detroit area, Razor allowed Helena to sit in the front.

The officers didn't travel as far as they were going. There was never a need to. Most of the people congregated toward the inner-city areas. With all the chaos, people found safety in numbers. Plus, some people tried to escape across the Canadian border once the new medical law was implemented.

That only lasted for a little while. Razor and Nick responded by setting up border patrols around the country. This left most of the people trapped in the inner-city areas.

It was odd having someone in the passenger seat. Razor was used to traveling alone when he wasn't with Nick. He kept looking over at her. Helena was staring out the window—taking in the view.

"It feels like ages since I've ridden in a car," she said, still looking out the window.

"It's much better now that there's hardly anyone on the roads."

"Lucky you."

Razor frowned. He couldn't tell if she was being sarcastic or joking. He looked at the road—trying to figure out if he crossed a line or something.

"I miss the old world," she sighed. "I miss the way things used to be."

"I believe everyone feels that way."

"Do you?"

"Yes and no," he said. He looked over at Helena and saw an eyebrow raised. "Yes, because it was a world that my parents could survive in. And no, because I was never accepted for who I am in the old world."

"You mean your ruthlessness."

Razor rolled his eyes and sighed. "If that's what you want to call it. Ever since I was a young boy, I always had this rage inside of me. I always thought it was good when I released it. But my mother, and everyone else, saw it as a negative. It always made me feel ashamed...like I wasn't good enough...but it's an advantage in this new world. It's praised and welcomed."

Helena frowned and looked back out the window. "That's not all there is to you. Your rage isn't the only thing you have to offer."

That statement made him think of his father. He was the only one who truly understood Razor—who truly accepted him. It was odd to hear someone else say that. It was comforting that those words came from Helena.

"My father used to tell me that," he whispered. Razor could feel Helena's eyes back on him.

"Because it's true," she turned her whole body toward him. "Yes, your rage may be welcomed and accepted in this new world, but if you ask me, it's being taken advantage of. It's being used for evil...to oppress the weak. I don't think that's fair."

"Then what do you think it should be used for?"

"To help those who don't have the advantage that you do. To help those in need. You've shown that you're capable of that."

"For *you*, I'm capable of that," Razor didn't mean to admit that. The words just slipped out.

"I'm sure that's not true. I see a lot of good in you."

Razor looked over at Helena.

Both of their eyes locked on each other. Razor was mesmerized by her beautiful brown eyes. He expected her to quickly look away, but she held him there with the intensity of her eyes. It felt like he was a prey trapped by his predator's stare. A shy smile crept upon her face, and Helena finally looked away. Her gaze went back to the window. Razor looked back at the road, a little shocked that they didn't run into anything by his distraction.

"So, I have to ask," she said after a few minutes. "Is Razor your real name?"

"A nickname. My father gave it to me."

Helena waited, expecting something more. She sighed. "You're really going to make me ask."

Razor chuckled. "It's Ryan...Ryan Thompson."

"Ryan Thompson," she was trying his name out on her lips. "Ryan, Ryan, Ryan." She frowned after a while—not liking the sound of it.

"I strongly prefer Razor."

"Me too."

The rest of the car ride was silent. Helena focused on the scenery and eventually drifted off to sleep. Instinctively, Razor concentrated on what he was going to report back to Nick. He was hoping that the doc was taking his advice and only provided people with food and shelter. It would be even better if Dr. Blackwell disbanded his following and went on his merry way. Where to exactly? Razor didn't know. But he was hoping that the doc was out of sight. Out of sight, out of Nick's mind. The trip would be much shorter and simpler if that happened. But Razor wasn't going to get his hopes up. When he tried to do right, things tended to be more challenging for him.

Helena had awakened once he reached the border of Niles. The welcome sign in view—battered by chaos and time.

"Welcome to Niles," she mumbled. "Who is out here again?"

"A doctor," Razor could feel her eyes on him. She was waiting for more information. He sighed. She was not one for being left in the dark. "He's a pharmaceutical scientist who is supplying medicine to debtors. He's gathered a following...a rebel group."

Helena gasped. "Is he a threat to you?"

"The DC has nothing to worry about."

"I said to *you*."

"No," he appreciated that she was concerned for his safety.

"You've spied on him before."

"Talked with him."

"I'm guessing that you were supposed to kill him."

"More or less."

"Why didn't you?"

"Because I actually admire what he's doing."

"Wow, seriously?"

"At some point, we need to rebuild civilization. The world can't go on the way that it's been. Bossman's ideal world isn't viable for the long run...Blackwell is the key to changing that."

Helena smiled at him. A little smugness in her eyes. "I told you there was some good in you."

Razor smiled. "If you say so."

"So, if you agree with what he's doing, then why are you staking him out again?"

"To make sure he's not doing something stupid," Razor reached the downtown area. "I told Bossman that he wasn't a threat, so I have to make sure the doc is falling in line with that...plus, Bossman is expecting more reports on him. It's one of the reasons why he left me behind."

"So, you have to do your job, or else he will come looking."

Razor knew what she was getting at. "I'll keep him away as long as I can."

"And when you can't?"

Razor sighed. She was worried, but he couldn't blame her. It wasn't something that he wanted either. "I won't let him hurt you."

Helena turned away from him. She looked at the buildings in the downtown areas. There was a pizza joint, and other various restaurants, one of them called the Nuggett. There were an old antique shop and an old post office. There were other unique, corky businesses too, but all their fates were the same—abandoned, rundown, and looted.

Razor parked in front of the theatre.

"I will do everything in my power to keep my promise," he turned to face her.

"And what if other forces won't allow you," she sighed. It was evident that she saw Nick being an issue.

"Well, that depends," Razor got uneasy. He really wasn't expecting to broach this subject so soon. "How do you feel about marriage?"

Helena's eyes widened as she snorted. "You can't be serious."

"Arms twisted...it would be the only way I can keep my promise.

Spouses receive the same benefits as the officers."

"So, I would still have food, shelter, and protection."

"And you won't have to do anything," he looked out the window, trying to see if anyone was coming. "But that's the worst-case scenario...the nuclear option."

Helena nodded and looked down. "Good."

"Don't think I'll be a good husband?" he teased, but it still kind of hurt to know that was something she didn't want. But how could she want that? They still barely knew each other.

"Not sure I'm ready to be a wife."

"It's just our last resort. We don't *actually* have to be husband and wife. I'm not expecting anything from you," his eyes narrowed. It looked like someone was approaching. He retrieved his binoculars from the glove department. Razor adjusted his binoculars and saw Dr. Blackwell come into view. "Shit, get in the back."

"What? Why?"

"Blackwell knows I'm here."

"You think he's going to hurt me?"

"No, if he sees you, then he will have something over me. Get in the back, please."

Helena made her way to the third row. After lying down on the floor, she placed some blankets and jackets on top of herself to conceal her like she did when they were in the city.

Razor took another look through his binoculars. He wanted to make sure that the doctor was alone. It appeared that he was. Razor made sure his knife was in its holster—in case the doctor decided to attack. Blackwell became more visible as he got closer. Razor noted how tired he looked.

Dr. Blackwell immediately opened the passenger door when he got near the truck. He slid into the passenger seat like it was the most normal thing in the world. Razor watched as Dr. Blackwell reclined back into the seat and sighed. The doctor closed his eyes. It seemed like he had the weight of the world on his shoulders.

"Nice to see you again, old friend," Blackwell said after a few moments of silence.

"Likewise, Dr. Blackwell."

"Please, call me Cole."

"I thought you preferred the doctor title."

"I'm only a doctor through a Ph.D."

Razor frowned at that news. "My reports stated that you examined and treated the sick and injured. All duties of a doctor. You had to learn that from somewhere."

"I learned through unconventional practices. I am not a traditional doctor."

"Nothing is traditional anymore."

"Point taken," Blackwell sighed again. "My father was a physician."

"What does he do now?"

"Nothing, he's dead. Died before my children were born...died before I even thought about having children," Blackwell opened his eyes and looked over at Razor. "I used to watch him with his patients when I was a little boy. I loved it. I admired the fact that he was healing people. But it wasn't until I was older that I realized it wasn't actually him that was helping patients, but the medicine he was prescribing them. They had the *real* healing properties...that's how I saw it anyway."

Razor wondered why Blackwell was telling him any of this. All he really wanted to know was if the doctor was being more discreet with what he was doing. He didn't care for Blackwell's history.

"I think I broke his heart when I told him I didn't want to be that kind of doctor. I wanted to be the one who made the medications. I wanted doctors everywhere to prescribe the drugs that *I* created for their patients. I would be healing them...it wasn't until just now that I realized that desire was preparing me for this new world."

"Now you really get the chance to heal people," Razor said sarcastically.

Blackwell laughed. "I'm afraid I bit more off than I can chew."

"Second thoughts?"

"No, I don't regret a thing...except for my inability to sleep," Blackwell sighed. "Are you here to kill me today?"

"No," Razor looked out the window. "Just making sure you're not doing anything stupid."

"I'm still helping people. But I've been encouraged by some of my members to do it more discreetly."

"Smart members. You told them about our meeting?"

"I did. It terrified the hell out of them."

"As it should."

"I will be discreet, for now, but I can't guarantee that I will always be that way."

"I strongly encourage you to try."

"Why?" Blackwell narrowed his eyes at Razor. "Why do you care what I do? Whether or not I get myself killed?"

Razor looked at Blackwell. "I actually admire what you're doing. There's not a lot of people who are willing to help others anymore...and I can't say I blame them. But the truth of the matter is, the world can't continue the way that it's been. It isn't viable. And if we keep this up, what's left of the human race will be extinct. Nick and Chase's bullshit beliefs will be our demise. The world needs people like you in order to survive...in order to thrive."

"Your kind words flatter me," Blackwell chuckled. "So, will you be here long?"

"Until I have enough information to satisfy Bossman. It shouldn't be more than a few days. I encourage you to keep your people away."

"Will do, but I won't tell them that you're here."

"I think that's best."

Blackwell sighed, reached for the door handle, and then paused. "It has its burdens, you know, trying to save the world."

"Doing the right thing always does."

"Until next time, my friend."

"Let's hope there won't be a next time."

Blackwell smiled as he opened the door. "There's always a next time."

Razor watched as Blackwell climbed out of the truck and closed the door. He kept his eye on him until Blackwell was out of Razor's view. Razor sighed and closed his eyes. Although he was trying his hardest, he knew his relationship with Blackwell was not going to end well. Good-hearted people usually didn't last for long.

"It's safe to come out now."

Helena ruffled around in the back. Razor could see the blankets and jackets get tossed around from the rearview mirror. Her pixie hair was disheveled. She made eye contact with him in the mirror.

"He seemed nice."

"We're going to camp out here for a couple of days," Razor looked over at the theatre.

"Here?" Helena frowned. "That's an odd choice. You think there's anyone inside?"

"Not sure," Razor grabbed a few more of his weapons. "But I'm going to check it out. Stay here."

"Should I get back under the covers?"

"No, but stay in the back."

"Ok...be safe."

Razor smiled at her as he left.

**

For the most part, their stay at Niles was uneventful. They camped out in the old theatre downtown. The place was called Ready Theatre. Helena kept mentioning how it reminded her of something from the 1930s. Razor wasn't sure if the theatre was, in fact, that old. Still, it definitely needed a remodeling before all of the chaos. No one was hiding out in the place, and it was clear why. There was nothing of value there.

Razor and Helena slept on a stage in one of the theatre rooms. He only left her once, and that was to look in on the Black Deficit.

"I wonder who came up with the name," Helena said, frowning. "It doesn't seem like that's a name that Cole would come up with."

"Cole?"

"Isn't that the name he prefers?"

Razor smiled at how casually she talked about all of this. "I shouldn't be gone for too long."

Helena sighed. "Ok, I'll just sit here bored without you."

"You'll survive."

"If you say so...be safe."

"You too."

Once he got to the warehouse, Razor couldn't focus. He cursed at himself. He needed to get it together. Realistically, he was going to be away from Helena. At some point, he was going to have to get used to that. There was still a job to do. And if his work started slacking, then Nick was sure to notice. He had to give a thorough report to Nick about Dr. Blackwell and the Black Deficit. Razor knew all of this, but he still found himself going back to Helena an hour later.

"Well, that was fast," she said from behind the concession stand. Helena had been spending the time trying to find any kind of candy there. Apparently, her treat of peanut M&Ms had activated her sweet tooth. "Is everything alright?"

"You have to come with me."

"Do you need my help with something?"

"I can't focus when you're away," he sighed. He hated to admit that to her.

A slow smile crept up on her face. "I didn't peg you to be such a worrywart."

Razor didn't say anything. He tried to avoid her gaze. It seemed like she enjoyed the notion that she had some kind of effect on him. Razor didn't know what to do with this fact. No one ever had so much pull over him.

"Alright," she walked around from the concession stand. "Doesn't seem to be any sweets here anyway."

The trip back to the Black Deficit's warehouse was a silent one. But Razor was determined to get the information that they needed to report back to Nick.

By the time they reached the woods, Razor had noticed that the members were gathered around the picnic area. Instead of Blackwell standing on the table, his two children: Jackson and Beverly, were commanding everyone's attention.

Razor and Helena lingered back—a few trees and bushes covering them from prying eyes.

"We are the way to the new world," Jackson was saying. "We are the way to a new civilization."

The members began to cheer aloud.

Razor frowned at the assembly. He warned Blackwell to be discreet, but what his children were doing was the complete opposite of that. What was Blackwell doing? Did he encourage this? The word of this little gathering was sure to get around. There was no way he could hide this from Nick. Razor cursed as he made his notes.

"The DCs are threatened by us," Beverly chimed in when the crowd quieted down a bit. "They send out their spies to look in on us because they know we are the future. They know that their reign won't last forever. We are heading into the black!"

"Into the black! Into the black! Into the black!"

"Enough!" Blackwell came into view. The crowd immediately fell silent. Some people recoiled back—as if they were caught doing something wrong. "Everyone, please go back to your duties and chores. I would like to have a talk with my lovely children privately."

The crowd quickly dispersed. They all headed back toward the warehouse. They mumbled along the way. Razor couldn't make out what they were saying, but he could sense some tension. He wondered if Blackwell told them about his presence after all.

Once everyone was gone, Blackwell turned to his children. "What the hell are you two doing?"

Surprisingly, the anger shocked Razor. Blackwell seemed like a calm, cool, collected man. It was odd to see him any differently.

"I told you we need to be discreet for a while," Blackwell continued.

"Because of that asshole Razor?" Jackson spat. "We're not afraid of him."

"You should be!" Blackwell quickly looked around—checking to see if Razor was there. "This is a serious matter. These are dire times, and none of this should be taken lightly. That is a good way to get these people killed."

"People will be killed either way," Beverly said. "Even more if we stand by idly."

"We are not standing by idly. We are helping. But in order to continue to do that, we need to be discreet for as long as we can. We are lucky to have been given this warning. We should not waste it."

"We're giving in," Jackson stated.

"We are playing the long game," Blackwell stared at his son. "We are playing smart to survive."

"We're being cowards!" Jackson glared at his father.

Blackwell sighed, closed his eyes, and pinched the bridge of his nose. Razor could see the veins bulging from the side of his head. He completely understood the doctor's frustration. His children were a handful and completely full of themselves.

When he finally opened his eyes, Blackwell backed away from his children. He looked at them for a moment and shook his head. "I was very wrong. You both aren't ready for leadership. Your way of thinking will get everyone here killed."

"You're the one who dragged us into this," Beverly defended her brother.

"You both are thinking like children. Not like 21-year-olds," he scanned the woods again, no doubt looking for Razor. "I'm done arguing with you about this. Go back to HQ now. And no more gatherings. I'm sure we'll get some kickback from this one."

Jackson opened his mouth to say something else, but his father quickly cut him off.

"I said now!" Blackwell didn't notice the way his children glared at him as they made their way back to the warehouse. He lingered behind, still gazing around the woods. He didn't speak until his children were out of earshot. "They think like children. Please, don't take their actions seriously...just let that be known."

Razor stood up from his hiding spot. The two men looked at each other in silence. After a while, Razor nodded and turned away. He looked down at Helena.

"Let's go," he waited as Helena slowly got up. She was hesitant. She made sure that Blackwell didn't see her face. They both walked out of the woods.

"I thought you didn't want him to see me," she said once they got back to the theatre.

"None of that matters now," he sighed. He was putting more blankets on their sleeping pallets. The hardwood floor was killing his back. He was sure that it was uncomfortable for Helena too.

"What's wrong?"

Razor looked over at her. There was concern on her face. "His children are going to get him killed."

She sighed. "I believe you're right. No wonder he seemed so tired in the truck. They look like they can be exhausting," she rolled her eyes and smiled.

Razor smiled back. He appreciated her trying to make light of the situation to cheer him up a bit. He started adding more blankets to her pallet. They were sleeping several feet away from each other. He was sleeping closer to the front of the stage—in case someone wandered in. Helena was sleeping in the back. She walked over and leaned against the wall.

"It's such a shame, really," she continued. "The things he's doing, what he's accomplishing, it's all so...hopeful."

Razor cringed at that word. It was such a dangerous phrase during this time. That was what he was trying to save the doc from. But now, Razor wasn't feeling so *hopeful.*

"We should probably get some sleep," he said, putting the last extra blanket on her pallet.

"We're leaving in the morning."

"First thing."

"Well, I enjoyed the view," Helena took off her boots and jacket.

Razor quickly turned his back to her. He made his way to his own sleeping pallet. He sat down and took off his boots and jacket. When he reclined back onto his pallet, he sighed. The extra blankets helped. The pallet was much softer.

"Night," Helena said.

"Good night."

Razor was in a deep sleep when he felt someone trying to wiggle their way into his pallet. He jumped up, expecting to find an intruder, but it was Helena. She was in a t-shirt and shorts.

"What are you doing?" his voice was groggy.

"Move over."

"Why? Is something wrong? Did you hear something?" this was so out of character for her. He looked at the back of the stage where her empty pallet laid.

"No, move over," she was forcing her way in, so Razor scooted over. Helena quickly lay down once she was under the covers. She was on her side, facing him. "I can't sleep. I haven't been able to since we got here."

Razor sighed and lay down on his back. He looked up at the ceiling; he could feel her staring at him. "I know the pallet isn't as soft as your bed."

"It's not that."

"Is something bothering you?"

"Just tired of feeling so alone."

Razor didn't say anything. He didn't know what to say. It was unclear what he should do, so he closed his eyes and tried not to think about

Helena lying next to him.

"Can you do me a favor?" she asked after a while.

Razor waited for her request—his eyes still closed.

"Can you hold me?"

Razor opened his eyes and looked over at her. Clearly, he must've heard her wrong. The confusion must've been on his face. Helena shrugged.

"Just trying something out."

A little shocked, Razor slowly pulled her into his arms. Instinctively, she rested her head against his chest and wrapped her arm around his abdomen. He felt her sigh with relief. Razor looked down at her and saw that her eyes were closed, a small smile on her lips.

"Better?" he asked.

"Much better."

Razor closed his eyes, amazed that Helena wanted to be in his arms.

~18~

Helena

As another three months passed, Helena and Razor were able to live in peace from Bossman. According to Razor, a few more things came up that needed Bossman's attention. Razor explained that this was very normal. It usually went that way when they were on the road—there were people everywhere trying to fight against the new medical law.

Whatever the case was, Helena was just happy that it kept Bossman away. They both didn't have to look over their shoulder for him. Plus, the safehouse was starting to feel like home to her, which she hadn't felt since her parents were alive. Ever since their death, Helena felt alone and scared. That was slowly no longer the case.

Since their trip to Niles, Helena felt closer to Razor. He was nothing like she expected him to be. He was very sweet to her. And caring. And loving. When he went out to handle tasks, he always brought her something back. Sweets. Books. Unique gadgets that she was convinced didn't exist anymore. And flowers in most cases.

When he first brought her back to the safe house, the place was run down—like most homes. But as time went on, Helena took it upon herself to spruce up the home a bit.

First, she started with her room. She managed to get some new linens for her bed and for the pullout that Razor slept on. The request for those things was very easy. She decorated the kitchen and bathroom with the flowers that Razor brought back. The different gadgets laid around various parts of the one-bedroom home. Some in the living room and others in her bedroom. And her books laid out on display on the coffee table.

Unfortunately, she could do nothing about the holes in the ceilings and on some of the walls. But she made sure she swept away any of the dust or debris that came in.

One day, Helena woke up to Razor fixing the wall in the kitchen. For some reason, this simple action made Helena's heart skip a beat. He noticed what she was doing, what she wanted, and did it with no questions asked. In all honesty, she wasn't expecting the walls and ceilings to be fixed. Why bother when the next earthquake would just rip it all down? But the house felt like a home, and Razor was helping her make it that way.

"You're fixing the wall," she stated as she walked out of her room. Razor didn't look at her. He kept his focus on the wall.

"It's hard to make this place pretty when there are holes," he mumbled with a couple of nails in between his teeth.

"So, you approve?"

He shrugged. "It doesn't hurt."

Helena smiled. "Thank you."

Razor fixed those problem areas in a day. Helena was happy when it was done. With it cleaned, decorated, and repaired, the safe house really felt like a home to her. This was the longest she had been in one place.

The longest she stayed anywhere was four months, and that was with Vicky and her crew. They never really bothered with making a place their own. They rarely even cleaned up some places. Helena always cleaned and cleared out the areas where she slept and spent most of her time. But those places never felt like home.

It was crazy that living with Razor made her feel that way. Never in a million years did she think that she would feel completely safe with one of the most ruthless men in the nation. But here she was, receiving flowers and gifts from him. Living with him. Eating with him. Surviving with him. And sometimes sleeping in his arms.

Whenever the feeling of fear and loneliness threatened to crush her, she would crawl into his arms, and everything would swiftly disappear. Some nights, she would feel perfectly fine and safe. And other nights, usually the nights when she found herself missing Jade, fear and loneliness consumed her.

When Razor wasn't out on missions and when Helena wasn't fixing and decorating the house, Razor continued his combat training with her. At first, Helena was hesitant to do it, but over time she began to enjoy it. He was the best teacher she could get. Their sessions weren't like her sessions with Johnathan. It seemed like Johnathan used that opportunity to touch Helena as much as he could. Usually, she recoiled from his touch when they weren't training, but she really couldn't do that when they were.

Razor seemed to be the opposite. He only touched her when it was vital. Most of the time, he was able to show her a technique by doing an example of it. And one of the biggest things that she appreciated was the fact that he gave her space.

That feat would seem impossible in a one-bedroom home, but it was possible. That was something Helena could never get from Johnathan. But oddly enough, she enjoyed Razor's company. She enjoyed his conversation. He was frank with her about things, sometimes brutally. Razor gave her a lot of the ins and outs of the DC and the way it works. Every time they talked about the DC task force, Helena expected him to suggest that she join.

To her, it seemed like the obvious thing to do. It would be easier to protect her that way—she guessed. But Razor never broached the subject. Helena wondered if he wanted that for her. Or if he thought she would be bad at it. There was no doubt that she wouldn't be able to handle it. She couldn't imprison innocent people because of their sickness.

To Helena's delight, Razor still allowed their runs. Although he kept warning her that the runs would have to stop one day, Helena enjoyed every moment of it. It was such a freeing and exhilarating experience. It was something that she really didn't want to give up, but she understood Razor's concerns. Especially when Bossman would be back roaming around. Everything he did and every rule he made were in the mind of protecting her.

"I have a confession to make," Helena said one day after their run. They were sitting at the kitchen table, eating dinner. Razor had made beans and rice.

Razor looked up from his food. "What's that?"

"I feel so safe with you," she admitted. "I used to feel so afraid. And so alone. Since being with you, I no longer feel that way."

Razor nodded nonchalantly, but Helena could see the satisfaction in his eyes. "That's great. I'm glad you feel that way."

That night, Helena joined Razor on the pullout couch. She snuggled up to his chest and watched as the moonlight peeked through the boarded window.

"What did you do before the end of the world?" Helena asked. She was convinced that Razor was different then.

"Stirred up a lot of trouble."

"How?"

"Got into a lot of fights."

"Because of your anger."

"It's always hard for me to control it."

"It seems like you've got a better handle on it now," Helena felt Razor press his lips against the top of her head. He did this whenever she paid him some kind of compliment. Helena's heart raced every time. She tried to calm the butterflies in her stomach as she pressed up against him even more.

"That's because no one's brought it out of me lately."

"You really think you're that bad?" she looked up at him when he remained silent. There was a grim look on his face. He just nodded curtly. "Why?"

"You have no idea what all I've done, Helena."

"Try me. What's the worst thing?"

"I killed a mother in front of her children...it was a terrible accident, of course, but I still hold myself accountable."

"That's why you tried to join the army."

Razor nodded. "During that time, I was just picking fights with anyone who crossed my path. I followed this dude back to his hideout and attacked him. What I didn't know was that his family was there. His wife tried to help him, and during my blinded fury, I pushed her. She crashed into some shelves, hitting the back of her head against it. Blood was pouring out of her. Her children were screaming and crying."

Helena could see the sadness and the regret on his face. She wanted to take the pain away from him. So, she leaned up and kissed his cheek. Razor froze at the action.

"You've been trying to make up for it ever since," she encouraged. Razor sighed but didn't say anything else. "I say you have a better handle on it," she hated that he didn't see his self clearly.

They lay there in silence for a while. Helena aimlessly ran her fingers across Razor's chest. He buried his head in her hair. She could still feel the shame and sorrow radiating off him. This was a subject she shouldn't have brought up. Helena decided to change it.

"Did you have any girlfriends?"

Razor instantly snorted—his mood shifting. "No."

"What? A handsome guy like you didn't have someone permanent on your arm?"

"No one could hold my attention...not pass the stress-relieving activity, at least."

"Stress-relieving activity?"

He chuckled. "That's what I call sex."

Helena stiffened in his arms. The topic of sex made her a little uncomfortable. It appeared that Razor noticed because he chuckled again and kissed her forehead. Instinctively, she relaxed a little. She hated to admit it, but she loved it when he was affectionate with her. It was usually random, and it left Helena feeling breathless every time.

"Did you have any friends?"

"A few, but they always ended on a bad note," he began to play in her hair. "What about you?"

Helena frowned. "I was a lonely child,...Jade was my best friend. It was hard for me to relate to anyone else. I was basically a loner."

"I'm sorry."

"Don't be," she sighed. "I think that's why it was hard for me to fit in with Vicky and her crew. I don't know how to act around other people…it's probably why I felt so smothered by Johnathan."

"You don't act that way with me."

Helena rolled her eyes. "You don't count. Besides, I'm beginning to see that you're a loner too. Loners know how to act around other loners."

Razor laughed. The rumble in his chest made Helena's head bounce. "I guess you're right about that."

After a few more minutes of them talking about each other's past, Helena eventually dozed off in Razor's arms—feeling secure and protected.

**

The next morning, Helena suggested a run as soon as Razor woke up. He was amused by her enthusiasm. He agreed to it, but after he checked in on his officers via the radio in the truck. Helena went into her room to get ready for their run as Razor headed out the door.

Once she had her running clothes on, she sat on her bed and continued to read one of the books that Razor had given her. It was classic, *The Great Gatsby* by F. Scott Fitzgerald. She wasn't a big reader like Jade, but Helena found it entertaining with nothing else to do. It was interesting to see how people entertained themselves in the 1920s.

When Razor finally came back inside, Helena was more than ready to go. As she went out of her room, she paused. She noticed the look on his face. Something was wrong. He wore an intense frown on his face, and she could see the muscles bulging in his arms. He threw his notebook on the coffee table and began to pace around the room, staring at the floor.

Helena cleared her throat, and he instantly looked up at her—as if he were noticing her for the first time.

"You should go ahead and take your run."

"Aren't you coming with me?" she asked, confused. Razor usually didn't like the idea of her running alone.

"No, I still have somethings to take care of here."

"Is everything ok?"

"Everything is fine," he went to sit on the couch. He flipped through his notebook, looking for something. Razor paused once he noticed that she was still standing there looking at him. He looked up at her and smiled. It was a weak one. "Seriously, everything is alright. Enjoy your run."

"Ok, I'll make it a quick one."

"You don't have to do that. Take your time."

His odd behavior was throwing her off. "Alright," she finally said. "I'll see you soon."

"Be safe."

Reluctantly, Helena left out for her run. Razor's odd behavior was confusing to her. He looked frightened for some reason. Did something go wrong with his officers? Did Blackwell and his rebel group do something stupid? Or did it have something to do with Vicky and her crew? Helena knew that Razor was still keeping an eye on them. He would update her on their whereabouts and what they were doing whenever he spied on them. After a while, Helena told him that she no longer cared to know.

The news always made her depressed. Not because she missed them, but because she could picture herself still with them. And when she was with them, she was miserable. Helena didn't want to feel that way again.

Plus, she couldn't forget the fact that they abandoned her when she needed them most. She couldn't forgive that.

Helena was determined to make her run short, no matter what Razor encouraged. Something was seriously wrong, and she didn't want him to deal with that alone. And although she struggled to admit it, Helena didn't like being away from Razor any more than he liked being away from her.

When she realized that, she intently went over the cause of that emotion, and when it really came down to it, the reasoning was clear. Helena was falling for him. And how could she not? Razor was handsome. He was sweet and caring. And above all else, he was the only one who made her a promise and kept it. Razor had yet to let her down, and she knew deep down in her heart that he would destroy the earth before he went back on his word.

Helena was halfway to the park before she turned around and ran back home. She needed to be there to help Razor with whatever was going on.

She got back to the house in impressive timing. She wasn't sure if she was feeling euphoric from her sprint or from the fact that she was in love, but Helena entered the house feeling like she was on cloud nine.

"Honey, I'm home," she laughed, but it stopped short once she saw a burly, menacing, looking man sitting in the armchair. Helena lingered between the kitchen and the living room. Razor appeared tense sitting on the couch.

The man turned toward her and smiled. "Ahh, you must be the reason why Razor's been away so long."

Helena didn't need a formal introduction. It became quite clear that this was Bossman; he was here. In their house. In their home. This was an awful situation. Helena wasn't sure what to do, but she could see by the look on Razor's face a plan was forming.

"How impolite of me," the man got up from the armchair and walked over to her. Razor quickly got up and closed the distance. "I'm Bossman."

Helena looked at his extended hand. Her heart dropped to her stomach. She took it. "Helena," she mumbled.

"Oh, I know who you are," his smile widened. "You were the lookout for those looters."

"She was already punished for that," Razor intervened.

"Oh, I know," Bossman laughed. "I told Razor I felt your punishment was a little harsh. It was the ones who attacked my officer that I truly wanted."

Razor took Helena's hand and led her to the couch. He made sure he was in between them—shielding Helena from Bossman. Helena tried to calm herself as they sat on the sofa. Her nerves calmed a little when Razor wrapped his arm around her waist and pulled her close to him. Bossman took notice of that action as he sat back down in the armchair.

"My friend, there was no need for you to hide her," Bossman said calmly. "Just bring her back to HQ. She will make a great officer. She clearly has a knack for scouting."

Helena could feel Razor's grip tighten around her waist. It seemed like that was the last thing he wanted for her. Helena finally understood why he never asked her to become an officer.

"I disagree," Razor said. Helena could see the veins protruding from his neck. "She doesn't have the heart or stomach for it."

Irritation rose in Bossman's face for a moment, but he quickly repressed it. "If you're not willing to make her an officer, then there's no place for her with us. You must leave her."

Razor took Helena's hand and looked at her. "All of that is irrelevant because I intend to marry her."

Helena smiled to give him confirmation. He was going to keep his promise to her. The tension in the room increased. Razor turned his attention back to Bossman. The two men glared each other down. Almost instantly, Helena began to get uncomfortable.

"I will make sure she receives *nothing* unless she becomes an officer," the threat was clear in Bossman's tone.

Helena could feel Razor shaking with rage. This was something he wasn't going to bend on.

Razor rose to his feet, fists balled. "Then, I'm out."

Helena looked at him in complete shock. Was he seriously threatening to leave the DC task force for her?

Bossman jumped up and tossed the coffee table across the room. Helena jumped further back on the couch. Razor instantly stood in front of her—blocking her from Bossman.

"You would do this because of *her*!" Bossman yelled.

"She's not becoming an officer."

Bossman stomped his way toward Razor. Razor met him halfway. The two men were seconds away from a physical altercation. Muscles were flexing. Veins were protruding. A fight was on its way. And these were the two most feared men in the nation, so it was unclear who would walk away unscathed.

Helena couldn't bear the thought of Razor getting hurt because of her—getting hurt because he was trying to keep his promise. She got up and grabbed onto Razor's arm, trying to pull him back.

"I'll become an officer," Helena said, breaking the tense moment.

Both men's faces softened. Bossman looked pleased while Razor looked stunned. This was how she could help Razor. She just wanted to make things easier for him.

"Delightful," Bossman smiled with satisfaction. He turned to leave but stopped. Bossman looked at Razor. "Oh, you won't be allowed back at HQ until the both of you are married...I think a marriage license should suffice," he turned his attention to Helena. "It was a pleasure meeting you, soon-to-be Mrs. Thompson. I clearly see what Razor loves about you. I will see you both at HQ, hopefully, soon."

Helena and Razor watched Bossman leave. Once he was out the door, Razor went outside—making sure that he was really gone.

After a few minutes, he came back in, still looking angry but a little relieved. Helena wasn't sure how to feel. But overall, she was horrified. How did this happen? How did he know where they were? Razor saw the look on her face and rushed over to her. He took her hand in his.

"I'm so sorry," he said. He caressed her face. Helena took notice of his warmth every time he touched her. "Please forgive me."

Helena frowned. "For what?"

"I've been stupid."

"How did he find us?"

Razor quickly removed his hand from her face and balled up his fist in anger. "One of my officers complained about me not being at HQ. Bossman got curious. He knew the location of your groups' hideout and came looking."

"Oh," Helena was in disbelief. She didn't know what else to say. She never realized how vulnerable their little home was.

"I was stupid. I should've moved us a long time ago…it's just," Razor avoided her gaze. "You seemed so happy here, and I didn't want to take that away from you."

Helena stroked the side of his face and smiled. "I think that has more to do with you than the house."

Razor smiled and then sighed. "I can still hide you. You don't have to marry me."

"I don't mind marrying you," she reassured him.

He shook his head, still not thrilled about the situation. "We can leave.

We can go far away from here."

"And go where?" his apprehension was confusing her.

"To Canada. Bossman doesn't have any reach there. I helped build the border patrol. I know how we can escape."

Helena was intrigued by the idea, but she was still hesitant. "I don't want to escape without Jade. I'm pissed at her, but I don't want to leave her. I know this world must be even worse for her with her asthma."

Razor sighed. "I understand. I'll look for her more intently. Once I find her, we're out of here...ok?"

"And in the meantime?"

"We get married...and go through with the rest."

Helena noticed the stern look on his face. "Me becoming a DC officer can't be that bad."

"The other officers will eat you alive."

Helena became afraid of the whole idea. What did she just get herself into? But what other choice did she have? Bossman left them with none.

"Hey," Razor caressed her cheek, seeing the fear on her face. "I will do everything in my power to keep you safe."

Helena smiled at him. "I know you will."

That night, they both ate their dinner silently. Helena was accepting the fact that she would become a DC officer soon. The thought of it was making her sick. She couldn't do those horrible things to innocent people. Her only silver lining was that she would be there with Razor.

If she got lucky, maybe she would be out on missions with him. Perhaps she could just ride along with him like she did in Niles. Hopefully, that will be the case.

Once they were done with their dinner, they began to clean the dishes. Razor washed while Helena dried.

"We need to leave out in the morning," Razor said as he passed her a plate. "It's a long drive to the capitol building."

"Why not a city hall?"

"Because that's the only place that legally does marriages."

"Really?"

"Hardly anyone gets married anymore," Razor passed Helena the last dish. "Not even DC officers. Usually, the spouses that receive benefits were spouses before the chaos."

Helena placed the last dish on the counter. "Well, I'm pretty sure everyone is preoccupied with trying to survive than getting married."

"Unless they're one and the same...like in our case."

"I told you, I don't mind marrying you."

Razor smiled. "Well, we should get to bed early. We have a long day tomorrow."

"Ok,...night."

"Night."

Helena packed-up her things and then got ready for bed. She was nervous, but she kept holding on to the idea that Razor was coming up with an escape plan for them—for all three of them. He was willing to save Jade too. Helena was astonished by the fact. She couldn't believe that he was doing all of that just for her. Sometimes she couldn't believe all the things he had already done for her. He was so much more than his rage. She hoped that he could see that.

As time passed, it became impossible for Helena to fall asleep. There was no way she could turn her brain off.

Before she knew it, she got out of bed and headed for the living room. She stood in her bedroom doorway for a moment, trying to figure out if Razor was sleep or not. It wasn't clear, so Helena just took her chance anyway.

"Hey," she nervously cleared her throat. "How about you join me in my bed tonight."

Razor didn't say anything. He slowly got up and followed her into the room. He was leery; Helena could see it written on his face. This wasn't the norm for her. Usually, she just wormed her way up to him on the pullout. It was always her choice. She came to him. That seemed to be the way he preferred it. If it didn't have anything to do with her safety, he allowed her to call all the shots. The only thing he ever asked was if she was sure.

Helena climbed into bed first, and Razor slowly followed. Helena moved as close as she could to the wall to make sure there was enough space for him on the full-size bed. Once he was in bed, she took her usual place with her head resting on his chest. He wrapped her in his arms and squeezed her tight.

"I promise, I won't fail you, Helena."

She could hear the worry in his voice. Helena wanted to instantly take that away from him. Reacting instinctively, she looked up and kissed him. His lips were soft and warm. At first, he was surprised, but then he kissed her back passionately. He hugged her tighter in his arms and pulled her closer.

Helena's heart was racing. She didn't want this moment to end. She loved the way his firm hands caressed her body. Helena pulled him on top of her. She wrapped her legs around his waist, and her hands went up his shirt—making contact with his abs. She felt him pull back slightly. Interpreting it as something else, Helena began to lift her shirt, but Razor stopped her.

"What are you doing?" he asked.

"What do you mean?"

He sighed. "Helena, I don't expect anything from you. You just being with me is enough."

"I know," she resumed to take off her shirt, but Razor quickly grabbed her hands.

"You don't have to do this."

"I *want* to."

"Or are you doing it because you're afraid?"

"We're getting married, Razor."

"I told you, it doesn't have to be that kind of marriage."

Helena sighed in disbelief. Was he really trying to talk her out of this?

"I just don't want you to do this for the wrong reasons," he explained.

"Trust me, it's not for the wrong reasons."

"Then what is it?"

Helena didn't say anything. At first, she resumed kissing him. Razor allowed her to.

"It's because I'm in love with you," she felt him freeze, shocked by what she just said. Helena pulled him even closer to her. "Besides," she said in between kisses. "I seriously doubt that we will have a lot of alone time in the future."

She could feel him giving in. He didn't resist when her hands went back up his shirt. Razor didn't even flinch when she took his shirt off him.

"Are you sure about this?" he whispered.

Helena bit down on her lip and nodded.

That was all it took. Razor swiftly took off her shirt. He was so fast that it left Helena breathless. He really was on his good behavior. His movements were quick. Before she knew it, all articles of clothing had disappeared. Helena couldn't get her heart to slow down as Razor kissed and nibbled on her neck.

"Are you sure?" he asked again.

Helena kissed him in response. She didn't know that someone who was known to be so ruthless could be so gentle. She enjoyed every single moment with him.

When it was over, Razor wrapped her back into his arms; his lips never left her neck. Helena drifted off to sleep, knowing that she made the best decision of her life when she chose him.

~19~

Razor

Razor kissed the back of Helena's hand as he drove toward Lansing. They had packed-up the truck with their belongings from the house and got on the road before the sun was fully up. He was expecting Helena to be sad about leaving, but surprisingly she was ok. She had left a few books and gadgets there, along with the bed linens that she got for her bed.

"So the next occupants can feel a little love," she stated when Razor was curious about her leaving them behind.

It was unclear how she was going to be in the morning. So much had been thrown at her yesterday that he would've completely understood if she was a bit emotional about leaving. Helena was being forced to become a DC officer, after all. Razor tried his hardest to not think about it. Every time he did, he was instantly filled with rage. For now, he wanted to remain blissful.

Helena loved him.

She had confessed on her own. Razor had already accepted the fact that she may never love him or look at him in that way. And he was ok with that. He was simply fine if she only cared about him. Razor found her company satisfaction enough. But she loved him. And not only that, but she also desired to be intimate with him.

Razor fought it as long as he could—confident that she was only making this drastic decision because of everything that happened earlier that day. Who could blame her? Nick basically put a gun to her head. So, Razor was determined to fight it. Then she said the magic words, "I love you." And Razor couldn't help but give in. Because he was definitely in love with her.

He woke up feeling no regrets, but he wondered if Helena felt the same. So, as they got ready to go, he made sure to give her space. He spent most of the time outside loading up the truck.

"Avoiding me, I see," Helena stated when she came outside to hand him a bag.

Razor avoided her eye contact, embarrassed that she was able to see right through him. "Figured you might want some space."

"That's what you interpreted from last night?"

It seemed like she got off on teasing him. Razor appreciated that. He smiled a little. "I was just giving you that option."

Helena pulled him to her. She got on her tippy-toes and kissed him. "I don't want space from you."

Razor smiled. "Yes, ma'am."

They got on the road shortly after that. Razor kept her hand in his'—validating that all of this was real. At times he caught her staring at him.

Other times, she looked out the window taking in the view. Razor fought off any thoughts about Nick but looking at Helena only seemed to make him think about Nick even more. He had to protect Helena at all cost. But it was feeling like he was feeding her to the wolves.

Razor couldn't believe how stupid he'd been. He should've kept moving Helena to different locations. If he'd done that, Nick would've never found them.

There was a strong urge to kill the officer who complained about his absence at HQ. Razor was never at HQ. It wasn't *that* rare for him to be gone for so long. He couldn't think of a solid reason why the officer would've complained in the first place. The only thing that came to mind was that the officer was trying to shirk from some kind of responsibility and blamed Razor for not being there.

Whatever the case may be, they endangered Helena's life, and Razor would make sure that they paid for it.

Now, Razor had to come up with an escape plan for them. Because he knew, before too long, he and Nick would no longer be friends. They would be on opposing sides. Razor could feel it. With his views on Dr. Blackwell and how he felt about Helena, their relationship was destined to come to a bloody end.

The first thing he needed to tackle was finding Jade. They couldn't escape without her. He couldn't really blame Helena for requesting that. Honestly, Razor would've suggested it if she hadn't.

"What are you thinking about?" Helena asked. She laughed a little. "You got a big frown going on over there."

Razor looked over and smiled a little. He kissed the back of her hand. "Sorry, I was just thinking about a few things."

"Care to elaborate?"

"Coming up with our escape plan and thinking of ways to find Jade."

"You have any ideas?"

Razor sighed. "Just one. Finding the last hospital she checked into and searching the surrounding area."

"That sounds promising."

"It's not solid, but it's something."

"You gotta start somewhere."

"You sure you want to do this?"

Helena frowned. "Becoming a DC officer?"

"And marrying me."

Helena sighed and rolled her eyes. "Do you not want to marry me or something? Geesh, you're really making a girl feel special here."

Razor laughed. "I wanted to marry you the day I saw you in that hospital," he looked over at her. "You have no idea how hard I had to restrain myself from taking you."

"Wow...*you're creepy.*"

"Sorry."

A sly smile spread across her face. She shrugged. "I'm stuck with you now."

Razor chuckled. "That, you are."

The rest of the drive was quick and uneventful. Razor was curious to see Helena's reaction to Lansing. It's been a while since he went with a first-timer. Usually, their responses were always the same: excited and angry. Knowing that the government was living lavishly while its citizens were suffering was a hard pill to swallow.

Helena gasped when the welcome to Lansing sign came into view. It was clean, shiny, and looked brand new. She gasped again when the downtown buildings came into sight. It was clear that the facilities were up and running with electricity. Plus, they weren't damaged and rundown like most of the buildings in the state—and the nation.

"This can't be real," she looked over at Razor in shock.

"It is."

"How is this possible?"

"The government put all of its resources into maintaining the nation's capital cities."

"While everyone else in the nation is suffering."

"Shitty, I know."

Helena looked back out the window in amazement, but there was anger in her eyes. She had the same kind of reaction Razor had when he first saw this place.

"Bright side, I guess," he stated. "Is that this is one of the perks you get being a DC officer. You stay in places like this for free."

"Fantastic," she grumbled.

Razor didn't have to guess whether or not she was being sarcastic. The sarcasm hung heavily in her voice. He honestly couldn't blame her. This was where the rich and privileged lived. They didn't truly understand what this new world was like.

Despite her initial reaction to the city, Razor wanted to make this day really special for Helena. It was their wedding day, after all,...forced or not. He desired to make her happy, so he drove to a place that he thought would put a smile on her face.

"I can't believe my eyes!" Helena shouted once she saw the sign. She turned to look at him. "There really is a functioning mall in existence...ugh, I'm kind of hating myself right now."

Razor laughed.

"I shouldn't be this delighted."

"You, of all people, deserve this."

She blushed. "Thank you."

There weren't that many functioning stores inside, but it was more than anywhere else. Razor watched as Helena looked around in awe. The lights were on, the AC was blasting, and there was even some music playing through the PA system. Razor could see the tears forming in her eyes.

"The many memories I am having right now," she broke off. Helena wiped away a few tears that hit her cheek. "And we're here because…"

"It's your wedding day," he headed toward a women's boutique shop. "You deserve to look nice on your wedding day."

Helena followed him. "I can't imagine what a dress would cost."

"Don't worry about it."

The boutique was dead. Razor expected that. Even in the rich part of town, who actually had the time to shop?

The store owner quickly approached them as they entered. She glanced at their clothing and immediately looked disappointed.

"Here to look…I assume," the owner said dismissively.

"Here to shop."

"Due to the rarity of these clothes, I *highly* doubt that *you* could afford it, officer."

"Commander Razor," he said casually, handing her his I.D. for verification. "And I believe that I can."

The shop owner's face dropped when she realized who he was—like most people outside the DC did. Razor loved and hated it. People quickly gave him their respect, but it was always rooted in fear.

"My apologies, Commander," she lowered her eyes. "But I fail to see what you would like here."

"It won't be for me, but for my wife," he gestured to Helena, who lingered a few feet away.

The woman looked at her, surprised. "Of course, she can select whatever she likes…on the house."

"I appreciate your generosity," he looked over at Helena. "Pick whatever you like."

Helena slowly walked up to him, doubt on her face. "I just take whatever I want...for free?"

Razor could see the dilemma in her eyes. "Is that not what you want?"

"Just seems wrong," she whispered.

Razor looked over to see that the store owner went to sit back down in a chair behind the counter. "This woman goes to sleep at night in a warm bed, with her belly full and a safe filled with money. She never once had to worry about surviving. Trust me, she's not losing out on anything."

Helena didn't say anything. She glanced back at the store owner.

Razor kissed her forehead. "This is your day. Get what you want. I'll be waiting outside," he didn't wait for a response.

No part of him felt bad for the store owner. She didn't have a care in the world—a luxury. If he had to scare someone to give Helena something nice, then he would happily do it. If she was forced to marry him, then he would at least make sure that she looked as beautiful as she could be.

It didn't take long for Helena to come out with something. Razor wasn't shocked. It wasn't that much stuff to pick from, which was why it was so rare and expensive.

His trip to the jewelry store was even a quicker one. Helena waited outside the store while he picked out two gold wedding bands. Helena's face was unreadable as they made their way out of the mall. Razor wanted to pry but resisted the urge. He wasn't sure if it was from his behavior or the store owner.

"I apologize if my behavior upset you," he said once they reached the mall's exit.

"I'm glad to see the rich still behaves the same."

"Was she rude?"

"Aren't they always?" she rolled her eyes and sighed. "It just reminded me of the times Jade and I ventured over to the rich side of Somerset. We enjoyed the peace and quiet but was looked down on because we didn't belong. This mall is nothing but the rich side."

"I'm sorry."

"At least I got some sweet threads out of it."

Razor smiled. "What did you get?"

Helena frowned. "It's bad luck for you to see it before the wedding...right?"

Razor shrugged. "The world is just bad luck right now."

"I guess you're right about that," Helena sighed and then quickly smiled. "But still. You can't see it until the ceremony."

"Fair enough."

Their next stop was to the hotel; it was just a few blocks away from the capitol building. The hotel looked brand-new. It was recently built just before the chaos broke out. The building was black, green, and white. The black, painted bricks made the hotel look modern and sleek, and the words Capital Hotel was painted in white and green.

"Fancy," Helena admired as they approached the building.

"You have no idea."

Razor quickly checked them in by showing his I.D. to the staff. They received the royal star treatment. Most of the staff thanked Razor for his service once they left them.

It had been a while since he last been to the capital. That time it was with Nick. They both were treated like gods. Razor loved it then. Unfortunately, he hated it now. Everyone he interacted with feared him. He was sure that Helena could see that. He wondered what she thought about that. Did she see him differently?

The staff gave them a lovely room on the top floor. The room was luxurious and cozy; there was a spacious bathroom with a clawfoot tub and a large shower. There was a little kitchenette, and the living room was right in front of the bedroom, which had a queen size bed in it. A flat-screen TV was mounted on the wall. Helena marveled at everything in the room and paused at the TV. Razor tossed her the remote.

"No way," she said, astonished. She screamed in delight when she turned the TV on and saw a sitcom playing. "Am I dreaming?!"

"There's nothing but reruns, but it's something."

Helena stared at the TV. "This is amazing."

"We should get ready," Razor didn't want to take her away from this delight, but they were there to do something. And the quicker they got it done, the better. Nick wasn't a man known for patience.

"Ok, but TV later."

"TV later."

"Promise?"

Razor laughed. "I promise."

Helena got ready in the bathroom while Razor dressed in the bedroom.

It wasn't anything too fancy. Razor just wore his formal uniform that they used on special occasions. It was rare that they got a chance to wear it. Razor recalled only wearing it once, and that was at a formal dinner with Nick and Chase.

Astonishingly, Razor was nervous as he dressed. He never thought that he would ever find someone who he loved romantically. He never even pictured himself being married. But here he was, getting ready for his marriage ceremony.

Once he was dressed, he paced around the room nervously. All these emotions were new to him, and he wasn't sure how to process them. His feelings for Helena made him feel vulnerable, and feeling vulnerable made him feel even more ruthless. No matter what, he couldn't let anything happen to her.

"Ready," Helena announced.

Razor looked up to see her standing in the living room area. Her skin looked light and fresh. Her hair was slicked down and wavy. Her lips were graced with a little gloss, and she wore a long black trench coat. Razor was a tad confused by her clothing choice.

"It's to cover up what I'm wearing," she laughed at his confusion. "I told you, it's bad luck to see me in my clothing before the ceremony."

Razor couldn't help but stare at her. Helena looked beautiful.

"Umm, are we still doing this thing?" she asked.

Razor cleared his throat and grabbed the rings off the bed. "Let's go."

"You clean up nice," she complimented as he walked past her.

Razor noticed how good she smelled. "You look beautiful," he held open the room door for her. Helena rolled her eyes as she walked out the door.

"You haven't even seen what I'm wearing yet."

"Doesn't matter. You look beautiful."

Once they got down to the lobby, Razor told one of the staff members that he needed someone to witness their ceremony. The manager was happy to send two bellhops with them. Razor led them all to the capitol building where he was set to get married.

**

Before he knew it, Razor was standing next to the justice of the peace who would marry them. The two bellhops sat in the chairs that were in the small room. One sat on the side of the groom, the other on the side of the bride. Helena hadn't entered the room yet. At the moment, she was out in the hall filling out a form a secretary required from her. The ceremony was to start when she was done.

Razor fought off his agitation. Each passing moment was agonizing to him. His nerves were on edge, and the day seemed to drag on. He wanted this and feared it all at the same time.

Then, Helena walked in with the secretary by her side. Razor was expecting to see some kind of fear or nervousness on her face, but she looked calm. She must've been able to read his reaction because a sly, confident smile spread across her face. Helena undid her trench coat, took it off, and handed it to the secretary.

Razor was hypnotized by the sight of her. She had on a white pants suit. The suit's jacket was low cut, and he could see a little bit of her cleavage. The pants clung to her hips, but the rest of it flowed, covering the black heels she wore. Helena was more than beautiful; she was magnificent.

The justice of the peace cleared his throat. "Shall we begin?"

It took a moment for Razor to answer him. He couldn't take his eyes off Helena. He nodded instead. Helena's smile grew even more prominent once she saw the way she was affecting him. She made her way to him. Once she reached him, Razor quickly took her hands in his'. She winked at him.

"I clean up nicely, don't I?" she teased.

"That you do."

"Do you have any vows prepared?" the justice of the peace asked.

Helena's eyes widened.

Razor shook his head. "Just keep it simple."

"Simple works best," Helena agreed.

"Ok, let us begin."

After that, the ceremony got a little blurry. All Razor thought about was how quickly he could keep Helena out of Nick's reach.

Their next step would be Helena's training. Razor remembered how intense it was. Most of the time, the cadets were forced to fight each other. Combat training was the primary thing the program focused on. Razor had trained her to fight, but he didn't prepare her to deal with cunning people. That was what most of the DC task force was made up of—cunning and ruthless people. Razor made a note to make sure that he was present during Helena's training. He wasn't going to make that an option for Nick.

"Do you, Ryan Thompson, take Helena Willer, to be your lawfully wedded wife. To love and to hold, through sickness and health, 'til death do you part?" the justice of the peace asked, bringing Razor back to the ceremony.

He stared into Helena's brown eyes. "I do," Razor slid the ring onto Helena's finger. She gave him a wink.

"And do you, Helena Willer, take Ryan Thompson, to be your lawfully wedded husband. To love and to hold, through sickness and health, 'til death do you part?"

Helena smiled. "I do," she gently slipped the ring onto Razor's finger.

"You are now joined to each other by love and respect. Two qualities you must always remember, even when times are difficult. I wish you the best of luck in your marriage, and it is my honor to introduce Mr. and Mrs. Ryan Thompson. You may now kiss."

Helena smiled and leaned over to kiss Razor. She closed in the small gap in between them as Razor wrapped his arm around her waist. She ran her fingers through his hair.

"Are you ok, Mr. Thompson?" she asked once she pulled away.

"I'm great," he looked over at the justice of the peace. "When can we get the marriage license?"

"First thing tomorrow morning, Commander. We just need your

witnesses' signatures."

"Great, thanks."

Once all the proper signatures were acquired and everything was in order, Razor, Helena, and the two bellhops headed out of the capitol building. Helena gave her trench coat to one of the bellhops to take back to the hotel.

"Hungry, Mrs. Thompson?" Razor asked.

"Starving."

"Come on, I know a spot."

They walked a few blocks to a small restaurant. Naturally, Helena admired each functioning building along the way. A few officers greeted and acknowledge Razor as they walked past. None of them acknowledged Helena, which Razor was thankful for.

They stopped at a restaurant that just had the word "Burgers" on the sign. Razor held the door open for Helena.

"It's not fancy," he explained as she walked inside. "But they have the best and *only* burgers around."

"I can never turn down a good burger."

They sat at a booth, and Razor ordered them cheeseburgers and fries. Helena glanced around the restaurant, taking in the old 1950s style décor. Surprisingly, quite a few people were eating in the place. Helena's eyes landed on him. He had been watching her for a while.

"Something is bothering my little worrywart."

Razor frowned at her.

"You went somewhere else during the ceremony," she explained.

"Caught that, huh?"

"Of course, I did."

"Was just thinking about our future."

"The whole DC officer thing."

Razor nodded. "You're not worried?"

"I'm terrified, but I really don't want to think about that *today*," Helena sighed. "You've gone out of your way to make this day special for me. The least I can do is enjoy it...and you should too. Let's worry about tomorrow...*tomorrow*."

"You're right."

"I know I am."

The waiter came with their food. Helena looked thrilled when her cheeseburger and fries were sat in front of her. She just stared at it for a while in complete disbelief.

"Are you going to take a bite sometime today?" Razor teased.

Helena picked up her cheeseburger and took a bite out of it. Her eyes instantly rolled back in ecstasy. She quickly took another bite of the burger.

"Don't forget to breathe," Razor laughed. He took a bite of his food.

"It's so good," she moaned in between bites. "I feel like I'm in heaven."

"I'm glad you're enjoying yourself."

They both devoured their food. Once they finished eating, Razor suggested they go to a bar to listen to a live band play.

"...I'm not old enough to get in," Helena admitted, sheepishly.

Razor rolled his eyes as he took her hand. "Let's go, Mrs. Thompson."

Helena didn't resist following him. Razor watched as she continued to look at the streets of Lansing in awe and wonder. The bar he wanted to take her to was just a few blocks away. Thankfully, it was a bar he never got into a fight at.

Razor noticed that Helena relaxed a little as the doorman held the door open without asking for I.D. As they entered the bar, Razor began to quickly regret his decision to come there. Just about every guy in the room had their eyes on Helena. And it was a lot of them. Noticing that he was tensed, Helena turned around and kissed him on the lips. The anger that was creeping in instantly vanished. Razor smiled at her—grateful. He wrapped his arm tightly around her waist and led them to a table near the stage.

A waitress quickly appeared as they sat down. Razor ordered them nonalcoholic drinks. He didn't want to get Helena drunk for the first time in public. And alcohol certainly wasn't great for his rage. Razor didn't want to ruin their wedding night by getting into a brawl with a guy who looked at Helena for too long. And that was bound to happen if he had some liquor in him.

There was a bluegrass band playing tonight. Helena tapped her foot and swayed a little in her seat.

"You like bluegrass music?" he asked before the band went into their next song.

"At this point, I like just about any music," Helena waited until she caught on to the beat before she started clapping along.

Razor just watched her—taking her all in. He never felt so lucky. There wasn't anything he didn't find beautiful with Helena. She was perfect. At least, to him. And he would kill anyone who thought otherwise.

After a few more minutes, the band began to play a slow song. To his surprise, Helena quickly rose to her feet and held out her hand. Razor looked at her, shocked.

"It's time for our first dance, Mr. Thompson," Helena teased.

"I'm not sure that's such a good idea," Razor never danced a day in his life.

Helena poked out her lips and pouted. "Please, for me?"

Razor sighed in defeat. There was no way he could say no to that face. He took her hand and slowly stood. "I don't think I'll be very good," he warned her.

"Don't worry, I'll lead," Helena flashed him a bright smile as she guided him to the small dance floor.

It took a moment for Razor to catch his breath. Her smile always did that to him. Surprisingly, Helena was an excellent dancer, and she led Razor with great ease. From the outside looking in, you wouldn't be able to tell that he never danced before.

"You're terrific dancer," Razor admired.

Helena smiled as she rested her head against his chest. "My dad used to slow dance with us all the time. He had to make sure his girls always felt like Queens."

Razor couldn't ignore the sadness in her tone. Forced or not, today was an important day for her, and she had to be missing her parents like crazy. He definitely was. Razor leaned down and kissed her gently. Helena smiled when he pulled away. Razor tightened his hold on her. He never wanted this night to end.

Their time at the bar went on smoothly, thankfully. They made their departure as the band was packing up. They headed back to the hotel.

Helena's trench coat laid on the back of the couch when they got back to the room. She went into the bathroom to change into her pjs while Razor took off his formal wear in the bedroom. He then turned on the TV and found a movie that was playing.

"*The Sound of Music,*" Helena said. She walked into the bedroom and sat on the bed.

"You like it?"

"Not really. My mom loved it, though."

"I can change the channel."

"No, I don't mind watching it," she reclined back and lay her head on the pillow. "It kind of resonates with what's going on today, don't you think?"

Razor shrugged as he joined her on the bed. "If you say so."

Helena rested her head on his chest like she usually did. Razor wrapped his arms around her and kissed her forehead. They watched the movie in silence for a while. Razor enjoyed the normalcy of everything. He was watching a movie with the woman he loved. So simple. So normal.

Despite it all, it was a great day. He had to appreciate that. Through everything else, this was something he could hold on to. When everything was going wrong, he could look back on this day and remember his happiness. It was about the only day he could remember being happy.

Helena shifted in his arms. He looked down to find her looking up at him.

"Thank you for today," she said. "It was perfect."

"You're more than welcome."

Helena kissed him. Razor enjoyed how affectionate she was with him. Of course, he kissed her back, his hands roaming her body. He felt her tugging on him; he knew what she wanted. Razor gently rolled on top of her. Helena's legs instantly wrapped around his waist—ensnaring him in her grasp. She pulled him close to her. Their kiss grew more intense— more passionate. Helena practically ripped his shirt off.

"Again?" he asked, amused by her aggressiveness.

Helena bit her lip and nodded, her hands never leaving his chest. "It's our wedding night, after all."

Razor smiled. He had no intention of fighting with her on this. There was no use; he wanted her just as bad. "Can't argue with that."

All his stress. All his worries instantly melted away when he was with Helena. He focused on the moment. The way her hands glided down his back. The way she bit into his shoulder blade. And her moans drove him wild. He was in utter bliss.

Razor watched her sleep once they were done. He kissed her forehead from time to time. This day was perfect, but tomorrow was quickly approaching, and it would be chaos from here on out.

Protect Helena, no matter the cost.

In the morning, Razor went to the capitol building to pick up their marriage license. At the same time, Helena packed up at the hotel. The certificate was ready for him, just like it was promised. Razor read over it. It all looked official. Nick should be satisfied with that.

When he got back to the hotel, he found Helena in the lobby talking to the store owner from the mall. Razor frowned in confusion. Helena handed the store owner the bag she carried yesterday. The store owner hugged Helena and walked away. Helena spotted Razor lingering at the entrance of the lobby. She walked over to him with a smile on her face.

"Hey."

"What was that about?"

"Oh, I was just giving her stuff back."

"Why?"

Helena shrugged. "What was I going to do with them? It's not like I'm going to have a chance to dress up like that again."

"But that was something special for you. Something for you to remember the day by."

"I have my memories. Besides, that's what our rings are for."

Helena had him there. But Razor just hated the fact that Helena gave that pretentious store owner her things back. Helena took his hand.

"There's no point of us keeping things we don't need. Our life isn't made for that."

Razor kissed her. "You're right," he pulled her close to him. "Let's put our plan in motion."

No matter the cost.

They departed from Lansing before the afternoon. They made their way to HQ, preparing themselves for the future.

~20~

Helena

Hold. *Hold. Hold.*

Helena stood at ease as she watched a fellow cadet charge at her. *Hold. Hold. Hold.* She could hear Razor's voice in her ear, giving her instructions on properly defending herself against her attacker.

Hold. Hold. Hold.

It had been four months since she's been in DC training, and Helena hated every second of it. Razor was absolutely right when he said that she wasn't a good fit as a DC officer. Most of the officers were cunning, heartless, and ruthless—the very opposite of what Helena was. But she had to put on a brave face, not for herself, but for Razor.

Ever since she's been there, Helena could see how stressed out he was, especially when it came to combat training. To make matters worse and even more intense, Bossman was there. Usually, he's never there during training. The last time he was present was when the program first started. Razor said that this was a clear threat. Helena couldn't see how.

Hold. Hold. Hold.

Helena didn't expect Razor to be there during her training. Both Razor's and Bossman's presence caught everyone off guard. Of course, her fellow cadets quickly learned that she was married to Razor. And Razor made it very clear how protective he was over her. It made the other cadets instantly hate Helena. She told Razor that he needed to back off a little, but he refused.

"It's my job to protect you," he stated.

"But this is combat training, Razor. You really can't protect me from that," she pointed out to him.

Most of the trainees refused to fight with her in fear of what Razor would do. But when he wasn't around, they made little snide remarks and couldn't wait for the moment when he was gone.

Razor didn't say anything, but he didn't leave either. Until one day, when he had to run a quick errand.

Their training sergeant quickly jumped at the opportunity and did an impromptu combat training session. Almost every cadet volunteered to fight with Helena. It shocked her. She knew that the cadets hated her, but she didn't think it was *all* of them. The sergeant chose one of the male cadets that hated her the most. But Helena wasn't afraid. Razor trained her well.

Helena didn't even break a sweat with him. The guy was wild and swinging all over the place. She hardly had to hit him. She simply just got out of the way before he could strike her. When she finally did use some defensive moves, Helena could see the cadet getting angry. Her blows were hurting him. At least this would make her fellow cadets respect her if nothing else.

Helena had the cadet's arm pinned back—applying as much pressure as she could. She was waiting for him to yield when he suddenly threw some dirt in her face. Blinded for a second, Helena struggled to get the dust out of her eyes. The cadet took that moment to tackle her to the ground. He punched her fiercely. Helena tried to block most of them, but he still landed some good blows. She was expecting the sergeant to call it off, but he didn't. The fellow trainees cheered as she blacked out.

When Helena finally came to, she was left alone lying on the empty training room floor. Razor and Bossman found her in the infirmary being attended to shortly after. She had a busted lip, a black eye, and somehow her cheek split opened, and it required stitches. Helena never saw Razor so furious. She explained to him what happened, and he went on a rampage. Helena chased after him as he went for the training sergeant.

Bossman laughed, following the whole way.

The sergeant tried to run when he saw Razor approaching, but Razor was much quicker. Before any of them knew it, the sergeant was getting tossed around the whole building. Everyone watched on in horror.

Helena was horrified. She kept screaming for Razor to stop, but this seemed to enrage him more. She never saw him so vicious. The sergeant kept crying and begging for mercy, but eventually, he fell silent. It wasn't clear if he passed out or was dead.

Razor then set his sights on the cadet with who Helena fought. The guy tried to flee, but Bossman blocked his path. As Razor began to extract his punishment to the cadet, Bossman walked over to Helena.

"You should go back to the infirmary and get that cheek looked at," Bossman suggested.

Helena didn't even notice that the stitches reopened. It was probably from all the screaming and yelling she was doing.

Bossman laughed and watched as Razor was practically beating the cadet to death. "It's going to take a while for my friend to calm down…you, my dear, have made him even more vicious."

Helena could see the delight in Bossman's eyes. She always thought that he viewed her as a liability. After seeing Razor's reaction when she got hurt, it seemed like he thought the complete opposite.

Helena walked back to the infirmary in disarray. That was something she never saw from Razor—him being completely ruthless.

She heard the rumors but seeing it in person was entirely different. She finally understood what he meant when he said that he loses control. It seemed like he didn't even hear her when she was screaming for him to stop. His eyes were vacant—like he was somewhere else. Razor was seeing red.

Helena sat in the infirmary with an ice pack on her lip as the nurse restitched her cheek. After that, she walked back to her room. As she passed the courtyard, she saw Razor doing something to the two men's bodies, and Bossman was doubled over in laughter. Helena was too afraid to look even further. She quickly walked past, hoping to go unnoticed.

When she got to her room, Helena fought back the tears. What did she get herself into? At this rate, Razor was likely to kill everybody. Even though these people were far from innocent, Helena didn't want their blood on her hands. She was afraid again. Not because of Razor, but because of what the program was making him do. Helena just needed to get through training, and then everything would go back to being the same.

At least, that's what she was hoping.

Helena cried herself to sleep. When she woke up, Razor was sitting at the edge of her bed, frowning and looking down at his hands. He looked sad to her. Helena sat up and reached out for his hand. He quickly took it into his'. He looked at her face and flinched.

"I'm sorry if I frightened you," he said. He looked ashamed. Like she just has seen the worst part of him. Razor kept his gaze off her, which was something he never did.

"I wasn't frightened...just shocked," Helena said. She didn't want to admit how terrified she was.

"It's been a while since I've gotten so angry that I blacked out."

Helena didn't say anything. She just looked down at their hands. She honestly didn't know what to say to him. Should she console him? Tell him that it was ok? The last thing she wanted was to judge him—make him feel ashamed.

Instead, she gently grabbed Razor's chin and forced him to look at her. She could see the remorse in his eyes. She leaned up and kissed him softly on the lips. Once she pulled away, he sighed, closed his eyes, and rested his forehead against hers. They sat like that for a moment. Helena missed this. Ever since she's been in training, she rarely had any intimate moments with Razor.

He placed his hand on her cheek as he backed away. "Are you ok?" he finally asked. His eyes were on her.

"I'm ok, just sore," Helena could see the anger quickly appear and fade from Razor's face.

"Are you hungry? Dinner was over 20 minutes ago, but they can still make you something."

"Yeah, I could eat."

Razor stood up, and Helena joined him. They walked out of her room and through the courtyard. Razor tried to block her view, but Helena forced herself to look. She stopped walking, too shocked to proceed.

The training sergeant and the cadet hung lifelessly from a tree. Both men were black and blue from the severe beating that Razor gave them. They both had the word "cowards" scribbled across their shirts in what appeared to be blood. Bossman sat at a table in the courtyard, admiring the view. Helena couldn't move. Razor stopped and frowned.

"I'm not proud of it," he admitted.

"Then why leave them up there?" she whispered in horror.

"To make others understand what the consequences are for fighting dirty with you."

Helena shook her head in disbelief. "You went too far, Razor."

"I not going to apologize for protecting you," he stressed. "If I didn't do something drastic, the sergeant would've kept testing how far he could go, allowing the other cadets to gang up on you."

Helena could see in his face that there was no way he was going to waver on this. She was his mission, and Helena knew how serious he took his missions. She sighed and reluctantly nodded.

"My friends," Bossman noticed them. "Come to admire your husband's handiwork?"

Razor grimaced.

Bossman laughed. "How are you feeling, Helena?"

"Ok, just a little hungry. We were on the way to get some food," she hoped he didn't notice how shocked she was.

"Don't worry about them," Bossman turned his attention back to the bodies. "We don't allow cowardly acts to fly around here. If Razor didn't punish them, I would've. And it would've been worse," he winked at Helena. She smiled weakly.

"It's getting late," Razor intervened. "I should get her some food and get her back to bed."

"I guess I should find me a new training sergeant," Bossman chuckled as he walked away.

Razor led Helena to the cafeteria.

Suddenly, she realized what she needed to do. She had to be on her A-game when it came to combat fighting. Otherwise, everyone would feel Razor's wrath.

Hold. Hold. Hold.

From then on, Helena made sure that another cadet didn't lay a finger on her. She didn't wait for them to yield. If Helena wanted to protect them, *she had to be ruthless.* She didn't stop until the new training sergeant yelled for her to. No one else looked at her sideways or made snarky remarks about her from then on out.

Helena passed her training with flying colors. She could see the relief practically rolling off Razor. Clearly, this was his biggest concern about the program. Maybe it would get better from there. That's what she was hoping anyway. Helena didn't think she could take any more of Razor's stress. But Bossman threw them both another curveball when it came time for her placement.

"I think Helena should come out with me for recon missions," Razor stated. "She can be my backup and lookout."

"I want her in the prisons," Bossman said casually.

Helena could see every vein popping out of Razor's body. He was shaking beside her—no doubt close to blacking out.

"I don't think that's a good idea," Razor gritted through clenched teeth.

"It's only temporary," Bossman said. "There are a few things I need you to attend to, and I need you ruthless..., and I mean *extremely ruthless.* You've shown me that you can be that way when you think Helena's in danger...no offense to you, Helena."

Helena stood there in disbelief. Bossman was using her against Razor. She was Bossman's leverage, and he was going to use that to get what he wanted.

"How many missions?" Razor demanded.

"Just a few, old friend...I assure you Helena will be fine. I've placed her to work the intake room."

Razor was still pissed, but Helena noticed that he relaxed just a tad. So, maybe her placement in prison wasn't *that* bad.

Helena was to be shipped off the next morning. Razor would leave for his mission after he saw Helena assigned to her position. She knew that he wanted to threaten the other officers there, but she didn't say anything. There was no point in arguing with him. Plus, after the curveball Bossman just threw at them, maybe Razor threatening the other officers was a good thing.

That night, Helena rested in her bed, wrapped tightly in Razor's arms. He kept kissing the top of her head from time to time as if he was trying to memorize her scent. They were silent for a long time, both trying to take in the moment. Helena focused on how warm she felt in Razor's arms; she focused on the strength of his embrace. The firmness of his hands. The way his beard tickled her face every time he kissed her. She needed to remember it all.

There was no telling when she was going to see him again. She wasn't counting on Bossman to keep his word. Besides, they didn't know how long "temporary" actually was.

"This is all just a test," Razor said so low that Helena wasn't sure if he was talking to her.

"For whom?"

"Me...he wants to see where my loyalty lies, the program, or you."

"Well, you have to make sure it's to the program then."

"No," Razor said firmly. "I have to show that it's both."

Helena sighed. "Ok," she looked up and kissed him, trying to ease away both of their fears. They both fell silent again. Razor tightened his hold on her.

"I got a lead on Jade. Her boyfriend Vincent is a bounty hunter now. I met up with him."

"Really?" Helena's heart started racing.

"Yeah, she had been surviving with him and his family about three years back. Vincent and his family were captured in a sweep, but Jade got away. His father died in prison, and his mother committed suicide shortly after that."

Helena gasped. She was horrified that Jade was almost captured and sadden by the news of what happened to Vincent's family.

"Apparently, he blames Jade for everything. He was angry when I talked to him."

"Why? What did she do?"

"I don't know," Razor shrugged. "But she wasn't responsible for his parents' death."

Helena was terrified by the news. Jade wasn't safe, and she was out there all alone. At least Helena had Razor. Who did Jade have?

"This is a good thing. I now know what area to search for Jade. This brings us closer to escaping."

"Ok," Helena sighed.

Razor released her from his embrace and took her face into his hands. He looked at her firmly. "You have to be strong in there. Keep your head down and do your work. Don't get involved in anything in there. Let the other officers do what they want...just don't get involved, no matter what."

"Ok," Helena was confused by his sudden intensity.

"Promise me, Helena."

"I promise."

Razor looked at her—studying her face. Finally, he wrapped her back in his arms. "Just be brave."

"I will," she was determined to.

**

One year later.

Hold.

Helena stood in front of the prison cell, waiting for one of the officers to approach. She had broken her promise to Razor, but how could she not? Since she's been there, Helena has done what Razor asked. She kept her head down. Focused on her work. Didn't get involved in anything. Allowed the other officers to do what they want. *Helena didn't get involved.*

Helena ignored the beatings and torture that the other officers extracted from the prisoners. She tried hard to ignore the screams that came from the women prisoners. Still, Helena cried herself to sleep every night since she's been there. She didn't do anything. And the guilt was eating her alive.

Hold.

Her job was to process debtors that had been apprehended. She put them into the system, gave them prisoner numbers and I.D., and issued them uniforms. From there, they would wait in the intake cells for the DC guards to come and get them and take them into the prison. Out of all the places she could be, this was the best place.

For a year, Helena was able to just do her job. She hardly interacted with any of her coworkers. And they seemed to avoid her too. Razor made it very clear that Helena was not to be messed with when she first came to the prison. She only saw him once every two months. Bossman was keeping him busy.

Because of that, Helena worked extra hard to be on her best behavior. She figured if she did really well in the prison, Bossman would reassign her to be with Razor or bring Razor back. So, Helena had to be good...until she saw her.

The girl was a debtor who had just been brought in. She looked to be around Helena's age—19 or 20. Helena could've sworn the girl was once a model. She had smooth, mocha color skin, incredible high cheekbones that went well with her short hairstyle, and beautiful hazel eyes. The girl was gorgeous, and Helena knew her time there would be hell.

Hold.

Helena could see instantly that something was wrong. The girl came in all bruised up, clothing torn and crying. Now, none of this was what caught Helena's attention. All of that was normal. Usually, that's how most debtors came in. It was *where* the bruises were on the girl. She had bite marks on her neck and near her cleavage area. Her shirt was torn so bad that it barely covered anything up. And Helena could see that her pants and underwear were ripped.

The whole situation was apparent; the girl was sexually assaulted on her way to the prison.

"Hurry up with this one, Thompson," one of the male officers demanded.

That was another red flag. They never demanded a rush on an intake.

Helena waited until the officers were gone before she talked to the girl. "Are you ok?"

The girl didn't say anything. She just cried even harder. It was clear that she was in hysterics. Helena didn't say anything. Instead, she pricked the girl's finger and ran her through the database. Her information quickly came up. Tatianna McBain. Tatianna wasn't a debtor but a provider (someone who got others' medical treatment under their name).

Helena walked over to Tatianna with a blanket, and she wrapped it around Tatianna. Helena noticed more cuts and bruises on her.

"Tatianna," Helena said. "Can you tell me what happened?"

The girl calmed down a little bit. She looked over at Helena. Helena could tell that she was confused by her kindness.

"They raped me," she finally whispered. "They...took...turns."

Helena knew that this happened often, but to hear it and see its aftermath just horrified her. And the officers, no doubt, had more plans for Tatianna. Helena couldn't allow that to happen. It was something about Tatianna that reminded Helena of Jade.

"Let's get you cleaned up."

"Please," Tatianna cried. She grabbed Helena's arm. "Please, don't let them take me."

Helena wrapped her arms around the girl. "I won't."

Hold.

The male officers came in four times, asking if Tatianna was ready yet. Helena lied to them every time, saying that something was wrong with the system. On the fifth time, they sneered and told her that they would be back. Helena knew that the fight was about to begin. She took her position in front of Tatianna's intake cell—guarding the door.

As expected, Declan came walking in 20 minutes later. He was the one who ran the prison and ran the group of officers who had their way with the prisoners. Helena never spoke to them, and they ignored her...until now.

"Thompson," Declan said, shaking his head. "What are you doing?"

"My job."

"Intake doesn't take this long. We know you're lying about the system being down."

Helena stood tall in front of the cell door—indicating that she wasn't going anywhere.

Declan sighed. "Surely, Razor told you how things work around here."

Helena folded her arms.

"Step aside, Helena. Don't make this difficult...trust me, you won't be able to handle it."

"The prisoner isn't ready yet."

A sly smile spread across his face. "Ballsy, I'll give you that. But I promise, you won't last long," he slowly walked out of the room.

Hold.

An hour passed before the next officer came in. It was a female officer. Helena couldn't remember her name, but she knew that she was a part of Declan's crew. The male officers weren't the only ones who had their way with the prisoners. The female officers partook too.

"Thompson, what are you doing?" the female officer put her hands on her hips. "The group has been waiting on this prisoner all day. Step aside."

Helena glared at her.

"Trust me, Thompson, this isn't what you want. Being married to Razor doesn't give you a pass."

"I'm more than just Razor's wife."

"What do you think Bossman will say about this? You know what his one rule is...no fighting amongst ourselves."

"I'm not planning on fighting," Helena stated. "But if you try to forcefully remove me, I will have no choice but to defend myself."

The female officer sighed and narrowed her eyes at Helena. "Have it your way then, but don't say I didn't warn you."

Helena watched as the female officer left the room. She knew what was about to happen next. Unfortunately, the next officer that walked into the room was going to attack. Helena wondered who it was going to be.

Hold.

Of course, they sent Trenton. Helena was on the verge of laughing. They were predictable.

Trenton was Declan's henchman. He was known to be rough with the prisoners and sometimes the officers. Helena hated him the first day she met him. She hated when he came to get the intake prisoners from her. He was rough for no reason. Trenton sometimes would laugh at her when he caught Helena's facial expressions. Helena had the feeling that he wanted to try to do something to her but refrained his self because of Razor. She would be lying if she said that she never fantasized about killing him. She thought of numerous ways she could do it.

"Thompson," Trenton said, grinning. "I've been waiting for you to slip up."

"I'm sure you have."

"I'll only ask you this once...step aside."

Helena could see Tatianna cowering in the corner of her cell. Her body language told Helena that Trenton was one of the officers who abused her. Rage filled Helena.

Hold.

"Not a chance in hell," Helena spoke calmly. She couldn't show her emotions. She had to focus.

Hold.

"I think I'll have a go at you first," he said, touching himself. "I've already had her."

Helena could see that he was aroused through his pants—a perfect target. *Hold.* She didn't move as he approached her.

"Imagine how heartbroken Razor will be once he sees what I've done to you."

Hold.

She wasn't sure if Declan, or even Trenton, realized it, but she spotted Trenton's weakness the first week she was there. So, she waited, allowing him to play into it.

As he got closer, eyeing her up and down and licking his lips, Helena slowly reached for her knife that was in her thigh strap. Trenton didn't notice.

"I warn you, Helena," he smirked. He was close to her—just an arm's reach. "I will not be gentle."

Helena smiled. "Neither will I," and she struck.

She jammed her knife into his penis—pinning it into his inner thigh. Before he had a chance to scream, Helena pulled out her other knife and slit his throat. Trenton dropped to the ground. Helena quickly went to retrieve her knives but left the knife in Trenton's penis. She wanted the message to be clear. Helena looked at the door. It appeared no one heard the attack, but she knew that someone would be coming in soon since they didn't hear her screams.

Helena unlocked the cell door. "Come on," she said as Tatianna leerily walked out the cell.

"Where are we going?"

"To the solitary unit."

"Why?" fear coated Tatianna's voice.

"So I can see them coming."

~21~

Razor

Razor's hands were bloody and sore. He sat on an old wooden desk in an empty room. The smell of blood, copper, and sweat filled the air. That was the signature smell of torture—to Razor anyway. The crying and pleas were the original soundtracks.

A man hung upside down in front of Razor, but he hardly seemed to notice him. Even though, just a few minutes ago, Razor was beating information out of him. Razor's hands were shaking. From adrenaline or rage? Razor didn't know. What he did know was he hated this. He hated every moment of this.

What he really wanted was to be beside his wife. They had been married a year, but he could count on his hands how many times they been together. Every other month—that's six times. Six times he's been able to hold Helena in his arms. Six times since he's been able to kiss her—take in her scent. Razor's been going crazy without her. He can only imagine how she was feeling.

Nick had been keeping him busy this past year. He had been hunting down Black Deficit members and torturing them for information. Unfortunately, Razor had been abnormally ruthless. In reality, he had no issue with the Black Deficit. However, this was why he was being taken away from Helena. So, unfortunately, they were left to feel his wrath. Razor was also angry with their leader.

Dr. Blackwell was supposed to be keeping things under wraps, but his group was now out fighting with DC officers. Of course, when Razor looked further into it, he saw that it was actually his children's doing instead of his. Razor quickly pointed this out to Nick, but he didn't care.

"His children's sins fall on him," Nick stated. "They've gotten their ideas from somewhere."

Razor didn't say anything else. The more he fought against Nick on this, the more he kept Razor away from Helena. Razor needed to get the job done. He was worried about Helena. What he was concerned about the most was the prison that Helena was placed at.

When he heard that she would be at Declan's prison, Razor just about had an aneurysm. The prison was brutal, especially the way Declan ran it. But Declan wasn't Razor's main concern. The one who Razor hated the most was Trenton, Declan's right hand. Trenton was known to be brutal to female prisoners and officers alike. Razor didn't want Helena nowhere near his sights.

During his last visit with Helena, Razor noticed the way Trenton looked at her. Razor knew what was running through his mind. Trenton was waiting for his opportunity. Eventually, Trenton caught Razor glaring at him, and he slyly walked away. It was then that Razor enlisted someone to keep an eye on Helena and Declan and his crew. The only other officer Razor trusted was an officer named Lucas.

Lucas was a rare case. He was someone who clearly wasn't cut out to be a DC officer, but he was there since the beginning. Usually, people like him didn't last that long. Lucas survived so long because he kept his head down, did his work, and didn't get involved in anything. Apparently, Lucas had been keeping an eye on Helena way before Razor asked him to. Razor was grateful for that.

"I'm surprised she lasted through training," Lucas chuckled.

"It was touch and go for a moment," Razor admitted.

"Well, she's been doing good with keeping her head down. But I'll keep a tighter watch on her...how often do you want me to report to you?"

"Is every day too much?"

Lucas laughed. "It's your wife, Commander. I'll report whenever you want."

"I appreciate it, Lucas."

"No problem."

But having Lucas keeping an eye on Helena didn't relieve the stress. Razor hated the fact that he had to enlist someone else to help him protect Helena. That was his job—his mission. Razor was dead set on not failing that, but the more he was away, the more he felt like a failure. Razor was determined to keep his promise to her. He would get back to her soon—no matter the cost.

In between the torturing, Razor was tracking down Jade's last locations. He found his self annoyed with the task. Jade was slippery. He would get there merely days after she left a specific place. She was smart. She never stayed anywhere for too long. The one time she did, a group of marauders came in. Razor found them beaten and injured. Pissed with just missing Jade again, Razor tortured information out of them. He was just about to follow up on the lead when Nick called him back to deal with a Black Deficit member.

The member wiggled in his chains, bringing Razor back to his current situation. Cole's children: Jackson and Beverly have been orchestrating some attacks on DC officers during sweeps. It was in some small-town areas, so the word hasn't spread much, but the act itself was a threat. They needed to handle it before word got around. Razor couldn't imagine how Nick would react if word spread that the Black Deficit was out doing rescue missions.

Razor got up and cracked his knuckles. He had to figure out where Jackson and Beverly were going to strike next. Razor approached the hanging man. The man wiggled around more once he saw Razor coming toward him.

"Please, no...no more," the man pleaded.

Razor punched him hard in the face. Then again. Then again. Then again. Blood poured out of the man's mouth and nose. The man's left eye was swollen shut and was already turning purple. He couldn't stop crying and moaning from the pain. Razor grabbed the chain that was wrapped around the member's legs.

"I'm going to ask you this one more time," Razor warned. He was beyond annoyed. He had been beating this man all day, and he wasn't giving Razor anything to work with. "What's the next mission?"

"I don't know!" the member cried. "Once you've worked a mission, they drop you and recruit another member. You never work them consecutively."

Smart. Razor didn't give Blackwell's children that much credit. That helped keep their plans secure for situations like this.

"I suggest that you think hard," Razor advised. "Otherwise, there's no need for me to keep you alive." The man cried harder when he heard this. "You have five minutes."

Razor walked back to the wooden desk and sat back on it. He watched as the man struggled to think of some useful information.

"I can tell you where our headquarters is," the member quickly offered.

"I already know the location."

"Shit," he moaned.

Razor continued to watch him. He hoped that the man could give him something. "What does Blackwell think of these attacks?"

"He hates them. He's been asking his members to stand down," the member pounced on the opportunity to give Razor something. "But sadly, his children already had the members riled up that they aren't listening to him."

"Where is Blackwell during the attacks?"

"Well, he's doing what you're doing...not torturing people, but asking where the next hit will be."

"Where was he seen last?"

"Benton Harbor," the man paused and frowned. Something came to his mind. "I do know that they're planning to stay in Michigan for the time being."

Razor stood up. That was something. Swiftly, he pulled out a map. He looked at the cities near Niles, MI. He focused on all the towns that were in Michigan. There was a pattern forming. Blackwell's children attacked in Buchanan, Benton Harbor, Edwardsburg, and Sturgis. They were staying close to Niles and not venturing further than 50 miles from their headquarters. Razor guessed that the next city would be either Dowagiac or Cassopolis. Both towns were their best bet since he knew that there were DC sweeps in those areas. This was something that Nick could go on. Razor's spirits lifted momentarily.

Then his emergency radio went off.

It was the radio he used with Lucas. Usually, Lucas gave his reports in the evening. It was the middle of the night.

Razor's heart dropped.

He was so involved with torturing the Black Deficit member, he didn't notice that Lucas didn't give him a report. Something was wrong. Razor knew this before he went to the radio.

"Code red, Commander Razor, please respond," Lucas radioed urgently. "Code red, Commander Razor, please respond."

"Razor here, Lucas, update me," Razor held his breath for the bad news.

"It's Helena, Commander," Lucas paused. "She's been fighting Declan's crew all night. There are about five officers dead, Trenton included."

Razor quickly got up and grabbed his things. "I'm on my way."

Rage burned through him.

This was precisely what he was trying to avoid. He knew Helena wouldn't be able to keep her head down for long. It just wasn't the kind of person she was. He was impressed that she lasted this long. But now she was there fighting off Declan and his crew. She was able to kill five of his officers. But with Trenton dead, Razor wasn't sure if Declan would back down.

Helena couldn't fight them off for long. She was bound to get tired soon; her survival was limited.

"Will you let me down..." Razor slit the member's throat before he could finish his sentence.

Razor was on the warpath to save Helena. There were sure to be several people dead in his wake.

~22~

Helena

Helena tried to catch her breath as she rested her hands on her knees. Four DC officers lay around her lifelessly. Their goal was to remove her from the cell door she was blocking. Tatianna cowered inside. Helena was thankful that she couldn't see her. Her tiredness would've probably alarmed Tatianna. If Helena grew tired, then Tatianna would suffer. No doubt the DC officers would've been pissed that they had to fight their way to her. Helena worried that she made Tatianna an even bigger target by protecting her.

Either way, Helena couldn't give in. Not now. So, she was ready to die to protect the innocent.

One thing she was thankful for was deciding to go to the fifth floor.

The solitary unit hall was narrow due to the metal balcony wrapped around in the center of the hall. The stairs were at the far end of the unit, so Helena could see her attackers coming. That wouldn't have been the case if she stayed in the intake room. The room was large and open. The fight would've ended quicker than it began. DC officers weren't known for fighting fair.

The second thing she was thankful for was the fact that Declan was refusing to use guns. One thing he didn't want to be seen was that his officers were fighting amongst themselves.

Helena finally caught her breath and stood up straight. She leaned her back against the door. It had been a long night.

Once they found Trenton's dead body, Helena heard over the radio Declan's crew going floor by floor looking for her. She was surprised that it took them so long to figure out she was on the fifth floor. Once they figured that out, Helena heard them going over the game plan to take her out. They waited for hours before they made their move—waiting for her to get tired.

Helena stayed sharp. She applied the techniques that Razor taught her for staying up. After a couple of hours, the first officer came. Before she knew it, four dead DC officers lay around her feet.

Helena waited for the next officer to come. Staying awake was no longer the issue. The adrenaline was pumping hard through her veins. Sadly, she was winded but no longer sleepy.

At the far end of the hall, Declan slowly came into view. He was there to talk her down; Helena knew that. Declan clapped as he got closer.

"I'm impressed," he admitted. "Astonished, actually. I never thought you could land a punch to Trenton, much less kill him. And so viciously, I might add."

"Guess you didn't know about his glaring weakness."

"I guess that's what I should've expected from Razor's wife," Declan sighed and looked at the dead DC officers. "He trained you well...but even Razor and his wife are prone to getting tired."

Helena stayed silent. Was Declan going to attack her after all?

"It's the middle of the night Helena, you've been fighting all evening. You can only last for so long," Declan took one last look at his dead crew members and then a final look at Helena. He sighed and walked out of the unit.

Before Declan fully descended the stairs, two officers made their way up. Helena took a deep breath and gripped her knife. One officer diverted to her right while the other went left. They were going to attack her at both sides, trying to lure her away from the door. Helena waited for them to attack. She wanted total deniability when asked if she struck first.

The officer to her right was the first to strike. Helena didn't notice it at first, but there was a taser in his hand. He went for her neck. Helena dropped to her knees, but she remained resilient. She refused to cry out in pain.

The officer to her left moved to attack. Still, Helena stabbed him in his upper thigh—making sure to hit the femoral artery. She quickly pulled the knife out, and the officer dropped to the ground, blood pouring out of him.

Helena then stabbed the officer who was tasering her in the gut. The officer screamed out in pain and dropped the taser. Helena twisted the knife and then yanked it out. The officer fell to his knees, and Helena slit his throat. The guy slumped to his side—eyes wide open, life slowly leaving them.

The smell of blood was thick in the air. Helena rested on her knees for a moment. She wiped the bloody knife on her pants. A puddle of blood from the officers was slowly coming toward her. Helena quickly grabbed the taser and a baton and stood up. She managed to push the two officers to the side to have more room when other officers came.

Again, Helena leaned up against the door, sheathed the knife back in her thigh strap, and placed the taser in her holster. She was so tempted to close her eyes, but she knew if she did that, then she would be a dead woman. Although she was pretty sure that she already was.

Minutes later, the female officer from the intake room came up, followed by another female guard. The intake room officer looked at her dead comrades. She shook her head in disbelief.

"Never send in boys to do a woman's job," she sighed. "I'm impressed, Thompson."

"Remind me, what was your name again?"

The woman looked at Helena like she was truly hurt. "Ava," she frowned. "You really should know the name of the person who's about to kill you, Helena," Ava and the other female officer charged at Helena at the same time.

Helena stood firm at the door.

The other female guard made it to her first. Helena smacked her hard in the face with the baton. She heard a crack; something was broken in the woman's face.

Ava came next. Helena thrust the baton into her gut and again in her face. The other woman got back up, face bloody, and went at Helena once again. This time there was a knife in the woman's hand. Helena quickly moved to the side awkwardly, causing the baton to drop out of her hand. The woman ended up ramming the knife into the door. Grabbing her hand, Helena twisted the woman's wrist as hard as she could. She waited to hear a snap. The woman screamed out in pain as Helena took her knife and jammed it into her chest. The woman stumbled back in shock. Helena kicked her, and she went flying over the railing. Her body fell hard on the concrete floor below.

Ava stared at Helena in shock, then she angrily charged at Helena again. The anger made Ava move faster. She attacked Helena with a baton. Helena was able to duck and dodge some of the blows, but just barely. Some of them made contact, like to her stomach and shoulder. Ava drew back to hit Helena again, but Helena caught the baton in mid-swing. The two women fought for the baton for a moment.

Then very quickly, Helena jammed her thumb into Ava's eye. Helena made sure she hooked it like Razor taught her. Ava screamed out in agony. She immediately let go of the baton and stumbled back. Helena took the opportunity to push her over the railing. Ava screamed all the way down. Helena looked down to see that she lay bloody right next to her friend.

Two more officers proceeded up the stairs before Helena could catch her breath.

This was it. This was the end of her.

Surprisingly, Helena wore a smile. She would go out fighting, and she found comfort in the fact that her death would be avenged. Their death would be much more painful than hers could ever be. Helena saw how Razor handled her being hurt. She could only imagine how he would take her death. Whoever she killed here tonight, their deaths would be mercy. Whoever survived would die a torturous death from Razor. That gave Helena strength.

The two officers immediately came charging. Helena took a taser to one officer as the other came at her with a baton. She endured the blows, and when the opportunity presented itself, she drove a knife into his gut.

The officer she tasered came at her again. Knife in hand, he charged at Helena. She managed to move out of the way, but not before he sliced her. Helena moved quickly; she grabbed a baton and went for his knife-hand. She managed to knock the knife out of his hand. Sadly, blood was pouring out of her. He got her good. She had to keep going; Helena was determined to take out more. She went for the officer's Adam's apple. The officer quickly paused—holding his throat. Helena used all her strength to kick him. The officer went flying off the railing.

Helena dropped to her knees. Her hand went to her side, where the officer cut her. Slowly, blood poured through her fingers. She took one of the officer's jacket and wrapped it around her tightly. Helena stayed on her knees. She focused on her breathing. Unfortunately, she wasn't going to last too long.

"A few more officers," she thought to herself. "Just take out a few more officers, then you can give up."

"Looking tired there, Helena," Declan said from the top of the stairs. "I wonder how much more you have in you."

"I guess we'll find out."

Declan smirked. "I guess we will."

More officers ran up as Declan descended back down.

Helena stayed on her knees. Different weapons surrounded her: knives, tasers, and batons. Fortunately, she didn't need to move. The officers just needed to get closer.

As the officers approached her, Helena slowly rose to her feet and screamed at the top of her lungs—a warrior's final battle cry. Two knives were clutched in her hands. Swiftly, she jammed a knife into an officer's groin. Another knife went into an officer's side and was quickly moved to his heart. She tasered another officer and shoved a knife into their throat.

An officer managed to cut her shoulder. Helena grunted in pain as she quickly bit the officer's hand. The officer pulled her by her hair, but Helena kept her grip on him. She tasered him in between his legs, and he quickly let her go. He stumbled back, and then someone quickly snapped his neck.

Helena was feeling woozy. The blood was seeping through the jacket she had wrapped around her cut. She was convinced that her eyes were deceiving her. Razor stood in front of her with rage in his eyes. She wasn't sure if it was at her or at the situation. He frowned at the blood that was coming out of her. Then he quickly turned his attention to the remaining officers that were there. Most of them were trying to flee, but they didn't get far.

Once the officers were dead, Razor scooped Helena up in his arms. Helena stopped him when he tried to walk away.

"I have to protect her," she weakly said, reaching for the door.

"Helena, you need these cuts looked at," concern was in Razor's voice.

"They will get to her once I'm gone," she heard Razor sigh, but he opened the door.

Tatianna cowered once she saw Razor walk in, but she glanced up when she saw Helena in his arms.

"Oh, God, Helena, are you ok?"

Razor had laid Helena down on the ground. Helena cried when she looked at him.

"I'm so sorry Razor, I really tried to keep my head down," she looked over at Tatianna. The bruises and bite marks still visible. "But I couldn't stand by anymore. It's not right. It's not who I am."

To her surprise, Razor smiled down at her and kissed her— passionately.

"I know," he said, looking down at her cuts. "I'm amazed you lasted this long."

"I'm sorry if I made things more difficult for you," she felt like she deserved his rage—his anger. Bossman was already making things hard for him. He didn't need that from her too.

Razor placed his hand on her cheek. "I heard what they did to her. I would've done the same thing too," another smile slowly crept on his face. "Nice job out there, Mrs. Thompson."

Helena knew that he was trying to cheer her up and get her to smile, but she burst out crying. She couldn't be away from him any longer, and she knew that was precisely what Bossman was going to do. Razor frowned at her reaction.

"I can't be away from you," she cried. "Not again."

Razor wrapped her in his arms and kissed her forehead. "Don't worry, Helena, there's no way in hell I'm leaving you again."

~23~

Razor

The female prisoner stood near Helena as a medic officer stitched up her cuts. Razor towered over them all. He was filled with shame as he saw how deep the cut on Helena's side had been. He was failing his mission, and he knew precisely who the cause of that was.

No more.

Razor was going to stand up to Nick. At the end of the day, Nick needed him more than Razor needed the program. He knew that he and Helena would live just fine without the DC task force. They weren't debtors. And Razor knew how to get medical care without "abusing" the system. He and Helena would be more than fine. So, if Nick wanted him around, Helena would be by his side.

That was final.

Razor looked over at the female prisoner. He learned that her name was Tatianna. She was pretty, which was very unfortunate.

When he first got there, Lucas met him at the gate. Lucas quickly informed him that Helena was protecting a provider who had just been brought in. Apparently, the girl was gang-raped during transport to the prison. Declan and his crew demanded that Helena quickly process her through. Razor knew they had more horrible things in store for the girl. Helena slowed up the processing and refused to let the girl go.

When Lucas told him that they sent Trenton after Helena, Razor had to compose himself. He had a nasty habit of sometimes taking things out on the person closest to him, and Lucas was the only person there. That wouldn't be fair to Lucas—considering everything he has done so far.

But Razor was shocked when Lucas reported that they found Trenton dead on the intake room floor, with a knife shoved in his penis and a slit throat. Razor was proud and terrified. Proud that Helena was able to handle herself. Terrified that she did something so vicious. The prison was changing her, and Razor didn't like it.

Lucas knew that Helena must've gone to the fifth floor, so he told Declan that he saw her in different areas to slow them down. None of them noticed that Helena took Trenton's radio, but Lucas did. He figured she had to be listening to Declan and his crew updates.

Although Razor had an idea of what to expect when he got into the prison, he still found himself stunned. Trenton was still lying dead on the floor—knife still in his penis and a massive slash across his neck. As Razor headed for the stairs, he saw three officers lying dead on the floor. Razor noticed that one of the officers was Ava—another one of Declan's favorites. One of her eyes was gouged out. Another officer had a knife sticking out of her chest, while the other looked like he died from the fall.

Declan stood at the bottom of the stairs. He looked surprised to see Razor there. Then Helena screamed. It seemed like a final cry. Razor quickly passed Declan and ran up the stairs to Helena.

Declan would pay later; Razor was going to make sure of that.

When he got to the fifth floor, he was amazed by the number of dead DC officers lying around Helena's feet. She was still fighting strong, but she was injured.

Razor went in to kill. He quickly snapped the neck of the officer who was pulling on Helena's hair. As he looked at her, something horrible hit him. He was slowly losing the woman he loved. The woman he loved was not a killer. She used to flinch at the thought of hurting anyone. But some officers had knives in their penises and eyes gouged out. There were officers with their throats slit, their guts out, and cracked skulls.

This program was slowly tainting her, and Razor hated it. He released his rage on the other officers that were there. Once they were dealt with, Razor picked her up, but she refused to leave. She still needed to protect the girl who was hiding inside of the cell. Razor sighed with relief. The woman he loved was still in there.

Now he watched as the female prisoner gravitated to Helena, no doubt afraid of everyone else but her. Once the medic officer was done stitching Helena up, Razor demanded that he leave.

"What now?" Helena asked. Her voice was raspy from her screaming and being up all night.

"We wait."

"You're not giving me to them...are you?" Tatianna asked. Razor saw Helena grab her arm protectively.

"My wife just killed about a dozen officers to protect you. I'm not about to undermine her by giving you to them."

Tatianna sighed. "Thank you."

Razor didn't need the thanks. At the end of the day, it was the right thing to do. Unfortunately, Tatianna's fate was inevitable. Even if Razor killed to save her. He nor Helena could be around her 24/7, and once there's an opportunity, an officer will pounce. They both were aware of this fact, but the two women held on to a sliver of hope anyway.

"So, what are we waiting for?" Helena asked.

"Declan."

"I imagine he would stay far away now that you're here."

"No, he has a point to prove. Whether I'm here or not," he said. "I just hope he comes quickly before Bossman gets here."

"Bossman," Helena shot up. Razor could tell that she was afraid. Tatianna's grip on Helena's arm got even tighter.

"It's ok," Razor walked over to calm her. "I had to tell him what was going on. I was in the middle of something when I got word of what was happening...everything will work out fine."

"He's going to punish me," Helena cried.

"He will not. Everyone says that you were protecting yourself. They attacked you first...trust me, you will not get punished. I will burn this place down before that happens," he hugged Helena and kissed her forehead. She relaxed a little, but she kept Tatianna close to her.

The cell door finally opened, and Declan walked through. Helena quickly pushed Tatianna behind her—instinctively determined to protect her. Declan smirked at her reaction. Razor stepped in between them—blocking Declan's view of Helena and Tatianna.

"Commander Razor, I must applaud you on your training capabilities," Declan peered over at Helena. "Helena took out some of my best people with pure ease. I greatly underestimated her."

"People tend to make that common mistake with Helena."

Declan sighed. "I think we need to talk."

"That we do," Razor turned to look at Helena. "Be back soon."

Helena nodded, but her eyes told him to be careful.

The two men headed out.

Declan didn't even bother to remove his dead officers. They stayed lying around the floor. Razor guessed that he wanted Nick to see how many officers Helena had killed. Declan was going to use that to paint an ugly picture. Razor wasn't worried about it, though. Declan wasn't going to be alive when Nick got there.

"So, I handled this all wrong," Declan admitted.

"You should've reached out to me first," Razor told him. "Not immediately sending Trenton after her."

"Actually, I shouldn't have to do anything but run my prison. Helena was holding up the process."

"By protecting a prisoner from being gang-raped again."

"Me and my men are allowed to do whatever we want."

"And does that make you all feel more like a man? Ganging up on an innocent woman?"

Declan laughed. "You know how it is, Commander. You know how these prisons are run. And you either fall in line or be punished...Helena needs to be punished. I'm reporting her to Bossman."

Razor smirked. "You *really* should've reached out to me first," Razor's knife quickly found its way to Declan's skull. Declan's eyes widen in shock. "Bossman is already aware of everything."

Declan's body slummed to the floor, joining his fellow comrades.

When Razor walked back into the cell, the two women were all but hugging each other. Helena tensed up when he walked in.

"It's ok, he's dead," Razor said. "He won't be hurting anyone."

"And Bossman..."

"I told you, Helena, you won't have to worry about him."

"What about Tatianna? I don't want her to suffer for my actions."

Razor kneeled in front of her and took her face in his hands. "I will work something out...trust me, please."

Helena closed her eyes and nodded. She was worried, but he honestly couldn't blame her. There were numerous dead DC officers scattered about the prison—majority from Helena's doing. But this wasn't the first time that several officers were killed by their own, and Razor was sure that it wouldn't be the last.

Razor and Nick were both guilty of killing their own. Helena wasn't going to be punished for doing the same. Razor kind of admired her restraint. At least she waited for the other officers to strike first. He and Nick weren't known for that.

Razor leaned in to kiss her. Helena kissed him back intensely—her hands gripping his hair. She didn't want to let him go. Razor chuckled as he loosened her grip.

"I don't think now is the right time for that, Mrs. Thompson."

"I'm sorry," she looked down sheepishly. "I just really missed you."

"I missed you more," Razor kissed her forehead.

The cell door opened for the second time, and Nick and Chase walked in. Razor stood up. He was a little annoyed to see Chase there. The more time he spent with the President, the more Razor didn't care for him. As years went by, Razor saw that Chase was an unqualified man who had no clue what he was doing. When he learned that Chase's beliefs on rebuilding civilization were actually Nick's ideas all along, it stunned Razor. Nick was a charmer. And he charmed the President into believing his views.

Chase relied heavily on advice from Nick, which made him incompetent and dangerous. Anyone in their right mind knows not to trust someone like Nick. Even though Razor and Nick were close, he never once fully trusted him. But because President Dooms relied on Nick's guidance, Nick was able to run the nation how he saw fit.

Nick looked elated when he walked in.

"Mrs. Thompson, I admire your handiwork. No doubt trained by the best there is. But I never thought the viciousness had transferred over to you too," he laughed and shook his head. "I mean, the number of officers I've seen with knives in their dicks...that is not the way I want to go."

Helena hung her head in shame. Now that she wasn't hopped up on adrenaline, she probably dreaded seeing what she left behind.

Nick looked over at Tatianna, who was hiding behind Helena. Helena shifted, trying to block his view. Nick laughed. "Is this the one who caused all the trouble?"

"She was gang-raped during transport," Helena stated boldly.

Chase gasped. "My God, Nick, is this how you're running things here?"

Nick feigned a look of shock. "Absolutely not, Mr. President. This kind of behavior is not allowed, and what Officer Thompson did here was the right thing. It was unfortunate that these men and women turned on her the way they did. Clearly, Officer Thompson was forced to defend herself and the prisoner. This was self-defense, and I applaud Officer Thompson's actions."

"As you should," President Dooms peeked outside of the door to look at the dead officers. "Those were horrible people."

"Clearly, I need to vet my officers more thoroughly."

Helena frowned at the men, and Razor rolled his eyes. She knew that she was being patronized.

Nick turned to Razor. "I see Declan has been handled. Good job with that...we need to talk, my friend."

"Not until Helena and the prisoner are somewhere safe."

"Of course. How about HQ?"

Razor nodded. That was probably the safest place for them. "I would like Lucas to accompany us."

"That's fine. Just let me go appoint someone new over the prison, and then we can get going."

Razor turned to Helena once Nick and President Dooms left the cell. "I think you should let me carry you out."

Helena frowned at the suggestion.

"You don't want to see it out there."

Helena took a deep breath and nodded.

Razor scooped Helena in his arms. She quickly closed her eyes before he got to the cell door. Tatianna followed closely by. Razor paused at the door and turned toward her.

"You might not want to look either."

Tatianna shook her head. "I need to see."

Razor shrugged and walked out. Tatianna followed. Razor watched her, curious to see what would appear on her face. He only saw one thing—rage. He understood it. Those people were there to do her harm, and it was a significant number of them—an overwhelming number. But Razor knew that's how it went for beautiful women in the prisons. The more attractive you were, the more popular you were with the officers.

Tatianna was going to be very popular with this group of officers. Razor knew that he couldn't entirely save her from this fate, but he could try to lighten it as much as he could.

He didn't release Helena from his arms until they were out of the prison. A truck was waiting to take them to HQ. They all got in the back and waited for Nick and Chase.

"I'm surprised to see the President here," Helena stated when they were alone in the truck.

Razor looked out the window and watched as the men approached, with Lucas following behind them. "Well, someone is threatening his leadership."

**

Once they got to the DC headquarters, Razor placed the two women and Lucas in his room. The room remained untouched. His bed was still pressed up against the back wall, and a desk and chair sat in the corner. Razor tried to convince both women to sleep and assured them that Lucas would watch them and make sure that nothing happens. Helena insisted on being awake.

"Rest, please. You've been up all night."

Helena sighed. "Fine," she looked over at Lucas. "But you better wake me if something goes wrong."

Razor smiled. He could see the threat in her eyes. "I'm sure that's the first thing that Lucas will do."

"It will be. I don't want to be on Mrs. Thompson's bad side," Lucas joked.

Helena took a spot next to Tatianna on the bed. "Wake me when you're done...as soon as you're done."

"Yes, ma'am," Razor kissed her forehead as she closed her eyes. He turned his attention to Lucas. "No one else enters this room but me."

"Copy that, Commander."

Razor joined Nick and Chase in the briefing room. The two men were sitting at the conference table looking over notes that Razor had taken on the Black Deficit and Dr. Blackwell. Razor didn't say anything to them. He sat down in one of the chairs across from them.

They didn't acknowledge him at first. Nick was mumbling something to Chase, who was listening intensely. After a few minutes, Nick finally looked up at Razor. He smiled.

"My friend, I will be moving Helena to a different prison in the morning, along with the prisoner she's so fond of."

Razor calmly folded his hands. "Helena isn't going anywhere."

Nick immediately stopped what he was doing. A flash of shock and anger ran across his face. After all these years, Razor had never defied him—until Helena.

"Razor," Chase chimed in. "We have Dr. Blackwell to deal with."

"I don't care. I'm not doing anything if my wife isn't by my side."

The two men stared at Razor. One in disbelief. The other in pure anger.

Razor didn't care. He stood firm. At this point, he had put the program in front of Helena, and it almost cost her her life. Razor wasn't going to make that mistake again. They needed him, and he was going to play into that to get what he wanted.

"Razor, citizens, and frankly some government officials, are looking at Dr. Blackwell as a strong possible leader," Chase stated in a rush. "They view him as being a better and more compassionate leader. They see him as the way of a new and better civilization. This is bad news for me and the program if we don't handle this quickly."

"I'm not doing *anything* until I get what I want."

"You're going to risk the fate of the mission over some pussy?" Nick spat.

Razor swallowed his rage. "I told you that she wasn't cut out to be a DC officer. You shouldn't have kept her away from me for so long. Because of that, you put Helena in danger."

"Did you not see what I saw? Helena handled herself well. Those officers weren't a match for her!" Nick rose from his seat. Razor followed.

"If I didn't get there when I did, Helena would've been dead. Yeah, she killed a lot of officers with ease, but it was an entire prison full of officers against her. At some point, she was going to lose."

The two men glared at each other. This was it—the beginning of the end. Razor could feel it. Their relationship was shifting, and Razor was ending up on the opposite side of Nick. And with the look Nick was giving him, Razor could see that he was coming to that same conclusion.

"Oh, enough!" Chase snapped. "Just let his wife be with him! What's the problem with that anyway? It appears that she could be useful out on the field...besides, do we really want another prison full of dead DC officers?"

Nick continued to glare at Razor. They both ignored what the President had said. Razor was determined not to bend. If they wanted to get him to do what they want, then they will give in. There was no other option.

"Nick!" Chase was shocked that this was still going on. "I demand that you give him what he wants!"

"Fine, Helena will be with you."

"No, I will be with her at whatever prison you're assigning her to," Razor pushed.

There was no way Helena was going to leave Tatianna in prison alone. Razor knew that. She already was barely letting the girl out of her reach, much less out of her sight. There was no way he could convince her otherwise.

"You're not going back on the road?" Chase was appalled by this news. Nick was even more furious.

"All interrogations can be handled at the prison," Razor pointed out. "Bring any Black Deficit members to me, and I will handle the rest."

"And Blackwell?" the President asked. That was the only person he cared about.

"Just let me know what you want."

"Kill him," Nick finally spoke again. "If you want your new little assignment, then you *must* kill Blackwell."

"Fine, once you get him, bring him to me. I will handle it from there."

"Great," Chase turned to Nick. "Give him his new assignment."

"I believe you said you had something else to report," Nick was trying to keep his voice even, but the anger was seeping through.

"I've narrowed down the potential areas that Blackwell's children could strike next. Dowagiac or Cassopolis...do we have a sweep scheduled for there?"

"Next week."

"Then that's probably when they're going to strike."

"That's excellent," Chase sounded chipper. "If we don't get Blackwell himself, then at least we'll have his children."

"It's a good lead," Nick reluctantly agreed.

"I think we have all we need to move," Chase seemed satisfied. "Well done, gentlemen. Nick, I will be waiting for you downstairs." The President left out the room with no further word.

Nick and Razor continued to glare at each other. Nick was the first to break the awkward silence.

"I never thought that some pussy could make you so weak," Nick spat, trying to get a rise out of Razor.

It took all his strength for Razor to ignore the insult. "Helena and I will report to the prison once I handle the Black Deficit member that I have hanging somewhere."

"Fine."

Razor headed toward the door before Nick stopped him.

"Word of advice, my friend...your work *must* be impeccable from here on out."

Razor opened the briefing room door and turned his back to Nick. "Copy that."

By the time Razor got to his old room, Helena and Tatianna were sound asleep. Even in her sleep, Helena had angled herself where she was blocking Tatianna. Razor sighed at the view. How was he going to convince her to go on this last mission with him? There was no way he could bring Tatianna along with them. He already pushed past his limit with Nick. If he pressed even further, one of them was likely to end up dead.

Lucas was sitting at the desk. He stood up when Razor walked in. "You're still breathing, so I'm assuming it went well."

"As well as to be expected."

"So, he reassigned her."

Razor shook his head. "He reassigned me."

"You? In a prison?" Razor could hear the laughter in Lucas's voice.

"I will now be in the prisons."

"Wow, that's going to be entertaining."

Razor chuckled and then sighed. "I need another favor from you."

"Sure thing."

"I have an errand to run before I go to the prison. I'm taking Helena with me."

"You need me to look after the prisoner."

"Never take your eyes off her until we get back."

"Copy that, Commander."

"Thank you, Lucas."

Razor went to wake up Helena. She rose quickly. She was relieved to see that he was ok.

"What's happening now?" she asked, rubbing her eye.

"I need you to go on an errand with me, and then we'll report to the prison."

"You're going to be there with me?"

"Would you be willing to be on the road with me?"

"The officers would eat Tatianna alive. I can't leave her."

Razor smirked. "Then I guess I will be in the prison with you."

Helena sighed. "I'm sorry."

"Don't be. As long as we're together, everything will be alright."

"...someone has to be with Tatianna while I'm away."

"I'm going to watch after her," Lucas said.

Razor could see Helena really eyeing him. He couldn't help but smile.

"Guard her with your life," Helena demanded.

"Sure thing, Mrs. Thompson."

Helena sighed and turned to wake Tatianna.

Razor allowed Helena to explain to Tatianna what was going on. As expected, she was reluctant to be away from Helena. Helena reassured Tatianna that she would be back as soon as she could. Razor told her that she could trust Lucas and that he would be looking after her. It took a while, but they finally convinced Tatianna that everything will be alright.

"Thank you so much for protecting me," Tatianna hugged Helena before leaving out with Lucas.

They were now out in front of HQ. Two trucks were parked nearby. One truck had Nick and the President inside, waiting to drop off Lucas and Tatianna at the prison.

"You're very welcome. I'll see you soon," Helena watched her leave. She sighed and turned to Razor once Tatianna was out of her sight. "What now?"

Razor walked over to the last truck. "We warn Blackwell."

**

"I don't understand what's happening," Helena admitted once they were on the road. Razor looked over at her. She wore a frown on her face. Of course, she hated being left in the dark.

"It's all just bad timing really," Razor looked at the empty road ahead of him. "Us...Blackwell. We're all running on borrowed time."

Helena sighed. "Razor, you're scaring me."

"Blackwell's children have been making attacks against the DC. They're making noise, and word is slowly getting around. Plus, the big wigs in Washington like Blackwell's ideas for the future, which is bad for the President."

"So..."

"They want to take out Blackwell, and they want me to do it...that's the price for me being in the prison."

"But you said we're warning Blackwell."

"We are, but if he's brought to me, I have no choice. Nick is going to be watching us closely. Blackwell's children, what happened with you at the prison, me refusing an order, it all has him on edge. And when Nick is on edge, he gets unpredictable and out of control. We have to tread lightly."

"I'm so sorry, Razor."

He looked over and saw the guilt on her face. He took her hand and kissed it. "Stop apologizing. It was always going to come down to this."

Helena smiled with relief. "Thank you...do you know where Blackwell is?"

"I have a hunch. Like me, he's been trying to track his children down. I figured out their pattern. Blackwell always shows up in the last place that they attacked, trying to find them. Their last attack was in Sturgis."

"Well, let's hope that he's there."

"Let's hope," Razor wasn't sure what he would do if he couldn't find Blackwell. He couldn't be on the road for long. Nick would grow suspicious.

If he couldn't find Blackwell, then Razor would have no choice but to go through with killing him when he gets brought to him. There was no matter of if. It wasn't just Nick who truly wanted him. The President wanted Blackwell too. Officers would be combing the streets for him. It was only a matter of time before he's captured.

Like Niles, Sturgis was a small town, so Razor had his first guess on where Blackwell might be. Once they crossed the city line, Razor headed straight to the downtown area.

They made their way down Chicago Street. Most of the shops and businesses were all run down—like everywhere else in the nation. The streets were dead. There was hardly anyone walking around. Everyone was probably hiding out or sleeping. It was early in the morning, after all.

Razor looked over at Helena. She was looking intently out the window—searching for Blackwell.

Eventually, Razor left Chicago Street and tried to venture away from the downtown area. He had no clue where he was going. He wasn't familiar with the city, but he needed to move quickly. He needed to deliver his warning.

"There!" Helena suddenly shouted. "By the police and fire station!"

Razor slammed on the brakes.

Sure enough, Blackwell was sitting on a bench in front of the Sturgis Police and Fire Station. His head was in his hands. He looked defeated. Razor quickly pulled up in front of him and got out of the truck. The truck was barely in park. Helena quickly got out after him.

Blackwell looked up, shocked. A weak smile spread across his face when he recognized it was Razor.

"My old friend, I guess it's finally time for me to die," he looked over at Helena. "At least introduce me to your wife this time."

"You need to leave, now," Razor went over and pulled Blackwell to his feet.

"I can't do that."

"There is an official hit out on you now. You've not only upset Nick but the President too."

Blackwell shrugged Razor off him. "Why? Because people are taking notice of how shitty this new system is. Are they now just realizing that this new way of life isn't viable? Am I to apologize for showing others a little common sense?!"

"You can't bring change if you're dead!"

"But my death could start the movement!" Blackwell looked unhinged. Razor understood the feeling. Everything seemed like it was spiraling out of control.

"Cole, do you really think your children can lead the movement the way you want?" Helena chimed in calmly.

Blackwell looked at her in disappointment. "No, Mrs. Razor."

"It's Helena," she smiled at him. "You are way too important to lose. You are our future. And my husband is trying to do the right thing and save you. Please, just listen to him."

Blackwell sighed and nodded. "I didn't want a war. I just wanted to help people...that is all. My children feel like they have something to prove."

"Well, even though you were just trying to help people, others were seeing you as a leader—a competent, compassionate, strong leader. You've become a threat," Razor said. "Your children trying to start a war with the DC task force only added fuel to the flames."

Blackwell took a seat back on the bench. He frowned at Razor's words. Helena sat down next to him; she placed her hand on top of his—for comfort. He looked over at her and smiled. He was grateful for her kindness.

"Sadly, I think a war is what it will take to truly extract change," Blackwell admitted. "But I don't see my children leading that. They're likely to die more than anything...the time of war may not be now, but it's coming Razor. And when it does...when that person sparks the flame, there will be no way to extinguish it."

"But that's in the future. And when it does happen, we will still need you there," Razor stated.

He agreed with Blackwell. A war was what it was going to take to remove those who were in charge now. But Blackwell's children were not the face of that. Whenever that person comes, Blackwell would be needed. He was the brains. The flame was the face, and the face can only get them so far.

"So right now, you have to stop your children from causing this war prematurely. Otherwise, it will be worse for everyone."

"And once I stop them?"

"Flee."

"To where?"

"Canada."

"You expect me to lead the revolution from another country."

"I expect you to survive until I come to get you."

"I'm not hiding like some coward!"

"If you're caught, they will bring you to me to be killed!" Razor shouted. He really needed Blackwell to understand the severity of the situation they were all in. "I will have no choice but to do it then."

Razor didn't know what Blackwell saw, but he quickly changed his tune. Blackwell sighed and nodded.

"Ok, what do I need to do?"

"Convince your children to stand down."

"I don't know where they are. I always get there too late."

"Try Dowagiac or Cassopolis," Razor said. "There are sweeps scheduled for next week, so that might be when they will attack."

"Ok," Blackwell stood up. "Thank you, I will do my best to talk them down."

Razor saw the sincerity in his eyes. "You really need to succeed, Cole...your life depends on it."

~24~

Razor

The past four months in the new prison was nothing but a big ball of stress for Razor and Helena. When they first reported, after they warned Blackwell, Razor found out that Lucas was killed, and Tatianna was sexually assaulted again. When he dug deeper, Razor discovered that it was Nick's doing.

Before Lucas and Tatianna were dropped off at the penitentiary, Nick put the word out for them to be targeted. Lucas tried to protect Tatianna but was outnumbered and killed in the process. Nick swiftly killed all the officers involved to cover his tracks. Razor could only find this information because one of the involved officers told a friend. That friend, in turn, told Razor.

Helena was enraged and crushed by the news. She wanted to attack any officer who looked at Tatianna. Razor had to refrain her from doing anything.

"The message is clear here, Helena," Razor had to lock her in a room to keep her from attacking another officer. "We can't mess up. Nick had Tatianna attacked because he knew it would anger you and make you want to fight. And if you fight, he knows that I will get involved. That would give him a reason to punish us."

Frustration and sadness covered Helena's face; she dropped to her knees and cried. Razor quickly wrapped her in his arms.

"This is so fucked up!" she cried. "Tatianna shouldn't be punished because of me."

"It's because of me," Razor admitted. "He wants to make sure I fall in line."

"It doesn't matter! Tatianna shouldn't be punished because of it."

Razor kissed her forehead. "You're absolutely right, but the more we intervene, the worst it will be for her. The best thing we can do is ignore it. If we ignore what they're doing, they'll eventually ignore her too. She's only interesting if we're interested in her."

"That's easier said than done."

"You just have to be strong."

Helena sighed in defeat—her spirit was slowly breaking. Razor entirely blamed himself for that. Because he loved her, she got dragged into this crazy fucked up program. She had been used against him and put into dire situations to get to him. And now, because of him, she had to do terrible things to innocent people.

Razor made sure that Helena participated in some of the beatings and tortures of the prisoners. They had to play along and make sure that word got back to Nick that they were falling in line. It killed Helena every moment she was there. At night, Razor would hold her as she cried herself to sleep. He hated his self. But he did what he had to do to keep them alive. In the end, the woman he loved was slowly dying.

They needed to escape. To live their lives somewhere else in peace. Sadly, with him overseeing the prison, Razor couldn't go out and search for Jade—the only hiccup in their escape plan. He hated to think of it, but he hoped that she would get caught. If she was in the system, he could get her sent to his prison, and they could all escape. But Jade was just one hiccup.

The second hiccup was Blackwell.

Unfortunately, he couldn't get his children to stand down. A big fight broke out between the DC officers and the Black Deficit members. Because of the chaos, no debtors were apprehended during the sweep. Nick was furious, but Chase was even more furious.

All the officers who survived the attack were immediately killed by Nick. Word spread like wildfire in the prisons. Even some prisoners were brave enough to cheer at the DCs demise.

Razor was on edge. Blackwell was sure to get caught soon. He hoped that he heeded his warning, and Blackwell was heading for Canada right now. Hopefully, Cole would take his children with him.

And to make the worst situation even worse, Jade's ex-boyfriend, Vincent, reported to Razor's prison as a bounty hunter. Razor hated him. Vincent was arrogant and full of himself. Plus, he was a major dick. He had the misconception that he was actually one of them.

To make matters even worse, Razor knew that Vincent was spying on him and Helena and reporting everything back to Nick. This wasn't Nick's doing. Nick would never like or trust someone like Vincent. Vincent was doing it on his own accord to get in Nick's good graces. Either way, Nick was getting intel on Razor and Helena, so they had to be careful.

Razor had assigned Helena to the solitary unit. Since Razor spent most of his time "interrogating" people there, he was able to keep an eye on her.

As time went on, he noticed some strange behavior from her. After encouraging her to remain uninvolved with the female prisoners, particularly Tatianna, Helena had become very aggressive toward them. One day she smacked a woman with her baton, damaging her face. Once the woman was attended to, Helena threw her into the solitary unit. It wasn't until later that Razor realized that the female prisoner was the current new favorite among the male officers. But with the woman now in solitary, the officers couldn't get to her.

Helena did this to a few more female prisoners, and it seemed to be vicious every time. Razor was suspicious about her reasoning for attacking these women, but he could never be sure. His theory was confirmed when Helena attacked Tatianna next. It was very brutal. She had cracked Tatianna's ribs, and she needed to heal in the solitary unit for a month.

Any female prisoner who became popular with the male officers were eventually attacked by Helena. Razor wanted to stop her but was too afraid. If he took this away from her, he didn't know how she would react. Something told him that she would just give in and start killing the officers. Razor found that this was the best scenario.

But over time, Helena started acting even stranger. She was slowly losing it. Not being able to save these women was killing her.

For a few weeks, there was a strange string of deaths among the DC officers. They were all dropping dead from what *seemed* like natural causes. The officers appeared to be sick with symptoms like nausea, vomiting, and diarrhea. Razor wasn't suspicious about this at first. With so many people confided in one area, sicknesses tended to spread around. But the illness was only happening to the officers. And it was a specific group of officers—officers known for sexually assaulting female prisoners.

"It's weird, huh," Razor said as he lay in bed with Helena. He was currently playing in her hair. He really missed the mint green color. It had grown out before Helena cut it into her regular pixie haircut. "That only those officers are getting this mysterious sickness."

Helena shrugged. "Karma."

"I guess," he sighed. He knew that she was the cause of it—probably poisoning them in some kind of way. The fact that she had temporarily stopped crying herself to sleep was a huge indicator. "I just don't want Bossman coming to poke around."

"Would he really come around because his officers are getting *sick*?" her tone was challenging. "They just need to watch what they eat...or drink."

Razor sighed again. She was right about Nick. There was no way that he would come around because some of his officers were sick. Helena was smart with her poisoning. Yes, the targeted officers were officers who sexually assaulted female prisoners. Still, they were also known for hanging around each other. So, it would make sense that the mysterious sickness would've spread among them.

Plus, the number of affected officers was so low that no one would even look twice at it. But it was the fact that Helena was so callous that made Razor so concerned.

"I guess you're right," he finally admitted.

"I know I am," she looked up and smiled at him, but it wasn't the smile that he was used to. She gave him a quick peck on the lips.

"I don't want to lose you, Helena."

She frowned, confused by his statement. "You won't."

Razor released her from his arms and sat up. "I think I already have."

"What are you talking about?" she sat up too.

"This isn't you, Helena."

"You just want me to sit around and do nothing?"

"I told you we're on thin ice."

"Then I would rather die doing the right thing instead of sitting by and watching other people suffer!" tears started streaming down her face. "I won't do it!"

Razor quickly wrapped her back in his arms. He kissed her forehead. "I'm sorry, Helena. This is all my fault."

He ultimately blamed his self for the situation she was in. Everything went downhill once Nick discovered her. He was slowly tainting her. Turning Helena into someone she wasn't. Razor never hated himself more. If he never fell in love with her, none of this would be happening to her.

"None of this is your fault, Razor. It's just the way of the world, sadly."

"But I helped make it that way."

"No, you didn't. You see that there's another way. That makes you different," she grabbed his face and kissed him. "You're better than you think."

Razor sighed. Despite it all, she still loved him. And gave him more credit than he deserved.

"I know it's hard for you to just stand by. But I'm begging you, please, be more discreet." There was no use in asking her to stop. The more he did that, the more aggressive she became. Maybe this would help.

"Don't worry," she sighed. "I've already got my point across."

Razor was confused by her statement. He didn't know what she meant by that. But he was grateful that she agreed to stop. He couldn't stomach the idea of something happening to her.

However, a few weeks later, he finally understood what she meant.

Nick and Chase came to the prison in a frenzy. There was another attack by the Black Deficit in Summerville, MI. Unfortunately, the assault left a lot of officers dead. Things were spiraling out of control, and the Black Deficit was starting to get known as a rebel group. This time, it was said that Blackwell was leading the attack.

Razor and Helena were stunned by the news.

Luckily, a Black Deficit member was captured from the fight. Nick and the President were bringing the member to Razor.

Helena and Razor were waiting in the torture room when Nick and Chase finally joined them with the captured member. Nick smiled when he saw Helena.

"Mrs. Thompson," he said slyly. "It's funny that my officers suddenly drop dead when you're present."

Helena shrugged indifferently. "Hazards of the job, right?"

"It is, but sudden illnesses?"

Helena gave him a blank stare. No one could pin it on her. Razor knew that, and so did Nick.

"Guess that was bound to happen," Nick mumbled.

"Diseases do tend to spread around."

Nick chuckled. "That it does," he and Helena stared each other down.

Razor was amazed and impressed. There was no sense of fear from Helena. In fact, she stood in front of Nick, daring him to accuse her of the officers' death.

After a moment, Nick laughed. "I'm beginning to see why you love this one, my friend."

"Yes, this is all nice," Chase chimed in, annoyed. "But can we please attend to the issue at hand?"

"You've been no fun lately," Nick sighed. He looked over at Helena and winked. He pulled the Black Deficit member further inside. He and Razor wrapped a chain around his feet and hung him upside down.

Razor turned away from the unconscious captive and looked at President Dooms. "Orders?"

"Find out where they're going to attack!" he yelled hysterically. "Blackwell was leading the charge at this one, and the officials were very impressed. My opponents have been itching to find a replacement. We've told the officials that our way is the *only* way, but they've been looking to refute that. And now there's a potential leader who isn't afraid to lead the fight. A compassionate leader who have viable ideas on how to reestablish society. Consider how bad this looks!"

Nick laughed.

Chase turned to glare at him. "What is so funny?!" he demanded.

Razor sighed and took a seat in a nearby chair. He motioned for Helena to join him. She walked over and sat on his lap. Razor wrapped his arms around her. He found that holding her sometimes fought off his annoyance, which was fortunate for those who were annoying him.

"You," Nick chuckled. "Consider how bad this looks!" he mimicked. "This only looks bad for *you*, Mr. President."

"It's your program he's making look like amateurs here!"

"And it's your views that he's contradicting! Me and my men are doing our job!"

"Then tell me, how many debtors have *you* and *your men* apprehended during those last sweeps?"

Nick growled.

"Exactly, so don't tell me that this only looks bad for me."

Before the President knew it, Nick had him in the air by the throat. Chase's eyes widen in shock and horror. He kicked around frantically, trying to get out of Nick's hold. Razor sighed again in annoyance.

Helena cleared her throat. "I believe there was a job you wanted my husband to do."

Nick looked over and smiled. Apparently, he liked Helena's new callous demeanor. He looked back at Chase. "Watch how you speak to me," he quickly dropped him.

President Dooms fell to the ground, coughing and trying to catch his breath. They all waited patiently for him to compose himself. After a couple of minutes, Chase stood and quickly brushed off his suit. He cleared his throat and looked over at Nick.

"Never touch me like that again," he spat.

Nick glared at him. "Is that a threat?"

"Call it what you want, but if you touch me like that again, trust me, it will be the last thing you do."

Nick walked toward him again.

"Enough!" Helena shouted. Nick stopped. President Dooms looked at her. "What information do you need?"

"The location of where they plan to attack next," Chase stated calmly. He looked a little embarrassed.

"Alright," Razor finally spoke again. He slowly stood—along with Helena. "I'll get it done."

"Thank you," President Dooms said. Nick glared at him.

"Now, both of you need to leave my prison," Razor was tired of them already, and they've only been there for 15 minutes.

Nick laughed at his bluntness.

"Fine, but I expect a report soon, Commander Razor," Chase walked out of the room without further comment.

Nick stayed behind. He looked at Helena and Razor and sighed. "Looks like you two have been doing well here."

"That's what you wanted, right?" Helena stated. She smirked. "I mean, that was the whole reason why you had Lucas killed and Tatianna raped...to make sure we fall in line."

Nick's eyes widened. Razor held his breath. Who was this woman? After a moment, Nick laughed.

"Well, it seems like you've lost your fondness for her...broke her ribs. That seems harsh."

Helena shrugged.

Nick looked at Razor. "I finally understand what you've seen, my friend," he walked out of the room. "Let me know if you get anything."

Razor nodded and watched Nick walk off. When he turned back to Helena, she had her hands on her knees, hyperventilating. Razor rushed to her side—confused by her sudden change in demeanor.

"Are you ok?" he asked.

"Let's hope that worked," she whispered, tears fell from her eyes. It appeared that she was talking to herself.

Razor had no clue what she was talking about. Apparently, she had some plan in motion and left him in the dark about it.

It appeared her mysterious plan worked. Before Nick left, he called off the officers who were targeting Tatianna. Because it seemed like Helena lost interest in her, there was nothing left to use against her—except for Razor. And they both knew that was hard to do.

"And you didn't tell me," Razor was a little disappointed that she didn't confide in him.

"I was afraid that you would talk me out of it," she brushed away a few tears.

"So, when you attacked her..."

"It was all part of the plan. But I had to do that to other female prisoners before and after her. He would've seen right through it if I just targeted her."

Razor sighed. "Helena, please, don't leave me in the dark again...I thought you were losing your mind."

She nodded and brushed away more tears. "I think I already have," she smiled weakly. "But I really am sorry."

Razor hugged her. "I promise, we'll get out of here soon."

**

Like most of the men Razor had beaten and tortured, the captured Black Deficit member pleaded and begged for mercy. And as usual, Razor sat on a chair in the torture room, looking at his bloody hands, and ignoring what the captive was saying.

This time Helena sat in the room with him. Razor thought it was vital for her to be there. She stood in the far corner of the room, trying not to look too much at the battered man.

As usual, Razor zoned out. Sometimes, he looked at his hands during these moments and reflected on all the damage they have done. They were evil. He always thought of them that way.

Then Helena placed her hands in them. She kneeled in front of him. Razor smiled a little. At least his hands were never evil to her.

"You ok?" she frowned. Concern filled her eyes and voice.

"Tired," Razor confessed. And he was. Tired of beating information out of people. Tired of being stressed out. Tired of trying to keep them both safe.

"Please...please, just tell me what you want," the captive begged.

Razor hadn't asked the member any questions yet. Once he came to, Razor immediately went to the beating part of the interrogation. Razor got up from the chair and walked over to the captive. He quickly punched him in the gut. The member groaned in pain.

Helena had her hand to her mouth, trying to hide the shock. Razor walked back over to her and kissed her forehead.

"Don't worry about him," he whispered. Razor didn't want Helena pitying this person.

The member was the reason why their current situation was so stressful. If Nick wasn't so paranoid about the rebel group and what they could do, he and Helena could be out on the road. They could've found Jade and escaped by now.

Angered even more, Razor went back over to the member and punched him again. And again. And again.

"Razor," Helena pleaded quietly.

Razor stopped when he felt her hand gently touch his back. He turned to look at her. He couldn't read her face. She looked into his eyes and then placed a hand on his cheek. After a moment, she diverted her eyes to the member.

"Miss, please," the member cried. "Make it stop."

Helena walked toward the member. Razor watched her as she kneeled in front of the captive—both of their faces at eye level.

"It will stop," she said calmly. "Once you tell us what we need to know."

The member cried even harder. Helena gently wiped away some of his tears and blood.

"What do you want to know?" he asked.

"Why is Blackwell leading the charge?" Helena asked. "The last we heard, Blackwell was against these attacks."

Razor stood amazed. He wasn't expecting Helena to take command. He just didn't want to leave her in the dark or recap the information to her. Never in a million years did Razor think that she would be asking the captive questions. But he mentioned that he was tired, so maybe she just wanted to help.

"I'm not really sure," the member cried.

Helena sighed. She continued to clean his face. "What's your name?"

"Ben."

"It's nice to meet you, Ben," she smiled. "I'm Helena...Ben, I really need you to think hard. Otherwise, my husband is going to get involved again. Why do you think Blackwell decided to fight now?"

The member cried harder at the mention of Razor. Razor cracked his knuckles for show. They really needed to understand what Blackwell was thinking and what he was up to.

Helena comforted the member, and eventually, he began to calm down a little.

"The only thing I can think of," he finally said. "Is that he's trying to protect his children."

Helena frowned. "How so?"

"Well, everyone knows that the President views the Black Deficit as a threat, and right now, people see Jackson and Beverly as the leaders."

Razor scoffed. "Jackson and Beverly are *not* the leaders."

"They're viewed as leaders now that they're the ones responsible for the uprising," the member countered. "Blackwell was slowly becoming a quack that was just spewing ideas."

"That's ridiculous," Razor said. How could anyone view Blackwell's children as leaders?

"I know," the member quickly said. "But it's hard to refute it when they're doing damage to the DC."

"So, Blackwell began to take charge to save face?" Helena asked, a little disgusted.

"No, to save his children. For a brief moment, there was a hit out on them."

Razor looked over at Helena. They both were in disbelief. This was news to them.

"So, Blackwell made sure he was seen at the next attack so the hit would be back on him," Razor stated. It was slowly making sense to him. He was right. His children were going to get him killed.

"Who put the hit out on them?"

The member looked at them in disbelief. "The President...don't you know?"

Helena slowly stood up. Razor gently took her by the elbow and walked her to the far corner of the room.

"What does this mean?" she asked.

"Not sure, but it appears that Chase put this hit out without consulting anyone, not even Nick...he would've told me."

"Considering how everything's been between you two, I don't think Bossman would've told you."

Razor shook his head. "Even though our relationship is rocky, he knows that I can still get the job done."

"But why put a hit out on Blackwell's children?"

"Just cause," Razor stated. Helena raised an eyebrow. "Blackwell is making a good impression with the government officials. If he is randomly killed now, everyone will know that President Dooms was responsible, but if he's killed during an attack..."

"Hazard of the job," Helena finished.

Razor nodded. "Chase wanted to force Blackwell out on the field...that would've been the last thing Nick would've wanted."

"What do we do with this information?"

Razor smiled. He knew what Helena was getting at. They had both just witnessed merely hours ago the discourse between the two men. Why not add a little fuel to the fire?

"I do my job and report it to Nick," they walked back over to the captive. Razor grabbed the chain that was wrapped around his legs.

"Where are they attacking next?"

"I don't know!" he began to cry at the prospect of pain. "I know Hartford, Portage, and Kalamazoo were in the mix."

"So, they're still planning on staying in Michigan."

The member quickly nodded. "Please...I've given you what you wanted. Please, don't kill me."

Helena looked over at Razor. He knew she was wondering if they had to kill him. Razor nodded at her. She sighed and looked over at the member.

"Let's get some tea," she smiled.

The member looked at her, baffled; the statement confused Razor too. The member nodded. Helena looked at Razor.

"Let's get him down from here. And I'll get us some tea," Helena didn't wait for a response. She walked out of the room.

Razor did what she said. He took the captive down and shackled him to a chair. Both men sat silently as they waited for Helena to come back. About 10 minutes later, Helena came in with three cups. She handed Razor two cups. He looked down and saw that both were filled with just hot water. He kept his face blank. It was unclear what she was up to. Helena walked the cup over to the member.

"Thank you," he said.

"You're very welcome, Ben," Helena walked back over and took a cup of hot water from Razor. She blew on it and took a sip. Instinctively, Ben took a drink of his tea. "How long have you been a member?"

Ben took another drink of his tea. "Six months. The Black Deficit is like family to me."

Helena took another sip of her hot water. She looked down at her cup. "I'm sorry you've been taken away from your family."

Razor could see her sadness at the mention of family. He played along with her and took a sip of his hot water.

"Are you going to kill me?"

Helena sighed. She took another sip. Ben followed. Helena looked at him. "I promise it won't hurt."

Ben frowned and finished his tea. "What does that mean?" his words began to slur.

Helena sat her cup down and walked over to him. Immediately, she kneeled beside him and placed her hand on top of his. Razor could see Ben's breathing increase. Fear was in his eyes. It finally dawned on him what was going on. Ben looked over at Helena in a panic. Helena's eyes were watery.

"It's ok," she whispered. "Just close your eyes and go to sleep...you'll be at peace."

Ben continued to stare.

"I'm sorry," Helena's voice cracked as a few tears fell down her cheek. "It's the best death I can give you."

Ben gave her a weak smile; he sighed and closed his eyes. Helena held his hand until he drew his last breath. She stood once he was dead. She brushed away her tears. Razor walked over to her and wrapped his arm around her waist. He kissed the top of her head.

"It was more than he deserved," Razor stated.

Helena nodded. Razor began to deal with Ben's dead body when his radio went off.

"Commander Razor, please respond."

Razor picked up his radio. "Razor speaking."

"Commander, there was another attack, but Blackwell has been captured. He's on his way to you now."

"Shit," Razor mumbled. He talked into his radio again. "Copy that."

Helena stood in front of him, wide-eyed. Razor frowned at her—a plan slowly forming.

"You got any more drugs?"

~25~

Razor

By the time Blackwell was brought to Razor, he was still unclear on what he wanted to do. If he fell in line and do what was expected of him, he and Helena would be in the endless cycle of being used by Nick and the DC task force. If he didn't go through with it, then he and Helena would most likely be killed. Razor was in a difficult situation.

When Blackwell was brought in, he was unconscious. Razor didn't have him hanging like most of his captives. Instead, Razor shackled him to the chair. They at least deserved a final conversation—despite it all, Razor could at least give him that.

Nick and Chase were on their way. They didn't want Razor to start anything until they got there. Helena stood in the room, watching him prepare. She shifted back and forth, looking at the door.

"What are we going to do?" she asked.

"Not sure yet," Razor glanced over the different weapons he had prepared in the room. It was all for show. He knew that Nick was going to want the theatrics of weapons instead of Razor's fists. He looked over at Helena. "Did you get the pills?"

"Yeah," she handed him a white bottle. "They're beta-blockers. I wasn't sure how I could use them...so, I moved to the deadlier stuff."

Razor watched her as she hung her head in guilt and shame. He pulled her to him and kissed her. "These are perfect."

"Ok, good," she glanced over the weapons table. "So, are you planning to poison him?"

"I'm not sure of anything yet."

"We shouldn't kill him."

"He left me no choice."

"President Dooms left you no choice. That still doesn't mean you should do it. Blackwell is too important," Helena looked him in the eyes. "I would rather live in a world with a compassionate leader instead of an incompetent one."

"We might not live at all if we don't go through with this."

"I'm ok with that."

Razor stared at her. Those beautiful brown eyes of hers were begging him to do the right thing. But the right thing would put her life at risk, and he couldn't allow that.

"At least let us inform Bossman with what we learned and see how things play out," she pleaded.

Razor sighed. He could give her that. "Ok, we can do that."

Helena smiled at him. It was the smile that he loved. "I love you."

"I love you more."

Helena laughed. "I think you might be right about that."

Luckily for them, Nick arrived at the prison first without President

Dooms. Seeing how they were literally at each other's throats the last time they were there, the two of them arriving separately made sense. Razor and Helena met him outside of the torture room. Nick looked tired and annoyed. He gave them a weak smile when he saw them.

"My friends, it's been a while," he greeted.

"Less than 24 hours, if I'm correct," Helena pointed out.

Nick chuckled. "It's been a long and exhausting less than 24 hours," he looked over at Razor. "Is he in there?"

"Yes, still unconscious," Razor said. Nick tried to walk in, but Razor blocked him. "Before we start, I think you should know what I got out of our last captive...well, what Helena got out of him."

Nick looked at Helena, surprised. He then looked over at Razor. "None of that matters now that Blackwell is captured."

"Actually, it does," Helena stated. "There was a reason why Blackwell was out in the field."

"Which is?"

"Someone put a hit out on his children," Razor quickly said. Nick wasn't great at hearing bad news, and he didn't want Helena delivering it.

Nick balled his fist. "What?" he asked through clenched teeth.

"Blackwell was trying to talk his children down, but word got out that there was a hit out on them. So, being a father, he put his self out on the front line to get the hit back on him."

"Who would put a hit out on them?" Nick demanded. "Who would be that stupid?!"

"Someone who viewed Blackwell more of a threat than you," Helena egged on.

"Chase," Nick gritted. Razor could see the rage in his eyes. "Because of that asshole, the Black Deficit is now a rebel group. And word has spread like wildfire! Because of his stupidity, hope has been given to these debtors, and they're feeling brave to revolt!"

"Shall we begin?" Razor asked casually. He could see the fury consuming Nick. Usually, when this happened, Nick became unreasonable and didn't listen to sound advice.

Nick looked at Razor and Helena. "You two start," he looked around. "And make it fast. I'm going to wait for Dooms."

"Copy that," Razor and Helena began to make their way to the door, but Nick grabbed Helena's arm. Razor tensed up.

"Thank you for bringing this to my attention, my friend," he said. Razor kept an eye on his hands.

Helena smiled. Her eyes were calm. "You're very welcome."

Nick nodded and released her. He looked back over at Razor. "Get whatever you can from him and end it. I'll be handling Dooms in the meantime."

They watched as Nick walked away.

"That worked better than I expected," Helena whispered once Nick was out of the solitary unit.

"This might work after all," Razor admitted.

When they got back into the room, Blackwell was up. He was looking down at the shackles that chained him to the chair. There was fear present, but Blackwell did his best to hide it. As they walked inside, Blackwell looked up and smiled at them.

"Old friends," he greeted. "It's nice to see you again."

"I wish it was under better circumstances," Helena sighed.

Blackwell sighed too. "You're right, Helena."

"Why didn't you do what I said?" Razor demanded.

"I tried, but they wouldn't listen. Once they attacked in Cassopolis, there was no turning back...I had no choice, Razor."

Razor responded by punching him hard in the face. Helena gasped, and Blackwell moaned out in pain. After a moment, he spat some blood out of his mouth.

"I'm really sorry," Blackwell said.

"Sorry, doesn't help me now," Razor hit him again. And again. And again. And again.

Helena turned away—unable to watch. But Razor did what he had to do. There was no way he could take it easy on Blackwell. Not now. After a few more hits, Razor stopped. Blackwell hung his head down in pain. Blood was pouring out of his nose and mouth.

Helena rushed over and tried to clean his face as much as she could. Razor could hear her whispering apologies to him. Blackwell smiled at her and touched her hand.

"You're too kind, Helena," he looked up at Razor. "I understand why you're angry, old friend. But if I didn't get involved, my children would've been killed."

Razor removed Helena away from Blackwell and resumed hitting him. "Now you have to die for me to save Helena."

It was that moment when the doctor finally broke down. He cried, not from the hits but from the situation they were all in.

"I sorry," he cried. "I never meant to endanger her life. I completely understand. You must do what you must do to save your love. There are no hard feelings for this old friend."

Helena made a sound. It sounded like a sniffle, and a gasped. Razor looked over at her. She was concerned. She wondered if he was going to go through with it. Razor wasn't sure himself. He was just angry and frustrated and was taking it out on Blackwell. Razor resumed the beating. Until someone pounded on the door. Helena quickly answered it.

"It's Bossman and President Dooms," an officer stated in a panic.

"They're fighting."

"Each other?" Helena asked in disbelief.

"Well, Bossman and President Dooms' new guards."

Helena looked over at him, shocked by the news.

"Go check it out," Razor said to her. "I don't want them in here."

Helena nodded and left with the officer.

Razor didn't want the President to get in there. If Chase made his way in, then Razor would have no choice but to kill Blackwell. This was his opportunity. The distraction could help him go through with his plan. Razor grabbed the pill bottle and poured some of the beta-blockers into his hand.

It was poetic that these were the pills that Helena had left. Because of his father's heart problems, Razor knew precisely how many tablets to give Blackwell to receive the desired outcome. He forced the pills into Blackwell's hand.

"Take these," he demanded.

Blackwell obeyed. "A more peaceful option..."

"You're not dying here today. You're too important for our future."

Blackwell frowned. Then Razor punched him so hard that he passed out.

Razor waited a few minutes. He could finally hear the fighting going on out in the prison. They were getting closer. He needed something dramatic to impress both men, should they come looking. Razor grabbed the machete off the weapons table. He struck hard and fast. It only took two strikes to cut Blackwell's left hand clean off. He quickly stopped the bleeding. Razor removed Blackwell from the shackles and laid him down. The room door opened as Razor was preparing the body bag.

Helena paused when she walked in, trying to hold back the vomit that was threatening to come out.

"Help me with this," he requested.

Helena nodded, and once she composed herself, she grabbed Blackwell's feet. "It's total chaos out there."

"What happened?" he and Helena lifted Blackwell's body and placed him in the body bag.

"Bossman confronted Chase. Chase admitted to everything and dared Bossman to do something about it. Bossman tried to attack, but Chase's guards got in the way. And then a fight with the guards and the officers pursued."

"Perfect," Razor grumbled.

Then another knock was at the door. Shortly after that, Vincent walked in with a smug look on his face.

"I was tasked with making sure you got the job done," he stated.

"It's done," Razor threw Blackwell's hand at him. Vincent squealed at the sight of the hand. Razor laughed. Vincent glared at him.

"I need more confirmation than that," he demanded. He walked over and checked Blackwell's pulse. A look of disappointment appeared on his face. "I'll report this to Bossman."

Razor zipped up the body bag and threw Blackwell over his shoulder. "Helena and I are going to dispose of the body...report that to Bossman too. They can keep the hand as a souvenir," he and Helena quickly left out of the room, not waiting for Vincent's response.

It was all working out better than they expected. Razor and Helena could actually save Blackwell.

There was hope for them yet.

**

Razor and Helena stood by the truck, waiting for Blackwell to wake. They both stared at the Detroit River—the Canadian border right in sight.

Razor was so tempted to take him and Helena across the border, but they still needed Jade. This wasn't the time for them.

Luckily, Nick and Chase were at each other's throats that Razor was positive he and Helena could fly under the radar. Especially now since the word of Blackwell's "death" had already spread like wildfire. It's been reported that the Black Deficit and Blackwell's children were already in mourning. Hopefully, this devastating blow will keep them at bay, and the rumors of them being a rebel group would cease.

Once Razor found Jade, they would go find Blackwell and prepare for the revolution.

It was only a matter of time before he and Nick would be back on bad terms. President Dooms was just the latest distraction.

Razor kept his gaze on the water. He would soon need to wake Blackwell. Someone could stumble across them if they stayed too long. The cover of darkness was good enough, but it was still a risk. No one could see that Blackwell was actually still alive.

Helena walked over to Razor. She wrapped her arms around him and buried her head in his chest. "You did the right thing."

Razor kissed the top of her head. "I know. Thank you for believing in me."

"I told you," she looked up at him. "You're more than your rage."

They felt movement in the truck, followed by Blackwell's screams. Razor and Helena quickly moved to quiet him. The shock of a missing limb was hard to take in.

"It's ok. It's ok," Helena tried her best to calm him.

"My hand!" Blackwell cried.

"I had to give them something," Razor explained. "They didn't see your dead body."

It took a moment, most of the time spent with Helena consoling him before Blackwell calmed down. Once he was finally able to listen, Razor filled him in on everything that happened. He also mentioned that word of his apparent death had spread. Sadness finally hit Blackwell.

"Thank you for everything you've done, my friend," Blackwell smiled weakly. "But I don't understand why you didn't kill me."

"I already told you, you're the future," Razor stated. "Once the war breaks out, you will be needed. So, stay alive and keep a low profile until I come to get you."

Blackwell nodded. "Just one last favor."

"And that is?"

"Keep an eye out on my children."

Razor grimaced at the notion. Blackwell's children were a handful. That was a mission he would surely fail. "Word has spread that I was the one who killed you. I don't think me keeping an eye on them would go well."

"I understand that," Blackwell pleaded. "Just please keep an eye on them."

Razor sighed. It was the least he could do. "I'll do my best."

Blackwell smiled. "Thank you."

"We need to get going."

They all walked to the border. Razor gave Blackwell some supplies that should hold him over for a few weeks. Helena gave him a hug goodbye.

"Be safe," she said.

"You too, sweet Helena," he hugged her tightly. He looked over at Razor. "Until next time, my old friend."

Razor nodded. "Until next time."

They watched as Blackwell crossed the border and was well out of view.

Razor sighed and looked over at Helena. "The search for Jade must be intensified."

~*Now*~

Razor

Who knew that finding Jade would be finding the flame? But here it was, one and the same. Razor looked over and saw her looking at the Detroit skyline in the distance. Jade was aggressively wiping away her tears.

"Goodbye, my little munchkins," he heard her whisper. "I love you."

Those words hit him hard. He was ashamed. If he had just escaped once he and Jade rescued Helena from Nick, none of them would be in this predicament. Raina and David would be alive. And Jade's heart and soul wouldn't be ripped out. But Nick kidnapping Helena had filled him with rage. Razor was so preoccupied with getting revenge that he made a series of errors that cost many people their lives—Blackwell's children included.

He should've stuck with the original plan.

Get Jade.

Flee to Canada.

Find Blackwell.

But he was convinced that he could lead the rebellion his self. He was wrong.

Razor was prepared to right his wrongs. Raina's, Levi's, and David's death would be avenged. Razor was going to see to that, but he needed to play smarter. They needed to find Blackwell. Razor looked over at the remaining survivors in their group: Tatianna, Keeper, Yoko, Calvin, Clay, Reagan, Junior, and Danita. Helena had gone over to console her sister.

Razor sighed and stood from the log he was sitting on.

"Get up," he ordered everyone. "We need to move out."

Jade turned to him—rage filled her eyes. "You fucking bastard!" she screamed. She rushed over and began hitting him—most were punches to his chest. "You took me away from him! You should've let me kill him!" she slapped Razor hard across his face. It was then that Helena grabbed Jade's hands.

"That's enough, Jade!"

"I hate you!" she spat at him. "I fucking hate you!"

Clay finally stepped in to intervene. He practically had Jade in the air. She struggled to get out of his arms.

For the first time, in what seemed like forever, tears hit Razor's cheeks. He deserved her hatred. He deserved her anger.

"I'm sorry. I fucked up."

Jade abruptly stopped once she saw his reaction. Helena quickly rushed to his side. She wrapped her arms around him—concern filled her eyes.

"I should've come here to begin with, but I didn't. And because of that, many people lost their lives," he quickly brushed away his tears. "I failed

Raina and Levi. And most importantly, I failed you. But I know how to make up for that...we need to find him."

Helena nodded in understanding.

Jade narrowed her eyes at him. "Who?"

"Blackwell."

Keeper walked up with a frown on his face. "Blackwell's dead. *You* killed him."

Razor shook his head and looked Keeper in the eyes. "He's alive."

Then they heard a group of footsteps running toward them.

The End

ACKNOWLEDGMENTS

This journey has been quicker than the last, but alas, it has been an incredible one. As *Surviving Red's* world continues the grow, the more in awe and amazed I am by it. We can only go more in-depth and grow from here.

Once again, I would like to thank you, the reader, for exploring this world that I have created. I hope that you will continue this journey as more books are released in this series.

I like to thank everyone who helped me put this book together, to the cover artist, beta readers, proofreaders, editors, my husband Fred, family, friends, and more. Your support has meant so much to me.

Lastly, but never the least, I like to thank God for continuing to guide me on this writing journey.

Until the next time,

Jana` Chantel

ABOUT THE AUTHOR

 Jana` Chantel is a writer from Detroit, MI. She holds a BA in Creative Writing from Grand Valley State University. Her work includes: *Into My Mind*, a collection of personal essays, and her debut dystopian novel, *Surviving Red*. She has written and filmed a sci-fi TV pilot with her husband entitled *Fault: Gamma*, which won the 2017 New York Film and TV Festival for Best TV Series Concept for a TV pilot. When she isn't writing, you can find Jana` on a film set with her company Thirty Four 26 Studios or working on a creative project with her husband with their company About Right Media Group. *Razor & Helena: A Surviving Red Prequel* is the second book in the *Surviving Red series*.

www.janachantel.com

Facebook.com/SurvivingRed

Instagram & Twitter: @survivingred